EARTHBORN

Earthborn

Lightning Strike

Book 1

Catherine Asaro

OPEN ROAD
INTEGRATED MEDIA
NEW YORK

ISBN: 978-1-5040-8786-5

This edition published in 2023 by Open Road Integrated Media, Inc.
180 Maiden Lane
New York, NY 10038
www.openroadmedia.com

This book is dedicated to Sharon Todd and David Dansky,
two gifted teachers who made a great difference in my life

EARTHBORN

1

NIGHT THUNDER

I felt the city tonight. Although Los Angeles never fully slept, it was quiet, wrapped in its own thoughts. Drowsing. Waiting for a jolt to wake it up.

Joshua met me when I finished my shift at the restaurant, and we walked to the bus stop together. It had drizzled earlier and a slick film covered the street, reflecting the lights in blurred smears of oily water. Above us a few stars managed to outshine the city lights and pollution, valiant in their efforts to overcome the amber glow that tinted the darkened sky. Sparse traffic flowed by like sleek animals gliding through the night, intent on their own purposes.

I could see Joshua's good mood. It spread out from him in a faint rose-colored mist that shifted with vague shapes, the form of unspoken words. I was used to seeing people's emotions, but with him it was even more vivid than with everyone else. He affected all my senses. His calm mood sounded like waves on a beach, smelled like seaweed, tasted like salt. The effect faded with distance; it would only last until he moved away from me. I never told him, of course. I never told anyone. I didn't want to sound crazy.

We sat on the bench at the bus stop and he put his arm around my shoulders, not like a boyfriend, which he had never been, but like the best friend I had known for six years, since 1981, the year that Jamaica became the fifty-first state and the Hollywood sign burned down in the hills above LA. Tousled yellow hair fell over his forehead and brushed the wire rims of his glasses. He was my opposite in so many ways, his curls sun-bright compared to my straight black hair. His eyes had always seemed like bits of sky to me, blue and clear where mine were dark brown, the color of loam deep in a forest.

A harsh jab punctured the bubble of our mood. I had no idea where the emotion came from, only that it cut like a knife.

"Tina, look." Joshua pointed across the street.

A red sports car was turning off San Carlos Boulevard into a side street. "What about it?"

"That was Nug driving."

I didn't want to hear Nug's name. "He can drive down the street if he wants."

"He was watching us." Joshua glanced in the other direction and his face relaxed. "The bus is coming."

Following his gaze, I saw the old bus lumbering toward us. Good. The farther it took us from Nug, the better. As we stood up, the bus pulled into our stop. I boarded and paid, then turned to look at Joshua. Standing by the bench, he waved good-bye, his hand disappearing from sight when the driver closed the door.

As the bus headed off into the night, I sat in one of its many empty seats and leaned my head against the window. The few other passengers seemed lost in their thoughts as they slouched in other seats. I wondered if they were going home to their families, to a world they understood. As hard as I had tried to fit in here, Los Angeles had always felt alien to me.

I had grown up in the Zinacanteco village of Nabenchauk, the Lake of the Lightning, on the Chiapas plateau of southern Mexico. I missed its cool evergreen forests, its bone-dry winters and rainy summers. My earliest memories were of my mother, kneeling barefoot at her *metate,* grinding maize in the muted hours that came before dawn, when the air felt as clear as the clang of a bell. She was a traditional woman of the Maya who followed the *baz'i* or "true way" of life—so how, at age fourteen, had she ended up getting pregnant by an artist from Mexico City? It went against every grain of her life. He had visited Nabenchauk only to paint our village, and he had left within a few weeks. I had never met him, my father, that unknown and long vanished artist.

When I was eight, my aunt and uncle died in one of the earthquakes that hit the highlands, leaving behind my cousin, their eleven-year-old son Manuel. My mother took him into her care as she mourned the death of her brother. The heart-parching loss also decided her; after years of struggling with the decision, she went in search for my father, taking Manuel and me with her. We left Nabenchauk and rode along the Pan American Highway to Mexico City, what I had thought then must surely be a golden paradise at the edge of the universe. The glamour soon became tarnished in the gritty realities of life. We never found my father, though my mother searched for years, following one dead end after another, until we finally ended up here in the city of sleepless, fallen angels.

Tonight the bus rumbled to the stop on San Carlos Boulevard a few blocks from where I lived. The drugstore on the corner was closed and deserted. I shivered, uneasy. I had hoped Mario and his men would be hanging out there so I could ask one of them to walk me home. Los Vatos de la Calle San Carlos, or just VSC; people called them a gang, with Mario as their leader, but to me they were like family. My cousin Manuel had died two years ago, and since then VSC had looked out for me. I could still hear Mario jiving with my cousin: *Oye, vato, let's go the show.* And Manuel: *Chale homes. I want to go cruising and check out some firme rucas.* The memory stabbed like a knife, and I pushed away the grief, unable to face that emptiness.

No one was around the drugstore, but the Stop-And-Go down the block was open. I could go there and call Mario. I would probably have to wake him up, though, if he wasn't here, and I knew he'd been getting up early, trying to find a job. The last thing he needed was for me to drag him out of bed at one in the morning. *It's only a few blocks,* I thought. *You can go alone.* I knew the neighborhood and everyone knew me.

I headed down a side street. Old buildings lined the road, tenements and weathered houses hulking in the night, shuttered and closed. Most of the street lamps were dark, but a few made pools of light on the sidewalk like isolated havens in a dark sea. Cracks jagged through the cement as if they were bolts of lightening frozen into the concrete and overgrown with grass. Debris lay scattered everywhere, chunks of rock, plaster, newspapers, candy wrappings, empty cigarette boxes. Somewhere curtains thwapped in the breeze. A tattered bag from some fast-food place blew along the street, then caught up against a building. The smell of damp paper tickled my nose.

When my mother had first brought us to LA, we'd lived in a suburb, a run-down one, sure, but it had been okay. Although we hadn't had much, she gave us a good home and more than enough love. After her death, Manuel and I had moved here to East LA, where we could better afford the rent.

As I walked home, an odd sensation bothered me. A . . . trickle? It ran over my arms as if it were the runoff from a torrent of air rushing by in a nearby *cañón*. Warm air. It felt pleasant. But that "canyon," it was in my mind, not the city. I was sensing someone—

There.

He stood about a block away, facing away from me, a tall man with short curly hair, blond maybe. He was tall, about six-foot-four. One of the only working streetlamps on this stretch of road was a few feet behind where I stood, so as soon as he turned he would see me. Not good. I didn't recognize him. I should leave—but what he was doing was so odd, I paused and watched.

He had a box that hummed and glittered with red, gold, and silver lights. He was holding it in front of his body as he turned in a circle. From the way he was dressed, I would have expected him to be hanging out, having a brew with his homies instead of playing with gadgets. When Manuel had run with VSC, he had dressed that way, a black t-shirt and jeans tucked into his boots. Except this guy had on a vest, not a t-shirt, and his clothes looked more like leather than cotton and denim. Too dull for leather, maybe, but I couldn't tell from so far away.

Thinking about my cousin brought me back to my senses. I backed away, intending to be gone before this guy saw me. But it was too late. He stopped turning and looked up from his box, right at me. At first he just stood there, staring, his mouth slightly open as if I was the big surprise. Then he started toward me, his long legs devouring the space that separated us.

That's it, I thought and spun around to run.

"*Espérate,*" he called. "*Habla conmigo.*"

What the—? I turned back, why I didn't know. I thought he had said *Wait, talk to me,* but he had such a heavy accent, I couldn't be sure. His voice sounded strange, too. On *habla* it had rumbled with a deep note, like a low tone on a piano. Even stranger was his effect on my heightened senses. The warmth I had felt earlier felt stronger, flowing over my skin, a river instead of a trickle.

He stopped and stayed put, watching me. I watched him back, ready to bolt if he came closer.

He tried again. "*Preguntar mi tu decir.*"

Well that made no sense. "*¿Que?*" I asked.

"*Me siento,*" he said. "*Yo español mal.*"

He Spanish bad? No kidding. "How about English?" I asked. He looked like a gringo.

"Yes." Relief flickered across his face. "My English, it is much better."

It was indeed, though he still had a strong accent, one I didn't recognize. On the word, "much," his voice had made that strange sound again, like a piano note.

"What do you want?" I asked.

He held out his palms as if to show he had no weapons. It meant squat. He could have a knife or a gun hidden anywhere. And he had that strange box in his hand.

"Lost," he said. "Help can me find you?"

I squinted at him. "What?"

He paused, his face blanking. It was odd, like the screen on a computer clearing. Then his expression came back to normal. "Can you help me?" he asked. "I am lost."

He wanted directions out here, in the middle of the night. How weird. "Where are you going?"

"Washington, originally."

Not good. Nug and his men hung around Washington's liquor store. They dressed in black like this guy, and he had on those wrist guards a few of them wore, like they thought they were some kind of barbarian warriors. He looked older than most of Nug's gang, but not all of them. Some of those guys had aged out of petty crimes and graduated to the big time. They did serious hurt to people.

I backed up a step. "You're a long way from Washington's."

"Yes." He tilted his head as if he were listening to something I couldn't hear. And then of all things, he said, "I decide it is better if I not come down in a continental capital."

Seriously? Washington, D.C., as in the capital of the country? Maybe he was zoned out on crack. He didn't sound wasted, though. His speech wasn't slurred or wandering, just strange.

Okay, I thought, curious despite my better judgment. "What's in Washington?"

"A reception."

"You mean like a party?"

He paused, then said, "Yes, that is an appropriate word."

I couldn't help but smile. "You're going to a fancy party dressed like that?"

"This is my duty uniform." He said it with a perfectly straight face. "My dress uniform is on the ship."

Hah, hah. Funny. I hadn't heard of anyone like him hanging around here, and surely I would have known about someone this bizarre. "What's your name?"

He was watching me with an unsettling focus, like I was the odd one rather than him. "I am Althor."

Althor. It sounded like a nickname. Nug's men all took one, though most were a lot less creative about it. "You mean like Thor? The guy with the hammer?"

"I am sorry, but I not know to whom you refer."

Whom? I hadn't known people actually existed who used that word. I had no idea if he was dangerous or not, but I had to admit, I hadn't met anyone this interesting in ages. Like maybe never. I motioned at his box. "What is that?"

"Transcom," he said.

"What does it do?"

"It transmit and receive waves. Right now I scan radio signals." He came closer, lifting the box so I could see it better. Startled, I backed away. As I stepped into the halo from the streetlamp, he stopped and stared as if he had just seen me. I suppose he had in a sense, given I had only now moved into the light.

"Gods," he said. "You are incredibly beautiful."

Normally that would've been nice, but not now. Not with me alone and out here in the middle of the night. I kept backing up. The drugstore wasn't far.

"Don't go." Althor started toward me again.

As soon as he moved in my direction, I spun around and hurried away. I'd never have thought I could move so fast in the stiletto heels of my waitress uniform, but it was amazing what you could do when you were scared.

"Wait," he called.

I hesitated, turning back, slowing to a stop. Why? Something about him was familiar, but I had no idea what. I felt his emotions far more than I ever had from anyone else. They flowed across me like a river of warmth with tendrils of mist curling into the night. His presence felt—good. Strong. So I stayed, poised and ready to run, watching him warily.

Althor made the one choice that would keep me from bolting. He backed away. He kept moving until he was standing in the light from the only working other lamp on this street. I could see him better now. His eyes were dark, black or brown, though it was hard to be sure. He had fair skin and curly hair that, as far as I could tell, was the same color as the bronze bracelet my mother had given me before she died. And that wasn't all. *El hombre era chulo.* The guy was *hot.* Just because he was good-looking, though, that didn't mean he was okay.

"You run with Nug?" I asked.

He tilted his head. "Who?"

"Nug. You know."

"I do not know."

"You must've seen him around. Tall guy. Anglo. Blue eyes. Buzz hair."

"I do not know this man." He considered me. "My uniform—you not recognize it?"

"I've never seen no uniform like that." I winced. "Any uniform." I hated it when I forgot English grammar didn't allow double negatives. Such an annoying language, not allowing you that extra negative to make your point.

Althor didn't seem to notice, though, probably because his English was even worse than mine. "I am a ****" he said.

I blinked. "A what?"

He repeated the word and it still sounded like gibberish.

"I don't understand," I said.

"Literally I think it translate as 'Jagernaut Secondary.'"

"What's a Jagernaut Secondary?"

"Similar to what you call naval captain." He thought for a moment. "Actually, I think Secondary comes closer to the rank in your air force. Major, maybe."

Yeah, sure. "You're a soldier?" And I was a space alien.

"I am pilot. ISC Tactical Fighter Wing."

Okay, that sounded cool. But still. "What's ISC?"

"Imperial Space Command."

Space Command, huh? That was certainly a step up from Washington's drugstore. This guy had to be blitzed. Either that, or he actually thought I was dumb enough to believe him.

"Sure," I said. "*De lengua me como un taco.*" No one actually said that any more, in this day and age, but a teacher had once told me the phrase and I loved it.

Althor squinted at me and his face blanked again. A moment later he came back to normal. Bewildered, he said, "You'll eat a taco if it's beef tongue?"

I couldn't help but smile. The literal translation did sound pretty strange. "It means, 'Yeah, right, tell me another one.'"

He seemed more curious than offended. "Does that mean you think I make this up?"

"Well, you know, I don't run into that many fighter pilots on my way home from work."

Althor smiled. "I guess not."

His smile caught me by surprise. No cruelty showed in it, no malice or anger. Nor was it a false smile or the too easy expression of someone who had never had reason to cry. His smile had history, complicated history. It was beautiful.

I thawed a bit. "So how come you're in LA?"

He considered me as if trying to decide whether or not I was a threat. I mean, really? Five-foot-two me in my waitress outfit, fluffy miniskirt and all. When he answered, the oddest thought came to me: he had just gone through extensive calculations in his analysis of whether or not to trust me. Close on the heels of that thought came another. *Calculations? Analysis?* I never thought that way. Sure, I had always liked math, unlike most of my friends, but for a moment it had felt as if I were thinking someone else's thoughts.

"I am in the wrong place," Althor said. "Actually, it looks like the wrong time. According to my ship, the date here is what I expect. But everything is too much different." He pointed to the streetlight. "For one thing, I never know this, that Los Angeles has such antique lamps."

I peered at the light. It was the same as most everywhere in LA: a bronze-hued pole with scalloped sides. It ended in a large, ornate hook that curled upward. Hanging from the hook was a glass lamp shaped like the bell on a Spanish mission. Books about Los Angeles always showed them.

"They're called angel bells," I said.

"Angel bells? They are beautiful. But I never hear of this before."

"You really must be new. They're as famous as the Golden Gate Bridge in San Francisco."

Althor frowned. "I have studied American history. If these bells are famous, I would know."

"Maybe whoever taught you history didn't know LA that well." More likely, if he was like the other guys in Nug's gang, he had slept through history class or never showed up at all.

"My 'teacher' is a neural chip," he said. "It has no record of these bell-lamps." He glanced around, taking in the debris-strewn street, broken windows, and crumbling buildings. "You live here?"

I didn't like him asking where I lived.

After a moment, when I didn't answer, he said, "Why do you live in a place like this?"

I stiffened. This was home. Yeah, it wasn't much, but it meant a lot to me. My voice turned icy. "Because I do."

He jerked as if my anger had struck him. "My sorry. I meant no offense."

His reaction was so odd, I forgot to be angry. Actually, his response *wasn't* odd, and that made it strange. He reacted the same way I did if someone's emotions hit me too hard. He backed off, easing up on the person he had hurt.

Less defensive now, I said, "Where are you from?"

"Parthonia, originally."

"Par-what?"

"Parthonia. The seat of the Skolian government."

"I've never heard of it."

Althor spoke wryly. "After everything else I find here, or *not* find, I am not surprised." He went to the nearest building and sat on its steps, planting his booted feet wide on the cracked sidewalk. "Everything here is wrong," he said, poking at his box. "I find only radio transmissions."

It was cool the way his box flashed with lights. As he tapped its faces, they glowed in different colors. He turned over his arm and pressed the box against his wrist guard. That was when I realized his guard wasn't all leather. Glowing wires crisscrossed parts of it, and other parts glinted like metal.

I moved closer to watch. "I've never seen wrist guards like that before."

"They have a new web architecture," Althor spoke absently, intent on his box. One of its panels turned green. "At least I can reach my Jag."

"Is that your car?" It seemed unlikely. He didn't look like someone who could afford those dream wheels.

He kept on working on his box. "My star fighter."

"Oh. Right." Maybe he was an actor rehearsing for a movie. More likely his brain had lost a few bolts. Oddly, though, nothing about him tripped my mental alarms, and my intuition about people was usually solid. "Maybe you're looking for the wrong signal."

He made a frustrated noise. "I check radio wave, microwave, optical, UV, X-ray, neutrino channels, everything. Nothing is right."

"Why come here to check?" I doubted East LA slums were high on the list of places for lost star fighter pilots to hang out looking for help.

"The Jag is doing the orbital scans," he muttered.

"I mean, why did you come to this street?"

Althor stopped poking his box and looked up at me. "I—well,

I don't know." After a pause, he said, "It seemed right. I am not sure why."

That sounded the way I felt when his river of moods trickled over me. "What are you looking for?"

"Something to make sense." He motioned at the deserted street. "This city, it looks like it is the wrong century. The date that my ship gives is correct, but this Earth, it is like no Earth I know."

Wait a minute! I knew what was going on. "You go to Caltech, right? My friend Josh is a freshman there. He told me about those games you guys play. That's what you're doing, isn't it? Role-playing."

"Caltech?" He squinted at me. "This means California Institute of Technology, yes?"

"I guess so. Josh never calls it that." Now that I thought about it, if Althor came from Caltech, what was he doing all the way out here in East LA, alone, in the middle of the night? Besides, he looked more like the guys who had terrorized Joshua in high school. One time, Nug and his creeps had cornered Joshua behind the gym. They tied his hands behind his back and lined up in front of him with their Uzis like a firing squad. The assholes had thought it was funny. Joshua had been so freaked, he hadn't come back to school for a week. He had been afraid to tell anyone besides me, but I told the guys in VSC and after that they looked out for him because he was my friend.

"I've heard of Caltech," Althor said. "I never went there, though. I graduated from DMA."

"What's DMA?" I asked.

"A military academy."

Sure, right. Though I had to admit, I loved the thought of Nug's gang trapped in a military school. Boot camp would be even better. I could just see a drill sergeant yelling in their faces.

Althor, however, was serious. He wanted me to believe

he had gone to a military academy. Maybe it was his dream. I understood that. Ever since I had graduated last year, I had wanted to go to college. I had no money for tuition, but I was saving. And dreaming.

During my junior year in high school, one of my teachers got excited when she saw the record of my test scores and grades. She said I was "gifted," that I had options for college, like scholarships. I had been thrilled, thinking maybe, just maybe, I could make something of my life.

Then Nug's gang had murdered Manuel and I had fallen apart. We all had. In school, the guys had stalked the halls, ready to explode, black armbands on their hardened biceps. School officials tried to have grief sessions for us, but we never went. We trusted no one except each other. Manuel had been my only blood family since my mother's death, so VSC became my people, surrounding me in the halls and classrooms. No one else dared come near me in those first days. I hadn't even realized I had missed the PSAT testing date until weeks later. At that point, I no longer cared. Life sucked and I was tired. If not for Mario, his sister Rosa, and the rest of VSC, God only knew what I'd have done. I might not be alive now.

I spoke gently. "It doesn't matter to me if you don't have a fancy degree. Just never give up your dreams."

"I do have degree," he said. "It's in inversion engineering."

He said it with such a straight face, I couldn't resist teasing. "Perversion engineering. Sounds exciting."

He reddened, like he thought he had made some embarrassing mistake in English. "*Inversion.*"

I liked the way he cared what I thought he had said. "So you're supposed to go to a party?"

"It is a reception at the White House for my mother."

"The White House, huh? She must be important."

"She is mathematician. But that was long ago. For many years she had been ****."

Although his English was improving, his accent still puzzled me. "I didn't get that last word."

His face blanked. Now that I was more tuned to him, I *felt* the change in his mind. He turned metallic. Then his human warmth returned, eddying around us and softening the banks of my barricaded emotions.

"Key," Althor said. "She is a Key. This is the closest translation I find."

That didn't sound like any of Joshua's games. Their characters were usually Ultimate Lords of Destruction or whatever. And I mean, seriously, who had their mother as a player?

"What does she do?" I asked.

"Sits in Assembly. She is liaison between the Assembly and the mesh networks."

"Oh." I had expected something more flamboyant, like sorceress or queen. Then again, maybe "liaison" was code. "Does that mean she's a warrior queen?" I grinned. "That make you a prince? If I kiss you, will you turn into a frog?"

A sleepy smile spread across his face. "Maybe you should find out."

I flushed. I had only meant it as a joke—well, okay, maybe flirting a little. But I wasn't coming on to him and now he thought I was. Why did I keep lowering my guard? After only a few minutes he was affecting me more than people I had known for years.

Althor could have reacted a lot of ways to my joke, and most would have had me backing off. Instead he held out his transcom as if he were a vaquero, a cowboy offering sugar to a skittish horse. "Want to see how it works?"

Ho! Clever man. One reason Joshua and I had become friends, despite all our differences, was because we both liked gadgets. He enjoyed making them and I liked to figure out how they worked.

So I didn't back away. Instead I said, "Okay." But I kept my distance.

Althor brushed his finger over the box and a panel turned silver. "This put it in acoustic mode." He showed me the other side of the box, which somehow had turned into a small membrane.

"Say something," Althor suggested.

"*Hola, cajita.*" I said.

The transcom answered with my voice. "*Hola, cajita.*"

I laughed, delighted to hear his transcom call itself a little box. "How did it do that?"

"Your voice, it makes longitudinal waves in atmosphere." Althor lifted the box. "This reproduces them." He tapped a code onto one of its panels and a note rang out. "That is frequency 552 hertz." He played another note. "What frequency? Can you say?"

"Almost the same as the first," I said. "A little higher."

"You have a good ear. It is 564 hertz." He had the box make a third note. "This one?"

"Same as the last." It didn't sound exactly the same, though. "I think."

"Not quite. It's 558 hertz." He pressed several panels and a tone came again, but this time it vibrated like a trilling bird with a whistle in its throat.

"Hey! That's cool." I grinned at him. "I know what you're doing. Making beats. Me and Josh read about it in school when we took physics." I had needed special permission to take AP Physics because the guidance counselors had put Josh and me on different tracks, him in college prep and me in the voca-tional program. But I talked them into letting me take the AP class. "Your box is singing those two notes at the same time, so they sound like they're vibrating."

He smiled his sleepy smile, seeming far more interested in my excited reaction than in the box. "Do you know what is the beat frequency?"

Well, of course. "Twelve hertz. And I can figure out the pitch of the beating note. It's that last one you played, the average of the first two, 558 hertz."

"That's right." Althor nodded as if it were perfectly normal for me to know all this buzz on beats, which raised my opinion of him by a big notch. He touched another panel and flute music floated out into the night as sweet as the down under an owl's wings.

"Pretty," I said.

"Want to try the transcom?" He pulled the box off his wrist and held it out to me.

Did Los Angeles have smog? Yeah, I wanted to play.

As I reached for the box, Althor shifted so his arm moved back in his lap, making me step closer to reach the transcom. Like an idiot, I stumbled over his foot and fell across his lap. He caught me, sliding his arm around my waist.

¡Maldito! Mortified, I grabbed the transcom and backed away from him.

"If you come over here," he invited, "I show you how it works."

I stayed put, keeping my distance. He was sitting on the third step of the stairs, his feet far apart on the sidewalk and his big elbows resting on his knees. Bits of plaster lay scattered around his feet, probably fallen from the building during the last thunderstorm. Given his looks and smooth style, he could probably have women scattered all around him, too, if he wanted.

Except he wasn't really smooth, at least not in that slick way a player talked when he knew girls thought he was hot and he wanted to get laid. Althor seemed like a nice guy. Sure, he had the moves, but underneath he was more like Joshua's techie friends than the slick guys who came on to me in the restaurant. I mean, really, who used physics as a pick-up line? Even weirder, who would have guessed it would work so well.

Another plus for Althor: he didn't push. When I backed away from him, holding the transcom, he stayed where he was, which reassured me more than anything else he might have tried. So after a few moments, I cautiously approached and sat on the other side of the steps, as far from him as possible, with about two feet of concrete separating us.

Althor reached over and touched a silver square on the box. The little panel turned gold.

I leaned away from him. "What are you doing?"

He sat back, giving me space. "I make it in electromagnetic mode."

"What does that do?"

"Right now, an antenna it creates." He swept out his arm, his gesture taking in the street, the buildings, even the sky. "Everywhere."

"I don't see anything."

"It uses the buildings." He dropped his arm onto the stairs between us, his fingers brushing my thigh. "And the effect, it is enhanced by changes in local air density."

I moved my leg away from his fingers. "I don't feel nothing."

"You can't feel it." Althor said. "Besides," he murmured. "There are better things to feel."

Whoa. His mood was a sensuous river, reminding me of the predawn coolness in Nabenchauk, those early mornings when I would sneak off for a swim by myself instead of preparing my loom for weaving like I was supposed to. I had known a secret curve in the lake hidden by fir-draped mountains. The mist hung over the water in veils, blue and shadowed, mysterious, impossible to ignore. That was what Althor felt like now. It was so distracting, I dropped the transcom. The box slid out of my hands, skittering under my fingers, and clunked onto the step by the spike heel of my shoe, its panels glowing like gemstones in a river.

A woman's voice burst out of the box. "—fourth caller wins two free dinners at Mona's Kitchen. So get your phone ready, folks."

"*¡Oiga!*" Flustered, I grabbed the transcom. My finger-nail clicked another square and the woman's voice cut off in midsentence, replaced by a man speaking an unfamiliar language. "Ah!" I jerked my finger away from the transcom. "What's it *doing?*"

Althor was staring at where I held the transcom between my knees. It seemed to take a great deal of effort for him to shift his gaze to my face. "What?"

I reddened and pulled my knees together, holding the transcom on top of them. "The box. What happened?"

"It picks up radio waves." He leaned in until his chest was against my shoulder, his hand braced behind me on the stairs. With his other hand, he touched the transcom and it went silent. Then he spoke next to my ear. "You haven't told me your name." His river of sensuality swirled around us, muddling my thoughts. I felt his moods more than I had with anyone else, even Joshua. With Althor it was so intense it would have both-ered me if it had been harsh. But it was nice.

"Tina. I'm T-Tina." I was talking too fast. "Akushtina Santis Pulivok." I had no idea why I gave him my full name. People here always thought it was strange.

"'Akushtina," he murmured. "A beautiful name. For a beau-tiful woman."

Ho! The surprise wasn't so much that he thought my name was beautiful, though that was strange too; the glottal stop at the beginning of 'Akushtina sounded harsh to most people who didn't speak Tzotzil Mayan. But what really hit me was that he pronounced it *right*. This guy who could barely speak Spanish and wasn't that much better in English, spoke my Mayan name perfectly.

Althor picked up a lock of my hair. "So long and soft and black." He had a musky scent, like catnip. "Why are you out here alone?"

I tried to ignore his smell, but it was impossible. It was like he was giving off those chemicals I had read about, pheromones or something, targeted at me. I put my hand on his shoulder and pushed him away. "I was coming home from work. My brothers are expecting me." He had no way to know I had no brothers. "They must be looking for me."

Althor took the hint and stayed back. He tilted his head, like someone straining to catch a sound he could barely hear. "How do you do that?"

"Do what?"

"Upload to me. Overwrite my thoughts. My internal mesh should be protected."

I wondered if he ever talked like a normal person. "I have no idea what you mean."

"I can't think straight." He paused, watching me as if for cues. Then he leaned in closer.

I stared at his lips. They looked full. Warm. He waited a moment more, and when I didn't push him back, he put his arm around my waist. My awareness of him intensified, the textures of his emotions mixing with his actual touch until I couldn't separate them. It was as if someone had painted a picture of us and then torn it in two, and now we were putting the halves back together. When he bent his head to kiss me, I slid my arms around his neck, acting before I had a chance to think that it was a lousy idea. Something here was *right,* something good, though anyone would say I was crazy to think that about this weird guy I had just met.

When it came to men, my cousin Manuel had been as strict with me as a father. No, he had been even worse, more like a priest. He had driven me crazy. I still had an idea what went on, though, enough to know Althor kissed differently than most guys. He flicked his tongue over my ear, the closed lids of my eyes, the tip of my nose. When he reached my lips, he kept one arm around my waist and held my head with his other hand, stroking my cheek with his thumb while we kissed.

It was a while before we separated. Finally he drew back and brushed my hair out of my face, watching me with an unexpected tenderness. "Where are your brothers?" he asked.

I looked at him, feeling the echo of his lips on my mouth. His scent was everywhere, like the fragrance of pine needles in a forest.

"Tina?" He touched my cheek. "Are you there?"

"*¿Que?*"

"Your brothers. Why they leave you to walk alone like this?"

"They don't." Which was true, seeing as I had no brothers. "I don't usually come out this late."

"Where are you going?"

"Home. Rosa usually gives me a ride, but her car is in the shop." That brought me to my senses. No matter how good I felt with this guy, he was a stranger. I pushed away from him and stood up. "I should go."

Althor blinked as if I had yanked him out of a dream. He rose to his feet next to me, moving more slowly, towering like an oak tree. "Already?"

"I have to work tomorrow." What did I do now? I didn't want to ask for his phone number. He might take it wrong. For all that he pretended he came from somewhere futuristic, this was really just dull ordinary 1987 Los Angeles. Some guys were okay with a woman asking for their number, but the way I had grown up, a girl never did that, not unless she was inviting a lot more than I intended. I wanted to—well, I wasn't sure. See him more, the way you did with a guy you liked.

His gaze was intent. "Tina?"

"I thought maybe—" I paused, leaving him an opening.

"Yes?" He watched as if I were turning into water, clear and cool, running through his fingers.

"I—Nothing." *Stop being an idiot,* I thought. He was probably way out of my league. Girls from the barrio didn't have boyfriends like him. I had even begun to wonder if he really was some kind of military pilot.

"I have to go," I said.

He started to speak, but then stopped. "You're sure?"

"Yes."

Again he had that odd look, as if he were losing something. All he said was, "*Adios,* 'Akushtina."

"*Adios.*" *Ask me to stay,* I thought, shielding that hope even in my own mind, as if that could make his rejection easier to bear. He said nothing.

So I headed home, trying to ignore the feeling that I was making the stupidest mistake of my life. After I walked about half a block, I looked back. Althor was still standing there, watching. He pushed his hand through his hair, leaving it tousled. I hesitated, but he didn't do anything else, so I turned away and crossed the street, then went around the corner. Once I thought I heard a footstep behind me, but when I glanced around, I saw no one.

I lived at the intersection of Miner and San Juan streets. As I came down San Juan, it was a relief to see the sagging stairs of my apartment house. Only three buildings and I would be home.

A pair of headlights flashed on across the street, coming from a parked car. A red car. *No!* I sped up, walking faster, practically running for my building.

The driver's side of the car opened and Nug climbed out. Actually, Matt Kugelmann was his name. Tall and lanky, with lean muscles, he moved like a werewolf on the hunt, muscles rippling under his sleek hide as he stalked through the streets with feral grace. I had never used the word feral before, but it came to me now and it fit perfectly. His head was shaved, except on the very top where yellow hair stuck up like a scrub brush. Although he was only twenty-four, he looked older. His face had a hard cast to it, as if he had baked in a kiln too long. But what made him ugly was the way he looked at you, as if in his view of the universe you meant nothing.

That was why I hated him, because people mattered less to him than the garbage he sold. He had ordered his people to kill Manuel for stealing crack out of his car. Worse, Nug was the one who had sold Manuel his first hit, to "help" him deal with his grief over my mother's death. And of course Nug had kept him supplied.

I wasn't going to reach home in time. I tried to run, but I tripped in the spike heels of my waitress uniform and fell, landing in a heap of blue and white ruffles.

A hand slipped under my arm and I looked up into Nug's face. "Hey, Tina," he said.

I stood up awkwardly, holding down my skirt, and stepped back, trying to free my arm. "Hi."

Nug didn't let go. "Just thought I'd make sure you got home okay." He pulled me with him. "I'll walk you the rest of the way."

"I'm fine now." I balked as we climbed the steps of my apartment building, and I managed to make him stop when we reached the landing. "Thanks, Nug. I'll see you."

He stepped closer. "Why are you in such a hurry?"

I backed up, into the wall of the building, wishing I could disappear. "Nug, go home, okay?"

"I saw you hugging Joshua at the bus stop." He touched the tip of his finger to my cheek. "How come you hang out with that dweeb? He's a loser."

"Don't call him that."

"Why?" Nug sounded genuinely curious. "Why would you bother with him? He doesn't even try to do you. I can't believe it. He must like guys."

I knew perfectly well Joshua liked women, especially tall ones with red hair. "I'm not his type. He likes brainy girls."

Nug laughed and traced his finger down my neck. "You don't need brains." He leaned his head down as if he were going to kiss me. "You're so fucking pretty."

I tried to duck under his arm, but he pushed me against the wall. "You know what you look like in that outfit?" he said. "Those models in that clothes catalog I get."

The thought of Nug ordering a clothes catalog was so bizarre, I almost laughed. "You mean like the Sears catalog?"

"Sears?" He smirked. "Hell, no. That place in Hollywood, I can't remember the name. Freedman or Frederick's or something. Man, those bitches are even hotter than the chicks in *Hustler*."

"Nug, I have to go."

"They got play clothes in there." He reached under my skirt and snapped my garter belt. "Like these."

I pushed his hand away. "Cut it out."

"You wouldn't believe what they got. I didn't know real girls even wore that stuff." He pushed my purse off my shoulder, and let it thunk to the ground while he pulled my arms over my head. He held my wrists against the wall. "Be nice to me, *chiquitita*. You don't know what Big Daddy might have to do if his little girl is naughty."

"Stop it!" I struggled to yank my arms away from him.

His voice hardened. "You gotta be nice to me." He let go of my wrists. "See, I know stuff."

I pulled down my arms. "Stuff?"

"Like you lied about your age to get that job." His voice grated as if it were the rasp of a weaving stick over a backstrap loom. "Like your papers are faked and you ain't here legal, baby. Like if you don't do what I want, I'll have to talk. You want to go back to taco land? What you gonna do there, Tina? Turn tricks in Tijuana?"

"Don't say that!" I pushed him away, hating it when he talked about me that way.

"Damn it!" He hit the side of the building with his fist, and flakes of old paint scattered around us. "Why don't you say, 'Yes, Nug. Whatever you want, Nug'? You always did whatever that shit cousin of yours told you to do, even going to Mass every Sunday. I mean, who freaking goes to church all the time? Well, he ain't here to keep me off no more. He's gone, he's not coming back, and V-Fucking-SC can't do shit." He grabbed my shoulders and shook them. "I'm king around here, baby. So don't play hard to get no more."

"No!" I gasped with the force of his motion. "*Stop it!*"

"You listen to me." He pushed me against the wall. "I'm done with your games. We're going to do things my way from now on. You do what I want, *when* I want, starting tonight. You got it?"

It was like a waking nightmare, one that no pinch would end. I had nowhere to go, no haven, no safety. "Nug, don't hurt me." I knew he would, that he liked it that way, but I didn't know what else to do. "Just let me go."

"Shut up!" He slapped me across the face so hard, it slammed me into the wall. My head rang with pain.

Something yanked Nug away from me. One moment he was hitting me, the next I was free and stumbling forward. As I caught myself, I looked up to see a startled Nug facing off with another man.

Althor.

"What's the matter with you?" Althor asked. "Can't you feel how frightened she is?"

"Who the fuck are you?" Nug said.

I didn't stick around to hear more. I ran inside the building and banged the door shut behind me. When I flipped the light switch nothing happened, so I ran down the hall in the dark, reaching for my keys—

No! My keys were in my purse, and my purse was outside on the landing.

I stopped, my heart thudding like the beats of a gourd drum. Then I went back to the door, walking soft, so very soft. Outside, I heard someone falling down the steps. Althor was bigger, but Nug was a better fighter than anyone else I knew. If I had to bet which one of them would win, I'd put my money on Nug, as much as I hated that idea.

A car door opened, followed by Nug saying, "You're gonna wish you never screwed with me." The door slammed and the engine started.

I hesitated. Nug wasn't one to leave a fight, not unless he thought he would lose. But against one man? It made no sense. I nudged the door open a crack—but in the same moment someone on the other side pulled it open all the way.

"Tina?" Althor stood there framed in the rickety doorway. "Are you all right?"

It was too much. I backed up and tripped over some torn

boxes on the floor. As I fell, I banged into the wall and dropped onto my knees. Pressing my fist against my mouth, I tried to stop shaking.

Althor came over and knelt in front of me. He started to reach for me, but when I stiffened, he dropped his arm. In the faint light trickling past the open door, his face looked strained, as if with pain, yet no cuts or bruises showed anywhere I could see.

"It's all right," Althor said. "He is gone." He stood up slowly, taking care not to jostle me, and offered his hand.

I avoided his hand and stood up without touching him. Then I stepped away, deeper into the shadowed building.

"I don't understand," Althor said. "Why does your brother treat you like that?"

"M-my brother?"

"That was one of your brothers, yes?"

"No." The thought of being related to Nug made me want to lose my dinner.

"Maybe that explains it."

"Explains what?"

"Why he had no caring of your fear."

"He likes people to be afraid of him." I clenched my fist at my side. "It makes him feel big."

Althor pushed his hand through his hair, and his arm shook, but it wasn't from his own reactions. I felt what he felt: He wasn't afraid of Nug, not at all. He was shaking from *my* emotions.

"How did you know I needed help?" I asked.

"I input it. Even from so far away." His forehead creased. "Can you always broadcast such a strong signal?"

He was doing it again, saying those strange things, and I couldn't take any more. I backed toward the stairs. "I'm not doing nothing."

Althor looked around at the shadowed hallway, taking in the scarred walls, the peeling plaster, the tags spray-painted in dark colors. "Tina, you should go someplace safer than this."

"*Está bien.* It's fine." I needed my purse, but I didn't know how to reach the landing where it lay in a crumpled heap just visible behind the edge of the door. A large pilot was in the way. Fighter pilot. Right. I wanted to laugh, then cry. Mostly I wanted to be safe in my apartment.

Althor watched as if I were a puzzle that was breaking his heart. Then he went outside and got my purse. When he came back, he set it down in the hall in front of me and stepped aside, giving me plenty of space. I grabbed my purse and backed away from him, clutching the bag. Then I headed for the stairs at the other end of the hall, practically running. As I went up the steps, I looked back. Althor was still standing in the same place. He made no attempt to follow, just watched me leave. I turned the corner and lost sight of him.

On the second floor, moonlight was coming through a dirty window at this end of the hall. Junk cluttered the hallway floor and black patches showed on the walls where a fire had scorched them years ago. A baby cried somewhere, a wail that broke off into softer sobs. Upstairs a man and woman were yelling. The musty smell was worse up here, but I didn't care. I was almost home.

I hurried to my door, which was halfway down the hall, and unlocked the top bolt, the bottom bolt, the police lock, and finally the door. As soon as I was inside, I locked it all back up. Then I sagged against the wood and started to shake. Once it started, I couldn't stop. I sank down to the ground in the darkened room, collapsed against the door, shaking and shivering, too drained to move anymore.

2

BLUE LACE

I opened my eyes to a sunlit room. It looked the same as always, with my TV table in the middle of the room and my bed against the wall to the right. Across the room, beyond the TV, the "kitchen" was no more than a narrow counter with space behind it for a stove and refrigerator. A barred window above the sink let sunlight sift through the gauzy blue curtains I had sewn.

My mother's dress hung above the bed, a wedding *huipil* she had never worn, a white dress she had woven with cotton, lace, and downy white feathers, embroidered with flowers in blue, red, and gold thread around the square neckline. It was gorgeous. Not only did it cover the peeling paint on the wall, but it also reminded me of Chiapas whenever I was homesick and lonely.

I rubbed my eyes and peered at my watch. 9:00 A.M. That meant I had seven hours until my shift at the Blue Knight. Exhausted, I changed into a white nightgown that came to my knees and crawled into bed.

Sleep, real sleep this time, settled over me like a quilt stitched from the clouds.

The sound of a dog barking outside woke me up. The clock on my TV table said it was two in the afternoon. I went to wash my face, and the bathroom mirror gave me a sobering reflection. I looked ten years older, with a bruise on my cheek where Nug had hit me. Maybe that was why Nug was aging so fast, because his ugly lifestyle had squeezed out his vitality.

He was right, though, the bastard. I was afraid to go to the police. My family had come to America in 1981, so we were eligible for amnesty under the Immigration Reform and Control Act of 1986. Unfortunately, neither my mother nor Manuel understood English well enough to keep our file up to date. I was trying to straighten it out, but since I was underage and without a legal guardian, I didn't want to draw attention to myself. I didn't understand all the bureaucracy, and I feared if I made waves, they would put me in foster care or pack me off to Chiapas where I had no family or prospects. Only a few more months and I would be twenty. *Just keep trying,* I thought. *You can do it.* I would save money for college, get legal, and have a real life without Nug killing my dreams with his fists or his body.

Right now, though, I had to get ready for work. I changed into one of my uniforms for the restaurant. They all looked the same, a blue laced-up bodice, a blue mini-skirt with fluffy white underskirts, and stiletto heels. I didn't much like the style, but the colors and cloth were pretty. I knew the only reason they gave me the job was because I looked good in their waitress outfit. Maybe they even knew I was underage. I just made sure I did my job well, never made waves, and smiled at the patrons, who gave me good tips. It didn't hurt, either, that I was better at math than any of the other waitresses.

When I was ready to leave, I opened the apartment door—
and almost jumped back inside.

Althor was outside, asleep.

He was sitting against the wall by the door, his knees drawn
up to his chest, his head resting on them as if he were an over-
worked bodyguard who had given in to exhaustion. Seeing
him in the light, I realized his hair wasn't blond after all. The
sun had streaked it gold, but underneath it was red, almost
purple. It reminded me of the merlot wine we served at the
restaurant. Even stranger, the color looked real, not like he had
dyed his hair.

He was older than I had first thought, too, well into his thir-
ties. The previous night I had assumed he was Anglo, but now
I had no idea what to think. His skin had a metallic tint, like
bronze or gold. It was subtle, so I hadn't noticed before, but with
the sunlight from the window down the hall slanting across his
arms, the tint became more visible.

I knelt next to him. "Althor?"

He opened his eyes and blinked at me, groggy and slow.

What the—? I knew he had *eyes;* I had seen them last night.
But when his lashes lifted, they uncovered nothing but a gold
shimmer. No pupils, no irises, no whites, no nothing. Just
gold.

"¡*Ay, carumba!*" I said. "I don't believe it."

His forehead creased and he looked around the hall for whatever it was that I didn't believe. As he searched, that gold rolled
up from his eyes like a retracting eyelid. Underneath, he had
normal eyes. Almost normal. They were an unusual color, like
grapes that grow in big, juicy clusters. I had heard about people
with violet eyes, but I'd assumed it meant dark blue. I had never
imagined the color could be so vivid.

Althor stretched out his legs and rubbed his eyes as if they were perfectly normal. He said, "It is late," and his voice resonated on "late" with a deep note, like the bass on a piano.

"You stayed out here all night?" I asked.

He massaged the back of his neck, working at the muscles, which surely had to ache given the way he had been sleeping. "The idea seemed like a good one."

I could hardly believe he had done that for me. "Are you all right? What happened to your eyes?"

He blinked at me. "My eyes?"

"The gold."

He shrugged. "The inner lids are like my grandfather's. He had—I am not sure what is the English word. Differences from birth."

Differences? Did he mean birth defects? I winced, hoping I hadn't offended him.

"Your day is so short," he said, yawning. "I need to reset my internal clock."

"It's spring. The days are long." I rubbed my finger along his biceps. The gold didn't come off.

He watched me touch him, his look turning sleepy. Bedroom eyes, my friend Rosa would say. Taking my hand, he curled his fingers around mine. "I was worried about you."

"I'm okay." I squeezed his fingers and said what I should have told him before. "Thank you for last night. I don't want to think what would've happened if you hadn't helped me."

He lifted my hand and pressed his lips against my knuckles, his teeth just barely touching the skin, not kissing exactly, more like biting. It was strange. But nice. I couldn't believe he was out here, though. I didn't know any other guy who would guard my door all night.

"You were watching over me," I said. "Protecting a girl you don't hardly know."

"Why do you call yourself a girl?" Althor started to reach for me, then paused. When I didn't object, he pulled me into a hug. I held him tight, my cheek against his ear, his curls tickling my nose. Closing my eyes, I willed that moment to last forever, as if I could preserve it in amber and take it wherever I went, to bring out for comfort whenever the loneliness became too much.

After a moment, I pulled back my head. "I have to go to work. If I'm late, I'll lose my job."

"Can I walk you there?" he asked.

I laughed, that kind of soft embarrassed sound you make when a person you want to like you acts as if he does. "Okay."

"I am sorry about last night. I should have asked then."

"I wanted you to."

"You did?" His teeth flashed in a smile. "I keep thinking, 'She will say something.' But nothing. So I believed you had not the interest." He hesitated. "I think, though, that your customs here are not like ours. That expectations for women and men are different than what I am used to."

I had no idea how to answer that.

We came out of the building into afternoon sunshine. For a moment Althor's face blanked. Then he came back to normal. "It is fourteen hours since I first meet you."

I hadn't realized that much time had passed. "Is that a problem?"

"No." He paused. "It is fine."

I could tell it wasn't fine. His tension created a pale mist around him. Yet despite that, he meant to stick around. It seemed a good sign.

As we walked along, an old Ford rumbled along Miner Street. Althor spun around as the car went by us and walked backward, staring until the Ford disappeared around a corner.

Then he swung back around to me. "Amazing! Another car, even more vintage."

Vintage? Then I realized he meant a classic car. How I knew, I wasn't sure. I must have overheard Jake, my ex-boyfriend, use the word. He was the best mechanic around here and seriously into old cars. English was his second language, after Spanish, but when it came to cars, he knew more than anyone else in either language.

I also noticed another oddness about Althor. Just a moment ago, his hands had been free, but now he held a gold box with rounded edges. Where had that come from? His clothes had no pockets, at least none I could see. Although the box resembled his transcom, it was different than what he had showed me last night. Yet even as I watched, this new box was changing color and becoming less rounded.

"Is that your transcom?" I asked.

He glanced at his hand. "Oh. Yes." The box's panels flickered, red, gold, blue.

"My friend Josh makes gadgets like that," I said. "Radios and stuff."

"I doubt he make a transcom."

"Are you still looking for signals?"

"No. I check my Jag." Althor paused. "I am check my Jag." He squinted at me. "I checking my Jag?"

I smiled. "I am checking my Jag."

His face blanked as if he were a machine. "Yes, that clarifies the syntax. I will set it as the correct grammatical construction. I am checking my Jag."

What the blazes? On those last sentences, his had spoken in perfect English.

His expression returned to normal and he continued in his heavy accent as if nothing had happened. "I don't use English much. It takes a while to reintegrate the programs."

"You mean, on your plane?" That made no sense, but it didn't sound any stranger than anything else he just said.

"My plane?"

"You said you were a pilot."

"It's not an airplane. It is a ship for space."

I couldn't help but laugh. He looked so serious. "Oh, Althor. If you really have a space ship, how is it up there while you're here?"

"I sent it back up."

"How?"

He lifted his transcom. "With this."

"How can that box make a ship take off?"

"The hull acts as an antenna." He spoke casually, as if his words were perfectly normal. "It receives transcom signals on a narrow bandwidth and sends them to the onboard web system."

Oooookay. Though I had to admit, it made sense in a bizarre sort of way. Not that I was any expert on space ship antennas. "And that box is flying your ship right now?"

"No. The Jag flies itself." He glanced around at the street with its potholes and broken manhole covers. "I think it is more safe in orbit than down here."

That seemed unlikely, especially if his ship had no pilot. Not that I really believed he had a ship. "It's not safe up there, either, you know. The military will find it."

He shook his head. "It has a *****."

"A what?"

He paused, thinking. "I believe the word translates as 'shroud.' The shroud, it polarizes a film on the hull of my ship. So the hull, it becomes a surface that reflects nothing. The shroud also projects false readings to fool devices. And its evasion programs monitor space around the ship, making it change course to avoid objects—" He broke off, staring past me, his mouth opening.

I turned to look, wondering what could be even more bizarre than what he had just told me. We had come around the corner into view of San Carlos Boulevard, an ordinary street, though bigger than most, with a lot of traffic, and also stores that lined both sides of the road. Everything looked normal.

"What's wrong?" I asked.

"The *cars*." He motioned at San Carlos as if he had found a pot of gold. "I've never seen so many in good running condition before. This is why the air smells bad, isn't it?"

No kidding. Who would have figured that smog would get him so worked up. "It gets even worse later in the day." I missed the clean mountain air of Nabenchauk.

"Your trees have no ****?" he asked.

"No what?"

He paused, flipping into machine mode and then back to normal. "Filters. Engineered molecules that sift pollutants out of the air and convert them to nontoxic chemicals."

"Well, no." What a great thought. "It sounds like a cool idea, though."

Up ahead, a bus pulled into a stop on San Carlos. My bus. Damn! If I missed it, I would be late to work. I broke into a run, and Althor strode easily at my side. We reached the stop just as the bus was pulling away from the curb. When I banged on the side of the bus, the driver gave us an annoyed glance, then relaxed when he saw me. He halted the bus and even smiled as he opened the door. It was a relief; not all the drivers would let you on after they left the stop. This guy was one of the nice ones, and he often drove this route, so he knew me.

I put my fare in the coin collector, then glanced back. Althor had followed me and was standing there watching with curiosity. If I hadn't known him, though, I would have only seen how he loomed, towering, unsmiling, his bare arms bulging with muscles, the metal on his wrist guards glinting. When the driver glanced at Althor, his smile vanished and his hands tightened on the steering wheel.

I spoke to Althor in a low voice. "Do you have the fare?"

"Fare?" He tilted his head. "What do you mean?"

The driver spoke curtly. "Either he pays up or he leaves."

"It's no problem," I said quickly. I paid for Althor, then took his arm and tugged him down the aisle before the driver could kick him off the bus.

The driver closed the door and pulled into the street. Everyone stared as Althor and I made our way down the crowded aisle. No seats were empty, so we stood near the back, holding onto the overhead bar while the bus bumped down the street. Althor gazed out the window, his fascination with the view making faint arcs of light around us, like translucent gold arrows looping through the bus.

After a while, when he had taken his fill of the sights, he turned to me. "What did you put in that machine at the front?"

"It's called money," I said dryly. "I take it you don't have any."

"Coins? Good gods, no." He didn't seem the least embarrassed by his impoverished state. "That is what those metal disks were? Actual coins?"

I gave him my most unimpressed look, the one I saved for guys who called me "girlie" when I was waiting tables. "Yeah, real honest-to-goodness coins." So okay, he wasn't the dream date. I didn't mind sometimes paying my own way; obviously he wasn't any richer than the rest of us. Even so. I had no intention of always picking up the bill. That didn't seem to fit him, though. Maybe I was naïve, but Althor didn't strike me as the deadbeat type.

We fell silent after that, and Althor went back to gazing at the city as we rolled along the hazy, sunlit streets of Los Angeles.

Potholes cratered the baked asphalt and the bus rattled along, making it difficult to talk. That was fine with me; I didn't want Althor to start in about space ships where people could overhear. He was no longer holding the transcom, though I had no idea where he had stowed the box, given the close fit of his clothes.

I was on time for work, thank goodness; we reached the Blue Knight restaurant at about ten to four. Out in the front, a blue and white striped canopy snapped in a crisp breeze. Robert, the doorman, stood at his post by the main entrance all decked out in his snazzy blue uniform with its gold buttons and ironed trousers. He was doing his best to look snootily aloof, which didn't work so well given that he was such a good-natured guy. The restaurant owners tried to make the place upscale, and they almost succeeded. It was still a bar and grille, nothing compared to the high rent places uptown, but fancier than most around here. I especially liked weekend nights, when a blues trio played in the bar, a piano guy, a dude with one of those huge upright basses, and a drummer who always wore sunglasses. They filled the smoky air with tunes from another era, and time when women wore long, slinky dresses instead of fluffy mini-skirts, and men in zoot suits carried trumpets instead of sub-machine guns.

I waved to Robert, and he waved back with a boyish grin, then remembered himself and straightened up, tugging his uniform jacket into place, doing his futile best to look snobbish. I took Althor around to the back entrance.

We went in the back door. It smelled good inside the building, like fresh soap and old leather from the seats out in the main room. Right away we ran into Brad Steinham, the manager, a big Anglo guy wearing dark slacks and a wrinkled white shirt with the sleeves rolled up to his elbows. He was helping the bartender carry boxes of what looked like cans and jars. They were clearing out one of the back storerooms, moving all the boxes into a different storeroom on the right.

"Hey, Brad," I said.

He glanced up, started to smile, then saw Althor and scowled. "You okay?" he asked me, as abrupt as usual. "You look tired."

"Yeah, I'm fine." I gave him my most reassuring smile. "This is my friend, Althor." To Althor, I said, "This is Brad. He runs the place."

Brad put down the box he was carrying and straightened up, looking over the giant I had brought into his restaurant. Althor nodded to him, sizing up Brad while Brad sized him up. And Brad *was* sizing him up, literally. He might as well have come right out and asked Althor how much he could bench-press.

Glancing at me, Brad motioned at the box he had put on the floor. "We sprung some leaks in two of the storerooms. Have to move everything before it rains tomorrow." He looked at Althor again and Althor looked back.

"You want a job?" Brad asked him. "My bartender has been moving the boxes, but I need him at the bar. You help us clean out the storerooms, I'll pay you five bucks an hour."

Althor blinked at him. "You are requesting that I provide manual labor for a wage?"

I almost groaned. Did he always talk like that?

Fortunately Brad just said, "That's right." He tilted his head at me. "Tina'll be here eight hours. You work that long and I'll pay you forty dollars."

"All right," Althor said. "What do I do?"

Huh. I wouldn't have expected Althor to agree so easily to such a grind of a job.

Brad pointed to the storeroom where we could see the bartender heaving up a box. "Follow him. He'll show you."

Althor went into the room and spoke to the bartender, a

dark-haired guy dressed a blue vest and grey trousers. The bartender nodded toward a stack of boxes, his face red as he struggled to pick up one from his own stack. Althor went where he pointed and easily hefted up two boxes, moving like a well-oiled machine. He carried them over to the other guy with no sign of strain and stood waiting for the bartender to show him where to go.

"Good Lord," Brad muttered. "Where do you find these hulks?" He turned to me. "No way can we finish both those storerooms tonight. If he works out with no problems, I can maybe give him a few more hours tomorrow."

"You're a prince, Brad." I hesitated. "Are you still thinking, too, about hiring Mario fulltime?" It had been a week since the last time I had asked him about Mario.

It was a moment before Brad answered. "I don't know."

"You said he did a good job that night he filled in for your bouncer."

"We'll see."

I couldn't let it go. "He's a hard worker. Really. He'd do right by your restaurant." Mario *needed* a job. He was trying so hard to turn around his life. His expertise was in fixing up old cars. He and my old boyfriend Jake loved working their magic on broken down wrecks; that was what made them such good friends. But none of the garages around here had any openings, a least not for him.

Brad blew out a gust of air. "Tina, he's got a rap sheet a mile long. Possession of a dangerous weapon. Carrying a concealed firearm. Assault with a deadly weapon. Felony battery. Attempted murder, for Christ's sake."

I knew how it looked. Most of the charges had come from a fight that went down between VSC and Nug's gang after my cousin Manuel died. The cops had busted Mario for carrying a Mac-10 machine pistol. They hit him hard for the gun because they couldn't make the attempted murder charge stick. They also wanted Mario and Nug off the street before the fighting went out of control. Both Mario and Nug had served time at Soledad, but no one had gone to jail for Manuel's death. The police never found enough evidence to make an arrest. Except I knew Nug had killed him. We all knew. I hoped Nug rotted in some dark place that made hell look like a party.

"They dropped the worst charges," I said. "Mario's done his time for the rest."

Brad spoke awkwardly. "I'll think about it."

I could guess what *think about it* meant. He wasn't going to offer Mario a job either, just like everyone else had turned down Mario's applications. How was Mario supposed to "rehabilitate" himself when no one would give him a chance? He was smart, strong, and loyal, and he worked hard. Yeah, he was the head of VSC, but that meant he was being a leader. A *good* leader. The other guys looked up to him and a lot of girls wanted him, not only because he was the big man in this part of town, but also because he treated people well and never beat on his woman. All that employers saw when they looked at him, though, was his hardened face, the tats on his arms, his worn-out clothes, and the knife scar on his cheek.

Brad motioned at Althor, who was walking with the bartender to the other storeroom. "How does your friend get his skin to glint like that?"

"I don't know." Right now, I wasn't feeling charitable enough toward Brad to say more.

"And purple hair." Brad shook his head as he walked away. "Sometimes I can't figure what you kids call style."

I watched Althor carry two more boxes out of the storeroom.

"Kid" was hardly accurate. He was a grown man well out of his youth. For once I was glad that when I was tired, I looked older than my age. If Althor knew I was only nineteen, he might change his mind about hanging with me. Not that I had any family left who would come after him. Nug had seen to that when he murdered my last living kin.

At midnight, I found Althor in one of the leaky but now empty storerooms. He and Brad were sitting on the floor with two of the other waitresses, Sami and Delia, the four of them drinking coffee and eating jellyrolls from Winchell's. Brad was actually beaming, wonder of all wonders, and Tami and Delia were flirting with Althor. *My* Althor.

"Hi." I stood awkwardly in the doorway, torn between being uncertain about Althor and wanting to shove Tami and Delia away from him.

"Hey." Brad grinned at me. "Look at this!" He spread his arms, indicating the empty room. "Althor finished *both* storerooms."

"That's great," I said.

Althor remained silent as Tami snuggled up to his side, her long blond hair falling across his arm. He wasn't paying attention to her, but for all I knew, that meant zip. She was older than me and as pretty as one of those girls in Nug's lingerie catalogue. Maybe Althor wanted me to get lost.

Whatever he thought, he just stood up. "Have you finished?" he asked me.

I nodded, trying to act nonchalant. "*Sí, estoy acabada.*" Then, flustered, realizing I'd answered in Spanish instead of English, I added, "I'm done."

Althor barely said good-bye to the others as he left. He didn't say much while we waited at the bus stop, either. Maybe he was irked at me for interrupting their party. Either that, or he was tired. Come to think of it, after clearing out two storerooms in one night, he was probably exhausted.

The bus pulled up and Althor followed my lead. He tried to pay with a twenty dollar bill Brad must have given him, but the bus driver just stared at him. So I pushed the money back at Althor and paid for him myself. After we sat toward the back of the bus, he put his arm over my shoulders and pulled me against his side. I rested my head against him, relieved finally to relax.

"Oh." Althor suddenly sat up. "I forgot." He pulled two bills out from under his belt and gave them to me. "Here."

Startled, I looked at the two twenties he had pushed into my hand. "Why are you giving them to me?"

He settled back in his seat with his arm around me again. "I've no idea what I would do with them."

"You don't know what to do with money?" That was a first.

He spoke drowsily. "In abstract, I suppose. I never carry any."

"I can't take this." I tried to give him back the bills. "It's your pay. You earned it."

"I don't need it. Really."

"How do you support yourself?"

"Salary, family . . ." He yawned as his voice trailed off. "How about you keep them for me?"

I hesitated. "Okay. Just until you need it."

Althor rested his cheek against the top of my head, wrapping his arms around me as if he were a boy going to sleep with his favorite stuffed animal. I almost laughed at the unlikely image. My eyes soon drooped closed, and I drowsed next to him.

I woke up in time to ring for our stop. Althor followed me out the back door, rubbing his eyes. Instead of trying to walk down the narrow steps on the bus, he just jumped over them, down to the street. We headed to my apartment in silence. At first I thought he was bored, that he was walking me home only because he felt obligated. I was so busy feeling self-conscious that it took a while for his mood to register. Finally it soaked into my mind that he felt clumsy too. It was odd; he seemed so confident, uncaring of what people thought of him. Except with me. Why?

As we walked up Miner Street, Althor grunted and massaged the small of his back.

"I can't believe you moved all those boxes in one night," I said. "You must be sore."

"That's what that man Brad said, too." He gave a wry smile. "Ragnar would say the hard work is good for me."

"Who?"

"Ragnar. Admiral Ragnar Bloodmark. A family friend." His face relaxed. "He's been my mentor since I was a small boy. Like a second father."

It was impossible for me to imagine having even one father, let alone two. "You're lucky."

"He could never replace my father. But he means a lot to me."

"Is your father a pilot, too?" Hey, his father could be an inter-stellar king. That would fit with Josh's games. It was harder and harder to believe, though, that Althor was playing a game.

"A pilot?" Althor laughed good-naturedly. "No, he is a bard."

"A singer?"

"That's right. He has a spectacular voice." His mood turned pensive. "My father and Ragnar, they don't have much liking for each other. They are opposites. Ragnar understood when I wanted to be a Jagernaut. He is a military man. My father, all he sees is that I might die."

I spoke softly. "That's because he loves you." I wished I could say the same about my nonexistent father.

Althor brushed his hand over my hair, and I picked up a

lovely sense, as if he wanted to make contact in some way he couldn't define himself, to touch me with a drop of the love his family had given him. I caught his fingers and kissed his knuckles the way he had kissed mine earlier today. As I let his hand go, his pleased surprise shimmered in the air around him.

Although we were silent after that, it was comfortable, neither of us feeling the need to talk. Eventually he started playing with his transcom. Once again, it appeared out of nowhere.

"Where do you put that when you're not using it?" I asked.

"In its slot." He sounded preoccupied.

"Slot?"

This time he didn't respond. As he worked with his transcom, his good mood vanished.

After a few moments, I said, "What's wrong?"

"The Jag," he muttered, intent on his work. "It has problems."

I wanted to ask more, but we had reached the steps of my building. I stopped, uncertain. Maybe *The Jag, it has problems,* was his way of saying, *Okay, I'm out of here.*

"Well." I stood awkwardly. "Thanks for walking me home."

Althor stopped fooling with his transcom and looked up with his full attention. "I should walk you upstairs." He paused. "To make certain you reach your rooms safely."

I wasn't going to make the same mistake I had last night, pretending I wasn't interested. So I spoke, soft and shy. "Okay."

As we entered the building, I flipped the light switch by the door. Nothing happened tonight either, which was no big surprise. We followed the hall and climbed the stairs in the dark, then walked to my room with only moonlight from the window at the end of the corridor to show the way.

I stopped at my door. "This is, uh, it."

Althor glanced around the scorched hall. "You will be safe here?"

"I'll be fine."

"Do your brothers wait inside?"

I hesitated, but then I said. "I don't got no brothers." Wincing, I added, "I mean, I have no brothers."

"Then why last night do you say you do?"

"I didn't trust you."

He touched my cheek, his gaze intent on my face. "And now you do?"

My instincts said yes, my logic said no. I knew I should listen to the logic. But I trusted my intuition. It never let me down. And I was so very tired of coming home by myself to that ugly little room.

I spoke shyly. "I was thinking . . . you might come in."

Althor slid his hand into my hair, his fingers slipping through the long strands. "I would like that."

I couldn't believe I was doing this. I was so nervous, I kept using the wrong keys on the door, but somehow I got it open. The light inside didn't work any better than the one downstairs, and the room stayed dark when I flipped the switch. So I went to the TV table and found the flashlight I always left there, just in case. When I pressed its switch, a circle of light formed around the table.

Althor came inside, shrinking the room with his size, but also chasing away the deepest shadows. Then he locked up the door. The police lock took him the longest, as he figured out how to set the bar in the floor and brace it against the door. I pointed the light in his direction, shining it on the wall when he turned around so the glare wouldn't blind him. It glinted on his skin in faint metallic highlights.

"I don't understand," he said. "Why does this building have no power?"

"It'll come on in a day or two." Kneeling down, I reached

under the table and felt around until I found the stand I had made out of an old birdcage. On the table, I nudged aside the TV and set the wire contraption next to it. Then I stuck the flashlight into the cage so it pointed upward, creating a make-shift lamp that cast a circle of light on the ceiling.

"Two *days*?" Althor was staring at me. "Why so long?"

"Our landlord is a creep," I said, standing up. "He takes forever to fix stuff." I went to the kitchenette and pulled my glass salad bowl off the shelf under the counter. Back at the table, I set the red glass bowl upside down on the stand, over the flashlight. The make-shift lamp shed a dusky rose light over the room. It was pretty, though it left the place too dim to see much. Tonight, it seemed romantic in a poverty-stricken sort way.

Althor came over and peered at my lamp. "That's clever."

I stood next to him, keenly aware of his height. "The lights go out so much I had to do something." I should have been nervous, but his size made me feel safe rather than frightened. But then he stepped even closer, and it was too much. He was different from anyone else I knew; his voice, body, clothes, everything was unfamiliar.

"It doesn't work that well." I was talking too fast. "The light I mean."

"Sometimes the night, it needs a softer light." He folded his hand around a length of my hair—and that's when I saw it. The hinge. A ridge ran from the bottom of his middle finger down the back of his hand to his wrist, forming a hinge that let him fold his palm lengthwise from fingers to wrist.

"What happened to your hand?" I asked.

"Hmm?" His eyes had that glossy look guys got when they were thinking about a girl. "My what?"

"Your hand. It has a hinge."

Althor froze, his warmth disappearing. He withdrew from

me, not visibly except for lowering his hand, but I felt his mood change as if he had turned away and walked across the room.

He spoke coolly. "My hands had a defect. When I was born. This is how they fix it."

I flushed, wanting to kick myself. This was the second time in one day I had put my foot in my mouth, asking him about birth defects. He hadn't cared when I asked about his eyes, but this was another story. His hand *bothered* him.

I had the oddest sensation then, as if Althor reset his mood, like a computer. He relaxed and lifted his hand, showing me how it folded in two from wrist to fingertips. He hinged his palm around my hand and slid his other arm around my waist, drawing me closer as if we were dancing. Then he bent his head and kissed me.

This was happening too fast. I had always been shy, even with boys my own age. I didn't understand why I was acting so different now, except that I liked Althor more than other guys, more than I knew how to say. All I could think was that Althor and I blended the way people should blend. And I was so tired of being lonely. No one would come near me because they were scared of Nug, but Althor seemed like he couldn't care less.

I put my arms around his waist. He felt good, so solid and strong.

Althor nuzzled my hair. "I like your perfume."

"I'm not wearing any."

"It must be you, then." He lifted his head. "Maybe we should sit down."

"Um, okay." I couldn't look at him.

He drew me over to the bed and sat on the edge, his booted feet planted wide apart. I stood awkwardly in front of him, between his knees, holding his hands in mine, staring at the floor.

"Tina," he said softly. "Look at me."

I raised my gaze, and he gave me that amazing smile, the one that lit up his square-jawed face, turning him from granite into sunlight.

"Don't you want to sit?" he asked.

I just nodded, too nervous to answer. I stepped around his legs and sat next to him, trying to figure out how to ask what I had to ask. While I was thinking, Althor nudged me onto my back on the bed and stretched out next to me, sliding his hand up to my waist. His grip was so big and my waist so small that his hand closed more than halfway around it. He went up farther and cupped my breast, along with a handful of ruffles, as if I had said, "Sure, you can touch me there," instead of what I wanted to say, which was, *Slow down.*

"So pretty," he murmured. "Who would have thought I would end up here with you?"

Ask! I thought. *Now.* But how? What wouldn't sound stupid? What did it matter if it sounded stupid? Better stupid than the alternatives. I pushed away his hand.

"Tina?" He lifted his head. "Is something wrong?"

"Do you have a—a thing?"

"A thing?"

"You know. A c-condom." There. I had said it.

His face blanked. Metallic. His mood wasn't a mood anymore; he seemed like a computer. Then he returned to normal. "I can't find 'condom.' What does it mean?"

"It's so I don't get—you know."

"Get what?"

"Sick. You know." Like from HIV.

"I am not sick."

"We shouldn't take chances. Besides, I don't want to get pregnant."

"You can't get pregnant."

"Why not?"

"It's true my ancestors were human," he said. "But they were taken from Earth so long ago, it is unlikely that you and I can interbreed."

I almost laughed. He was certainly original. I didn't know any of my friends whose man had tried *that* line. "Althor, if you don't have any with you, we have to get some. I'm not trying to lead you on, but I won't go no further without it."

"Is maybe possible I could get you pregnant," he admitted. "Not likely. But maybe possible."

"Yeah. Maybe possible."

"This is not something you would like?"

I stared at him. "Althor!"

He squinted at me. "I take it that this mean 'no.' You don't want a baby if I am the father."

"Of course not!" It was hard to believe he was serious. Even odder, he was looking at me as if I had just done the role-reversed equivalent of a guy telling a woman, *I'm going to bed with you because I want to get laid, but no way would I ever consider you good enough for anything more.*

"My mother raised me without a father," I said. "I don't want a child until I know the father will stay with us."

His expression relaxed and things were right again. "I understand. But I have no 'protection.' You have none either?"

"None. Sorry."

He tilted his head toward the television. "Can we order it from your console?"

"My what?"

"Your mesh console. On the table."

"That's a TV. You can't order things from it."

"TV?"

"Wait. I know what we can do. I'll be right back." I scrambled off the bed and hurried to the door, tugging my skirt back into place.

"Tina, wait."

I turned to see him sitting on the edge of the bed, his elbows resting on his knees. "You will come back?" he said.

He thought I might skip out, leaving him alone? That seemed more like what I would think about him rather than the other way around. "I'll be right back. I promise." Then I undid the locks on my door and sped out into the hall before he changed *his* mind and decided I was too much trouble. I had no idea what to make of him; he wasn't acting like any guy I knew.

Bonita and Harry's apartment was on the same floor, three doors down. I knocked, praying Bonita answered instead of her husband.

The door opened just a crack, showing a narrow view of a woman's wary face above the links of a door chain. "Tina?" she asked. "What are you doing up so late?"

"I was wondering if you could help me," I said.

The chain rattled and the door opened, revealing a sleepy Bonita in her white nightgown and a fuzzy pink sweater with pearly buttons. A black braid fell over her shoulder. I didn't know her that well. We said hello when we saw each other in the hall, but given our different work schedules, that wasn't often. She had always seemed to like me, though.

I spoke awkwardly. "It's—uh—I needed to ask . . ."

She took my arm and pulled me inside. "What's the matter, honey? Are you all right?"

I managed a smile. "I'm fine. Really." Awkwardly, I added, "I need sort of a favor."

"A favor?"

"Do you have—I mean, I guess Harry would have them . . ."

"Have what?" She stifled a yawn. "It's late, Tina."

My face heated with a blush. "A condom."

"Oh." She was suddenly wide awake. "Are you sure?"

"Well, it's better than if I don't have one."

"That's not what I meant." She watched me closely. "Is it Jake? Tina, honey, don't let him push you into anything."

"It's not Jake." He had been my first and only boyfriend, and we had broken up months ago. "I'm sorry. I shouldn't have woken you up." I felt more foolish by the minute. I backed toward the door. "You go back to sleep. I won't—"

"Wait." Bonita laid her hand on my arm. "Stay here. I'll be right back."

She disappeared into her bedroom and reappeared a moment later with a box. Putting it in my hands, she folded my fingers around it. "Tina, think before you rush into something." Her expression reminded me of my mother. "Why don't you stay here tonight? You can sleep on the couch."

I shook my head. "Thanks, Nita. But no thanks." I backed out the door. "*Muchas gracias.*" Then I was out in the hall and running back to my apartment. It was a relief when I heard her door close in the hall behind me.

Althor was still sitting on the bed when I came back in and locked up the door. His curiosity tickled my nose like pepper. I sat next to him, too embarrassed to say anything, and showed him the box of race horses. He eased it out of my clenched hand and fooled with the box until he had it open. Pulling out one of the little foil squares, he tilted his head, then turned the packet this way and that, studying it as if he had never seen one before.

"What do we do with this?" he asked.

He wasn't making this easy. "When it's—well, that's the time. You know. With us and all. That's when you do the thing."

He laughed good-naturedly. "I am slow tonight. I have no understanding of what you just say."

My face burned. "I'll show you. When it's time."

"All right." He put the foil back in the box and set it on the floor near the head of the bed. As he turned to me, the tickle of his curiosity faded from my skin. He replaced it with a real tickle, the touch of his finger as he trailed them along my arm. I watched his handsome face, sure I looked like a deer in the headlights.

Althor eased us down until we were lying together on the bed. He held me close while he fumbled with the laces on my uniform. He pulled at the fastenings, pushed the strings, and scraped the holes, but he couldn't get them untied. Finally he gave a frustrated exhale and said, "Does it come with manual explaining how it works?"

I laughed, a shy sound, then pushed my hand between us and undid the laces. When he pulled down my top, the cool air raised goose bumps on my breasts. Then it was warm again, as he hugged me. While he worked on my skirt, I fumbled with his vest, having no more luck unfastening it than he'd had with my uniform. I couldn't find any hooks, snaps, buttons, ties, or anything. My hand just slid over the leather. At least, it looked like leather. It felt too smooth, like nothing I'd ever touched.

Finally Althor rose up on one arm and ran his finger down the front of his vest. It popped open, just like that, simple as you please. I had no idea how he did that, but there it was. Or wasn't. His chest was beautiful, all muscles and smooth planes with a dusting of gold hairs. His nipples glinted even in the dim light, more like metal than the rest of his skin. I touched one, expecting it to be cold, but it wasn't. It felt warm, like real skin.

Althor took his time taking off my outfit, turning the process into a sweet seduction. Except he left on my stockings and garter belt, playing with them as if he had never seen such clothes. To me, they were just the annoying blue lace stockings that came with the uniform. I mean, seriously, who wore those anymore. The way he touched them, though, you'd think he was seeing exotic lingerie in a style that was over two hundred years old.

Watching him undress almost made me forget how nervous I felt. *Mi hombre guapo.* His body was all muscles, wide at the shoulders and narrow at the hips like those Greek gods we had studied in school. When he lay down and pulled me close, I told myself I wasn't nervous. Really. Honestly.

Althor spoke against my ear. "What's wrong?"

"I'm okay." I wrapped my arms around his torso and ran my hands down his spine, from his neck to waist, exploring his muscles, his back, his socket—

His socket?

Whoa. He had a *socket* at the base of his spine. I probed the circle with my fingertips. It was less than half an inch in diameter.

Althor kissed my ear. "That's for a psiphon plug."

I had a sudden image of a gas station attendant siphoning fuel into his body. That was just way too strange. In the midst of my confused thoughts, Althor lay me down on my back, ever so gently, shifted his weight on top of me, and started trying to do his thing.

"Wait!" Flustered, I said, "Althor, wait! The thing."

He held still. "The what?"

"The—the condom."

"This?" He reached down and took a foil packet out of the box on the floor. "You must show me what to do. I have no data stored in my memory for this."

His memory? Good grief. I was making love with a guy who thought he was a computer. I wasn't one to kiss and tell, which was good, because if I ever told my friends about this, none of them would believe me.

When I pushed his shoulders, he hesitated, and confusion sparked around him like fireflies in a dusky night. Then he figured out what I wanted, and he sat up on his heels. I sat up too, self-conscious and embarrassed. I took the packet from him and tore open the foil, then pulled out the little circle of latex.

"Here." I offered it to him. "You put this on."

He squinted at the circle. "On?"

I touched him where he was so obviously glad to see me. "There."

Althor exhaled as if I were torturing him. "I see." His voice turned husky. "You do it."

Ay! I couldn't keep touching him. Could I? Or maybe I could. So I rolled the horse onto him, and it was nice. Sexy. I knew guys had a lot less sweet words for what we were doing than "nice," but that felt right to me. We lay down again, holding each other. Except being with Althor wasn't anything like I had imagined for my first time. In fact, it wouldn't work at first. He knew what he was doing, though. He finally guided himself with his hand—and it *hurt*. But the moment I tensed up, he took it more gently, and after that, things were better.

The sparks created by his mood intensified. In the past, when I had experienced emotions from other people, I was the only one who knew. It just happened; I couldn't control the process. This was different. Althor was *directing* those sparks as if they were part of his seduction.

"Tina." His breath was warm against my ear. "Let me in."

Let him in? Hadn't I already done that? His mood intensified—

Words flashed in my mind like a message. Path established. Upload commenced.

I jerked, stifling a cry. Althor murmured soothing words in a language I didn't understand.

Another message flashed in my mind. Download.

Althor's mood suddenly hit me with so much intensity, I felt as if I were drowning. He moved on my body, sure and steady, his peak swelling like a Baja wave during a storm. Then he groaned and shoved me down into the mattress with his hips, driving out my breath. His orgasm broke over us both like a tidal wave crashing into shore, and the sparks blended into an erotic blur. My mind hazed over, nothing more than sensation, no conscious thought . . .

It was a while before I became aware again of the room. We were lying together in a daze as the sparks winked out one by one, like fireflies leaving the beach after the wave receded. Althor lay on top of me, breathing deeply, his thoughts quiet and sated now, Baja drowsing in the moonlight.

Eventually he said, "Am I too heavy?"

"It's fine, Thor." I felt wound up, an instrument that had been tuned and then not played.

"Thor?" He raised his head and kissed my nose. "No one has said my name that way before."

"Thor was the god of thunder. He had a magic hammer and he threw thunderbolts at the Earth."

"Thunder, eh?" Rolling onto his side, he pulled me into an embrace, fitting my curves into his angles. "I promise not to throw any bolts at you."

I snuggled closer. "You just did."

He laughed sleepily. "So do I become a frog now?"

I smiled. "That's okay. You can stay a prince."

"Ah, Tina, you are so refreshing."

"I am? *Por que?*"

"Most people fawn all over me."

I could see why. Even so, a lot about him still made no sense. I slid my hand around his waist, touching the hole in his spine.

"It's a psiphon socket," he said. "It is how I am installed in the Jag."

"Installed?" That made no sense. You installed parts. Not people.

"The sockets connect to the biomech web in my body," he added.

Sockets, as in plural? "You have more than one?"

"Six. My neck, wrists, back, and ankles."

"But why? What do they do?"

"They link me into the Jag." He spoke as if his bizarre words made perfect sense. "Through the Jag's EI brain, they link me into the Kyle mesh. I can do wireless, too, but a direct connection is more secure."

That was certainly a mouthful, whatever it meant. "Not many people can do that."

"This is why Jag pilots are so few." He yawned. "You know."

"I do?"

"Like you." He closed his eyes. "Like me. So few of us exist . . ."

"I'm not a pilot."

"I meant with the Kyle. Not everyone wants to study . . ."

I still had no idea what he meant by Kyle, but I was pretty sure I wasn't like him when it came to studies. "I'm not in school. But I'm saving for college. I'm going to apply to Cal State."

Althor opened his eyes. "No academy?"

"Well, no." That sounded like a place where rich kids went. "I just work at the restaurant."

"But you have had neurotraining, yes?"

I squinted at him. "Althor, I have no clue what you're talking about."

He stared at me, wide awake now. "Who taught you to control your mind so well? Or to manipulate neural webs the way you did with mine on the street yesterday and here tonight?"

"No one taught me anything."

"You teach *yourself*?"

"Althor, don't." I couldn't bear it if he did the "sexy, dumb Tina" bit. "What, is it such a big surprise I have a brain?"

"Not at all," Althor said. "Many Kyle operators have a high intelligence. It comes from the increased concentration of neural structures in our brains."

"Kyle what?"

"You are a Kyle Affector and Effector."

"Oh. Yeah. How did I forget?"

"Tina, I am not making this up."

What to say? If I asked more and he was playing some game with me, I would look like an idiot. He was just being crazy. He didn't sound crazy, though. He was too outwardly directed, too aware of other people and interested in them. He also had a sense of humor about himself that people who were nuts, or pathological like Nug, didn't show. Besides, his being crazy wouldn't explain the socket in his spine.

"What did that mean, the 'upload' and 'download' thing you said?" I asked.

"That I said?"

"Well, not said. Not exactly." I hesitated. "This sounds silly, I know, but it was like I saw the words in my brain."

"In English?"

"Mayan, actually. Glyphs." It had looked like Tzotzil, my first language. Very few women in the village of in Nabenchauk where I grew up had known Spanish. Learning it hadn't been considered womanly back then. I had been in the US for so long, though, that now I spoke both Spanish and English more often than Mayan. I even often thought in Spanish. But at the deepest level, I was still a woman of the Maya.

Althor just said, "My spinal node must be translating for

you." He rubbed his fingers over the back of my neck. Then he turned over my hand so he could see the inside of my wrist. "How could you receive the signals? You have no bio-mech."

This had gone on long enough. "Althor, I really don't know what you're talking about. It all sounds made up to me."

"Gods." He dropped my wrist. "It's a crime."

"I didn't do nothing wrong. I mean anything. I didn't do anything wrong." Damn! He must think I was an uneducated nobody.

Althor spoke quietly. "I meant it is a crime that you go unnoticed because no one in this absurd place sees what a marvel you are."

I didn't know what I expected him to say, but that wasn't it. "I'm no different from anyone else." If I admitted otherwise, people would think I was a freak. I already spent so much time alone, unable to bear emotional contact with other people, flooded by their moods. I could shut it out sometimes, if I concentrated, but it was hard. Except with Althor.

"Tina, you *are* different," Althor said. "It is not a bad thing. You are an unusually strong Kyle transmitter and receiver."

"I still don't have any clue what that means."

"I am not sure how else to describe it."

I tried to stop feeling defensive. "It's okay. Just tell me the best you can."

He thought for a moment. "People like you and me are called Kyle operators. Or sometimes psions. We have microscopic organs in our brains that most people don't have. Those organs are called the Kyle Afferent Body and Kyle Efferent Body. The KAB and KEB."

"Okay." It still sounded loco, but what the hell. A reason had to exist for why I was different, and I hadn't heard anything better.

"We also have specialized neural structures in our cerebral cortex," he said. "They are called paras. They respond to the neurotransmitter psiamine, which only Kyle operators produce. It's a chemical your brain makes." He touched my temples. "Your KAB picks up electrical signals from the brains of other people and sends them to the paras. They interpret the message into neural signals that your mind understands as thought. Your KEB does the reverse, that is, it sends signals from your brain to the brains of other psions."

"You mean like we're radios?" That actually sort of made sense.

"In a sense. To be exact, you'd say that the quantum distribution of your brain has an unusually strong coupling constant with the distribution created by the brains of other people, especially other Kyle operators."

I squinted at him. "Could you be a little less exact?"

He laughed softly. "Your KAB receives signals. The KEB transmits them."

"What's in the signal?"

"Whatever is in your mind."

"In my mind?" I didn't like that. My thoughts were personal.

"Don't worry." He brushed his fingers over my temple. "We can almost never decode data as complicated as human thought. Perhaps a simple thought, but only if it's unusually intense and sent by another psion. Usually we just pick up moods, and even for those, it's only if those emotions are on the surface of someone's mind. And just to do that much, we have to be close enough to the other person that our brain waves can interact with theirs."

He made it sound so normal. "Sometimes I see what people feel. Like a mist. Or I hear their mood. I might even feel it, not in my mind but on my skin."

He blinked. "This is strange."

I couldn't help but laugh. "Right. And everything you told me was ordinary."

"I meant it's unusual for a psion to associate senses with moods. The neural pathways to the sensory centers of your brain must be tangled up with those to your Kyle centers. So the emotional input you receive triggers sensory responses."

Just like that, he made the strangeness that had haunted my entire life understandable. "How can you know all that about me?"

"You know how," he murmured. "You feel it too. It's your mind. Why do you resist? You are beautiful, like light. You shine, so lovely and bright and—and I don't know the words. I am near you and I feel soothed. Healed. I had not known even that I am injured, yet now I am healed."

Such pretty words. Even if we were both off our rockers, he was kind in his craziness. "You're okay, you know that?"

"Maybe not so much." He gave me a guilty look. "I didn't do much for you, did I?" He slid his hand between my legs. "I can still help. Just tell me what you like."

Ay! I couldn't *talk* about it. I pushed his hand away. "I'm fine. Really."

"You're so tense." Althor peered at his hand. "What is that?"

"What is what?"

He looked up at me. "Is this your time?"

"My time for what?"

"Your menstrual cycle."

Why did he ask so many embarrassing questions? "No."

"Then why do you bleed?"

"I'm *bleeding*?"

"Tina—you have done this before, haven't you?"

"Done what?"

"Been with a man."

So. The Question. "Uh, actually no. But you don't have to worry. I'm nineteen. No one will send the cops after you." I grimaced. "VSC would beat you half dead if they knew, but I won't tell them."

He stared at me. "You are only nineteen?"

This wasn't going so great. "Yes."

"Earth years?"

"Yeah, Earth years."

He flopped onto his back. "I ought to be crack-whipped."

I couldn't help but smile. "I will if you want. But I've never done that either."

He gave me a startled look. "I hope not."

"Althor, with you tonight, that was nice." It was, in fact, one of the nicest things that had happened in a long time. I wasn't ready to tell him that, though.

"Very much," he murmured. His smile faded. "According to my people, you're considered too young to make such a decision."

I was getting annoyed. "I am not a child."

He spoke wryly. "Most of our young people say the same." He touched my cheek. "You do seem more mature."

"Thank you." I hesitated. "Are you going to leave?" As soon as the words came out, I wished I could take them back. They made me sound needy.

"Well, no." He had an odd look, uncertain, even vulnerable. "I'd like to stay—but only if you feel good about it."

"It'd be okay with me." More than okay, but I was trying to play it cool.

After that we lay quiet. I drowsed next to him, listening to his breathing as it deepened into the rhythms of sleep.

3

THE BULLET MAN

After my shower, I stood in front of a window in the apartment and brushed my hair, long strokes from the top of my head all the way to my waist. While I brushed, I gazed outside, between the narrow bars that protected the glass pane. Water splattered out from my hair, cooling my skin and making spots on the glass. The sun had risen high enough that shadows no longer stretched across the vacant lot outside. The smog wasn't bad yet; the day still had a fresh look, new and clear. Mounds of rubble cluttered the lot, including the splintered boards the kids upstairs played with. Beyond the lot, an old Mustang rumbled by on the road. A homely dog dashed along the sidewalk after the car, barking at it with the oblivious joy of an animal that needed no more than sunlight and the freedom to run.

I turned around to look at my bed. Althor lay there, fast asleep on his back, one of his long legs hanging off the mattress with his foot on the floor. The pillow covered his head, leaving only his mouth visible. I laughed, not only because he looked funny but also because it was wonderful to wake up with him here.

I eased the strap of my blouse into place and slid my bracelet around my wrist. I'd change into my waitress uniform at work. Right now, I had on my favorite outfit, worn especially for Althor, including a lacy white blouse with red and pink roses I had embroidered myself, just as I had done for so many dresses during my childhood in Nabenchauk. My skirt was the color of dark pink roses, what my cousin Manuel had called "the color of a giggling white girl's ass after you slapped it." When I'd asked how come he knew that about giggling white girls and why it was all right for him to do things that he would threaten to put me in a convent for if I even thought about, he told me to go do my homework.

The electricity was still off, so I made hot chocolate using the Sterno plate I kept on the kitchen counter. I carried two mugs to the bed, the fragrant chocolate steaming, curling tendrils into the air. It reminded me of the cocoa my mother had made in my childhood, what I would always remember as the aroma of early morning in the Chiapas highlands. I sat on the edge of the bed and set the mugs on the floor. Then I tugged the pillow away from Althor's head.

"Wake up, sleepyhead," I said.

He grunted and pulled the pillow back.

I laughed, pushing it away. "You have to wake up. I have to go. I have an earlier shift today."

He made a muffled noise of protest. This time, though, he did open his eyes, revealing the gold shimmer I remembered from the last time he had woken up, outside my door. I couldn't even see the whites of his eyes.

"Hey," I said. "Your eyes are doing that thing again."

"Hmmm?" As he sat up, the gold retracted, revealing his real eyes. He looked around the room, his forehead furrowed. "It is morning? I didn't realize I had fallen asleep."

"You konked out like a log."

"A konked log?" He peered at the mugs on the floor. "That smells good."

I gave him one. "Why does that gold cover your eyes?"

"It's an inner eyelid. I don't really need it." He swung his other leg off the bed and sat next to me with the blanket pulled over his lower body. "The sun on a planet my ancestors colonized was too bright, so they engineered the extra lid to protect their eyes. For me, it only comes down when I'm asleep. Or if I feel threatened."

Well sure, the planet his ancestors colonized. Then again, maybe it wasn't that much stranger than my mother's tales of our ancestral spirits. Those had always seemed real to me.

"Your English is a lot better this morning," I said.

"It is?" He took a sip of his chocolate.

"Your accent is almost gone."

"I'm not sure why. I guess it took me a while to adapt to this archaic form of the language." He lifted the mug as if toasting me. "This is good."

"Thanks. But hey, my English isn't archaic."

"For me," he said, "we're speaking a form of English nearly two centuries old." More to himself than to me, he added, "My language mods must have better integrated their codes with my other systems while I slept."

"Don't do that," I said.

"Do what?"

"Talk about yourself as if you're a computer."

"I am a computer. Or more accurately, a mesh node."

"Althor!" I had *not* slept with a computer.

He took another swallow of chocolate. "With such an

extensive biomech web, technically I'm not considered *homo sapiens*. Not a man."

I smiled. "You feel like a man to me."

His expression warmed, making me think about last night. Lying back down with him would be so easy, and if I didn't distract myself, I'd never make it to work today. So I picked the least erotic subject I could think of.

"What does biomech web mean?" I asked.

He tilted his head. "You want the whole description?"

"Sure." If it was as unsexy as all that business about Kyle and KABs, it would divert my misbehaving mind from thoughts that would make me late to work.

"I have nodes at the base of my brain stem," he said. "Biothreads network my body and connect those nodes to the sockets in my wrists, ankles, and spine. When I jack into my ship, it sends signals to my nodes through the sockets. Wireless works, too, if I'm close enough. My nodes send the signals they receive to bioelectrodes in my neurons." He had the strangest tone. Or it wasn't strange, and that was what made it odd. He spoke as if what he described was ordinary. "If one of my nodes sends a value of one to an electrode, the electrode fires the neuron connected to it. If the node sends a zero, the neuron doesn't fire. My brain interprets the firing of my neurons as thoughts. So my nodes translate signals from my ship into thoughts I understand. It works in reverse, too, translating my thoughts into code for my ship. Bioshells protect my neurons and neurotrophic chemicals patrol my brain, preventing and repairing damage."

I stared at him for a full five seconds after he finished, wondering what the hell he had just said. Finally I said, "Wow."

He looked a little self-conscious. "You did ask."

"Is that what makes you so strong and fast?"

"Not at all." He took a swallow of his drink. "Bio-hydraulics inside my body enhance my skeleton and muscles. It gives me two to three times the speed and strength of a normal man." He drank more chocolate. "A microfusion reactor powers the system and my metal-alloy skin helps me dump excess heat."

"You have a *nuclear reactor* in your body?" No, I absolutely could not believe that.

"Microfusion." He didn't look the least concerned. "It's only a few kilowatts; my body couldn't take more power."

"Do you pilots ever, uh, blow up?" He could give a whole new meaning to the phrase *Going nuclear.*

"It's almost impossible." He set his empty mug back on the floor. "Too many safeguards."

I could hardly imagine what he described. "That's some story."

"It's true, not a story." He was quiet for a moment. "Sometimes when I go into combat mode, my natural brain does almost nothing. Reflex libraries in my nodes control my actions while my brain 'watches.' It can be unsettling."

"It sounds so strange." Too strange to believe.

Althor smiled at my skeptical tone. And then he *moved.*

He just touched my shoulder. That was all. But he was so fast, his motion blurred. It happened in a fraction of a second, and then his arm was back at his side.

"Hey!" I gaped at him. "Do it again."

Zip! In and out, he touched my shoulder.

"That's so cool!" I said. "Can all of you move that fast?"

Althor grinned, his teeth a flash of white. "Of course. It strains my natural skeleton, though." After a pause, he added, "At least what I have of a natural skeleton." A cloud passed over his mind, dimming his mood. I could see the effect, as if the room darkened. "Anyway, I try not to overuse the enhanced modes. They're mainly for hand-to-hand combat."

"You're a gadget." I let my gaze rove over his beautiful body. "I like gadgets."

He laughed, and the sun came back out. "I'm glad."

"But I don't get it. Why not just put your brain in a machine, one that doesn't mind a reactor with more power?"

He lifted his hands, the palms facing me as if he were fending off the suggestion. "I have no wish to be a brain in a robot." With a grimace, he added, "Besides, can you see me walking into a diplomatic reception at the White House as an armored machine?"

I had to admit, it didn't make for friendliest image. "Won't they wonder why you never showed up at that party?"

"No one knew I had leave from my squad to attend the reception. The permission didn't come through until after the rest of our delegation had left for Earth." He paused, his face pensive. "I never did find out what held it up." Then he added, "Your Allied president gave the reception in honor of my mother's visit to Earth."

Wait a minute. "The what president?"

"Allied." He set his mug on the floor. "The President of the Allied Worlds of Earth."

"There is no Allied Worlds of Earth. This is America."

"Not the one I was expecting." He picked up his wrist guards. They had looked huge and bulky lying on the floor, but in his large hand, they didn't seem as big. "Isn't there a world government here?"

I wasn't sure what he meant. "I guess you could say the United Nations. But they aren't a government, not like in the FSA."

"FSA?" He snapped open one of his wrist guards. "What is that?"

"Federated States of America." I watched with fascination as he fastened his metal-studded guard around his lower arm, clicking a prong on its inner side into the socket in his wrist.

"Federated?" He looked up at me. "You mean the United States, yes?"

"I guess." I was pretty sure it meant almost the same thing, but I'd never heard anyone call them united rather than federated.

He scooped his clothes off the floor and stood up while he pulled on his trousers. The black leather moved with him and molded to his body as if the cloth were figuring out the best fit for him. "Is LAX operating here?" He fastened up his trousers. "I might be able to get more information there."

"You mean the airport? I'm sure it is."

"Airport?" He pulled on his vest. "I meant the Los Angeles Interstellar Spaceport."

"Sorry. No spaceports."

He stopped and stared at me. "Has your Earth colonized Mars yet? The moon?"

"No, afraid not."

Althor slowly sat on the bed. "And this is the twenty-fourth century?"

"Well, no. Today is April 23, 1987."

"According to my ship, it's April 23, 2328."

The overhead lamp suddenly came on and the TV blared out. Jumping to his feet, Althor whipped a knife out of his boot. The blade flashed like lightning, throwing sparks of light everywhere, over the walls, ceiling, floor.

"¡Oiga!" I stood up and grabbed his arm. "It's all right! The electricity just came on."

The instant I touched Althor, he spun around, raising his knife above me in a blur of speed—

He stopped with the knife only inches above my head. I looked up, frozen, afraid to breathe.

Althor lowered his arm. Behind him on the TV, a

weatherwoman was telling us today would be sunny, hot, and hazy.

"I'm sorry." My voice shook. "I didn't mean to startle you."

He regarded me steadily. "Tina, never touch me when I'm in combat mode. That includes any time I move faster than normal."

"Okay." I had heard about soldiers who couldn't turn off their battle reactions. "But you stopped yourself."

His expression softened. "For you, yes. But I can't guarantee I always will in time." He glanced at the TV. "When did you start the picture box?"

"I pushed it last night while I was getting the flashlight." I went over and turned off the sound, leaving the image of the woman talking. "I must have hit the 'on' button."

Althor slid his glittering knife back into his boot. "I need to get back to my ship."

I could guess what that meant. Despite what he had said about honor last night, I doubted he would hang around. I didn't know how much of what he said was true, but he obviously hadn't made up everything. I'd have to be deaf, dumb, and blind not to see he was way out of my league.

And yet . . .

I understood now what my mother had meant when she told me about my father, why she had acted so unlike herself, sleeping with a man she barely knew. She had told me that she and my father were the same, that his spirit was as sweet as maize, brushing across her like the breath of an owl. She called it the *ch'ulel* and *chanul,* his inner soul and its animal spirit companion; Althor used words like neuroscience and quantum wave functions. Regardless of what they called it, the result was the same, that bone-deep connection I felt with Althor.

Except my father had left my mother and never come back.

In Nabenchauk, people lived in large families, including elders, the young, and married couples with children, all together in houses made from logs, saplings, and thatch, built much as my people had built houses for thousands of years, to withstand hurricanes and heat, grief and joy. But my family had shrunk over the generations, bleached of fertility like sun-scoured bones, though none of us understood why. I was the last of our line, the sole survivor of a dying heritage. Most times I managed to push back the loneliness, but after last night I knew it would be so much worse if—or when—Althor left.

"Tina, don't." Althor was watching me as if he hurt inside. "I'll come back." He came over and pulled me into his arms. "I just have to figure out what's going on."

I laid my head against his chest and slid my arms around his waist, seeking his mind. I tried deliberately this time, hoping to find the link we had made so easily last night. His moods came to me as if they were a wind rushing over the parched land-scape of my mind. For all that he seemed stoic on the outside, vivid emotions filled him: worry for his situation, desire for me, memories from a life far more privileged than anything I had ever imagined. He felt so guilty for making love to me, it was tearing him apart. He wanted to protect me, love me, cradle me, and it confused him. I was fine with him being older, but he felt terrible.

Behind all those emotions, his loneliness created hollows, like empty aqueducts in the desert, dry for so long that the arid years had parched and cracked their sides. Many women pursued him, but he rarely responded with more than casual interest. It wasn't because he didn't want more; he longed for companionship in a way he would never let show. But his lovers left him with the same emptiness I had felt with my old boyfriend Jake, as much as he and I had loved each other. Althor wanted someone who could answer the touch of his mind.

Someone like him.

He drew me closer, murmuring in another language. We stood that way, holding each other.

Suddenly Althor's arms went rigid. "That's my ship!"

I pulled back. "What?"

"My *ship*." He was staring over my head at the television.

I turned to look. The picture showed a blurry shot of what looked like an aircraft, though it was impossible to make out details. It seemed way too small to be a jet plane.

Althor strode to the table, then dropped to his knees and poked at the TV knobs until he found the volume control. A newscaster's voice filled the room. ". . . discovered in orbit early this morning. The Anglo-Australian telescope took this picture when observers detected a change in the scheduled operations for the expanded space shuttle *Challenger II*. Instead of following its schedule, the shuttle loaded the craft into its cargo bay and brought it into Yeager Military Flight Test Center in California. An unconfirmed source claims the craft is a small hypersonic drone with orbital capability that malfunctioned and had to be retrieved."

"What the hell?" Althor grabbed his side, at the waist—and pulled out part of his body.

I almost screamed. For an instant, I thought he had ripped out his own flesh. Except the rounded cube he held was solidifying into his transcom. On his right side, just above his hip, a membrane was closing over a large socket in his body.

"Oh, God," I whispered. I didn't know how much more of his strangeness I could take.

He jabbed at the transcom, making lights blink. "I can't reach my Jag."

I stared at him. "Are you saying that plane they found is your ship?"

Althor looked at me. "They must know it's no plane. They'll recognize its extraterrestrial nature." He hit his knee with his fist. "Gods only know what they'll think. A Jag carries enough artillery to wipe out Los Angeles in a second."

He could destroy a city that big? "Why would you bring a ship like that here?"

"I told you. I was going to a party."

This was surreal. "You need a *warship* to cruise a party?"

"It's part of me. I can't just leave it home."

I was having trouble breathing. "I thought you said it was hidden."

"It was." He stood up, towering over my TV. "It must be in worse condition than my tests detected. Otherwise it could easily evade capture. But how could my diagnostics miss damage that serious?" Grimly he added, "Unless it was deliberate sabotage." He clenched his transcom. "The Jag will scare the holy hell out of your military. For all they know, I'm the advance scout of a hostile force."

"You haven't done anything hostile."

"Tina, I left a heavily armed warship spying on your planet." He raked his hand through his hair. "A craft probably as far ahead of military technology here as your military is ahead of natives with bows and arrows. They have no idea what they're dealing with."

"Meaning what?"

"Most likely scenario?" He gaze never wavered. "They tamper too much with the ship and it detonates itself. Given the weapons and antimatter onboard, it would take a good chunk of California in the explosion."

I couldn't believe what he was telling me. "You must be able to do something."

He started pacing in front of the TV. "I'm hoping it disguised itself. The Jag could pass as a planetary shuttle without interstellar capability if your military doesn't know what to look for."

"You could contact the people who took it. Tell them that you and your ship aren't hostile."

His expression softened. "Ah, Tina."

I scowled at him. "What does that mean? Ah, Tina, you are so silly and naïve?"

"Why would they believe me?" He stopped in front of me. "The only way they'll let me near the Jag is if I cooperate with them."

I wasn't exactly sure what "cooperate" meant, but it didn't sound drastic. "Can't you do that?"

His voice tightened. "I would never willingly divulge information to your military. Besides, they still wouldn't let me near the Jag. They have no reason to trust me."

I watched him uneasily. "What do you think they'll do?"

"Move the ship to a more secure installation. Except that might draw unwanted attention." He stood thinking as the TV droned in the background. "If I were them, right now I'd be searching for a mother ship. The longer it takes them to figure out that no one knows I'm here, the better." He started to pace again. "One of my top priorities would be capturing the pilot."

"That doesn't sound good."

Althor went and sat on the bed. Propping his elbows on his knees, he rested his forehead on his hands and closed his eyes. I felt his mind straining. Whatever he was doing, my mind interpreted it as a translucent image, water on the ground pooled around him but growing thinner as it stretched away, until it evaporated into nothing.

I waited.

After several minutes, he looked up at me. "It not work."

"What are you trying to do?"

"I fly this Jag many years." His accent was even heavier now than when we had first met. "My mind reach it, in limited sense, even with no physical link. But the more distance I have from ship, the less it link with my mind. It is too much far away for me to reach."

I could barely understand him. "What happened to your English?"

"My English?"

"You're a lot harder to understand."

His unease shimmered in the air. "I never separate from my ship. My mind, I leave it as subshell on Jag's EI brain."

"It's what brain?"

"EI. Evolving Intelligence. The Jag and I, we are one brain. I am human component. Creativity. Ingenuity. Imagination." A bead of sweat rolled down his temple. "Most times, when I leave the ship, I centralize my codes into my own brain, so my mind no longer runs as a system on the ship." His English was beginning to improve again. "This is what separating from the Jag means."

"But you didn't do it this time." Because he hadn't expected to meet me.

He raked his hand over his hair. "A large part of my mind, it is still in ship."

"But you were fine just a few minutes ago. Your English was great."

"My mind was in a—I am not sure how you say—in a subshell."

"A what?" I felt as if I kept saying that, over and over.

"You know what is supercooled liquid?" Althor asked.

"No," I wanted to shout my frustration. "I don't know 'what is' half of what you say. I'm sorry if I seem slow, but I don't understand."

"You are not slow. Far from it." His accent was fading. "Supercooled means this: If you lower the temperature of a liquid below freezing and it doesn't freeze, it is supercooled. But if you shake the liquid, it will suddenly freeze, all at once. My mind does something like if I am cut off from Jag. I am in subshell. So I think normally. But the shell, it is unstable. One disturbance and it collapse."

"And when you tried to reach your Jag, that made the subshell collapse?"

"Yes."

"You sound better already."

"For now. It is a patch. Only temporary." He exhaled. "I need information about that Yeager Base."

Finally something I could help with. "I'll call in sick today. We can go to the library. Maybe we'll find something."

He had a bleak expression. "I hope so."

The San Carlos branch of the Los Angeles Public Library was in a strip mall between the One Day Cleaners and a bowling alley. As Althor and I walked to the mall from the bus stop, heat rose all around us from the sidewalk. The afternoon sunlight had lost its morning freshness and was too bright, giving it a tense quality, like glass under stress.

It was a relief to open the library door. Cool air wafted over us. The librarian, Joe Martinelli, was dusting the counter where people checked out books. A husky guy with gray hair and glasses, he had looked the same in all the years I had known him, ever since Manuel and I had moved to East LA. The place was otherwise empty today except for an elderly man and woman, both of them relaxing in armchairs at a round table where they were reading the newspaper.

Martinelli glanced up as I walked inside. "Hi, Tina—" He

broke off, his gaze flicking past me, and his welcoming smile vanished like a cigarette stubbed out in an ashtray. The older couple were suddenly putting down their newspapers, taking up their belongings, getting ready to leave.

Puzzled, I followed their gazes. Damn. Althor was looming in the doorway, well over two hundred pounds of solid muscle, dressed from head to foot in black, his bare arms bulging, leather and metal guards on his wrists, his face impassive. He looked ready for a federal lockup.

I spoke to him in a low voice. "Could you try to look less threatening?"

"How?" He was glancing around the library, checking out the place. "This is the way I look."

I had no answer for that. So I just took his hand and brought him over to the counter where Martinelli was watching us.

Martinelli gave me an odd smile. "Got a late shift at the bank today, Tina?"

Huh. Weird. He knew I worked in a restaurant. I didn't understand why he had that strange look, either, as if his face were too stiff for his smile.

Then it hit me. Martinelli was frightened for me. He was trying to give me a way to send him a message if I were in trouble but couldn't talk.

I gave him my most reassuring smile and motioned to Althor. "I'm not working today. My friend is visiting. From, uh, Fresno."

Martinelli nodded coolly to Althor and Althor nodded back, the two of them taking each other's measure. When Martinelli turned back to me, though, he didn't look quite so tense. "What can I do for you?"

"Do you have any books on Yeager Flight Test Center?" I asked.

If he thought that was a strange request, he didn't give any sign. I often asked him for books on subjects that seemed odd to many people, like Maya history. Sometimes he recommended novels for me, books so much better than the stupid textbooks they gave us to read in school because the kids in my English class were supposed to be too slow to understand real literature.

Martinelli always knew what I would enjoy. One of my favorites was Rudolfo Anaya's *Bless Me, Ultima* about a boy guided by his *curandera,* the shaman who acted as his mentor. I loved the language, how he described a way of life so alike and yet so different to what I knew. It took me longer to read the English classics Martinelli gave me, but it was fun and helped me learn new words. Manuel had never understood why I spent so much time reading outside of school, but he figured if it kept me out of trouble, it was okay. I liked *Pride and Prejudice* because Elizabeth and Mister Darcy were so ridiculously polite about pretending they didn't like each other when really, they wanted to hook up so bad, they were dying to do each other. *Romeo and Juliet* was good, too, as long as I had the edition that explained their language. They were talking in poetry, their version of rap. Who would have thought "O Romeo, Romeo, wherefore art thou Romeo?" actually meant, "Romeo, why the hell do you have to be a Montague?" *Lord of the Flies* was grim but made sense, another story about two rival gangs, this time in a turf war on a mostly deserted island.

"I'm not sure what we have about Yeager," Martinelli said. He motioned toward the card catalog. "Take a look there. If you don't find what you need, let me know and I'll see what I can find."

"Great," I said. "Thanks."

Althor and I went to where Martinelli pointed, Althor peering at the card catalogue as if it were some strange beast from a bad horror flick. I didn't see why. It looked ordinary, just a wide file cabinet made from wood, except it had nearly a hundred little drawers instead of a few big ones.

"What is this thing?" he asked as we came up to the catalogue.

"It has the cards you use to look up books," I said.

He bent down to squint at the label on the front of a drawer. "Why cards? Can't you check the mesh for what you want?"

I blinked at him. "The what?"

He straightened up. "You have no mesh?"

"I guess not." I didn't see how a mesh would get him books, but I doubted he meant a fishing net. Maybe his people used computers. Sometimes I dreamt about the future, and my imaginings always had a lot of computers, big machines that took up entire buildings, even cities, huge and flickering with lights. Joshua said he thought computers would be little in the future, not big, but that didn't make for daydreams anywhere near as impressive as the monster machines.

I pulled out a drawer toward the end of the catalog, one with the letter Y on the front, and carried it to a nearby table. As I sat down, Althor pulled over a chair and sat down to watch while I flipped through the cards in the drawer, looking for titles with "Yeager" in them.

"Why does that man behind the counter dislike me?" Althor asked.

"He thinks you're one of Nug's friends." I took a piece of paper from a pile on the table and wrote down the numbers for some books. "They come in here and bother him."

"Nug? What is that?"

"Not what. Who. Matt Kugelmann. You met him the night before last." I stopped flipping cards and sat staring at the table. "He killed my cousin Manuel."

Althor spoke gently. "I am sorry."

Every time I thought I was over Manuel's death it turned out I was wrong. I missed him so much, it felt like someone had cut away a part of me. Sure, he had been strict with me: no swearing, no late nights, no alcohol, no cigarettes, no drugs, no running with anyone he didn't like. Nor had he been much on talks about life. But I had heard the words he didn't speak in the way he treated me, words like respect, honor, loyalty. Love. That was before the crack had silenced him. It had been his way of dealing with my mother's death, but it had taken him from me too.

"Tina?" Althor asked.

I looked up at him. "It's okay."

"You say this a lot." His gaze never wavered. "It's okay you live in a building unfit for animals, it's okay this man murdered your cousin. It is not okay. You deserve better. A lot better."

"I'm just trying to get by."

"Where are your parents?"

I felt like a wire pulled too tight. "I do fine on my own."

"Tina—"

"You're lucky to have a father," I spoke too fast, needing a new topic, anything that didn't bring all that pain.

Althor seemed ready to say a lot more on the subject of my crappy life, but he let it go. Instead he spoke wryly. "My father and I, always we argued. Ragnar understood me better."

Ragnar. I remembered the name. "That's the admiral who encouraged you to join the military, yes? Even though your father didn't want you to."

"It was my choice to join." He tried to shrug with nonchalance, but it didn't fool me. "My father isn't always rational about Ragnar."

"What does your father do?"

"Lose his temper." Althor shifted in his chair. "Once, when

I was a boy, Ragnar came to see me. He is my doctor, after all. And he and my mother are friends. They have known each other for decades. My father, when he saw Ragnar talking to my mother, he exploded. Most times my father is a calm man, but with Ragnar, he becomes irrational."

Well, maybe. But it sounded to me like coveting thy neighbor's wife wasn't unique to us Earthbound humans. Then again, it could be completely different from how it sounded.

"Anyway," Althor said. "I went into the military because I wanted to become a pilot."

I spoke carefully. "I need to ask you something."

He watched me curiously. "Go ahead."

"Don't soldiers kill people?"

His good mood faded. "Yes."

"Have you?"

He spoke quietly. "Yes."

I shifted in my chair. "How many?"

"I don't know."

I didn't want to hear this, not at all, but I couldn't stop. "Is that because you were in your ship so you couldn't see or because you killed so many you lost count?"

He met my gaze. "Both."

"*Both?*"

"Tina, people die in wars." The air around him seemed to mute his words, as if he were speaking through pain that he couldn't express. "Our enemies killed one of my uncles, the man my parents named me for. Althor Valdoria was a military hero. My father's brother. I think part of the reason I went into the military was because I wanted to avenge my uncle."

I thought of my cousin Manuel. "Revenge is no good. They kill, you kill, they kill, you kill. It never ends."

"That wasn't my only reason for joining the military. I feel—"

He stopped, as if searching for the right word. "Obligated. To protect my people."

That reminded me of Manuel. Honor and family had mattered to him. Country, too. If we had been legal, he would have enlisted in the Marines.

"I understand," I said.

Althor's voice gentled. "Last night was the first time I felt relaxed in so long. With you." He took my hand. "I felt at peace."

"With me? Why?"

"I don't know." He grinned, his teeth flashing white. "After all, you want to turn me into a frog."

I laughed, relieved to leave the shadows of our pasts. "You'd make a handsome frog."

He spoke dryly. "A frog who needs his ship."

"We'll find it." I indicated the catalogue cards. "It looks like most of these books are in the same place." Pointing out the shelves a couple of rows from where we were sitting, I added, "Why don't you go look while I keep going through the cards?" I wrote down a few more call numbers and handed him the paper. "Try these."

"Cards," Althor grumbled. "Paper books. Shelves. It's barbaric."

"You have a better idea?"

"Go home. Relax. Have the mesh look up book and deliver a microspool to your lounger. Plug in spool. Choose font, graphics, holography. Or have book read itself to you. You are done, life is good." He continued to grouse in his own language, but he took the paper and went to the stacks.

I smiled, then bent over the catalog drawer again.

Someone spoke next to me. "Hey, Tina. You got a new boyfriend?"

I looked up with a start. Nug was standing there, wearing his ragged old jeans and a faded jacket. String and Buzzer were with him, two guys who looked like their names: String was tall and skinny, and Buzzer looked like a stocky old buzzard.

"That's right," I said. "He's coming right back."

Nug's smile oozed across his face. "New guy, looks like."

I didn't like it when Nug smiled. "From Fresno."

"Fresno?" Nug laughed. "Shit. That's worse than coming from Cleveland."

"What do you want?" I asked.

"Talk nice to me, sweetheart." Nug stepped closer. When I tried to scoot my chair away from him, he caught my arm. "What's the matter?" He wasn't smiling now. "You can't take that pretty nose of yours out of the air for two fucking seconds?"

Martinelli spoke from behind the counter. "Leave her alone, Matt."

Nug glanced up, his lips twisting in a scowl. He did let go of my arm, but then he put his hand inside his jacket—and pulled out a 9-mm Luger.

Martinelli froze. So did I. Nug looked ready to tear holes in the sky, as if he had been winding up since his fight with Althor. He stretched his arm straight out, pointing the gun at Martinelli. "Shut up, old man."

No. *No.* I should have known something was wrong, with Nug wearing a jacket when it was so hot. I rose to my feet. "Don't hurt him. Nug, please."

Nug ignored me and glanced at String. "Make sure he doesn't bother us."

"Yeah." String strode to the counter and hauled himself over the barrier while Martinelli backed away from him. When String drew his knife and tilted his head toward the back wall, Martinelli retreated and String followed him.

Nug turned back to me. "Well." He smiled again and it

didn't look any better now than it had the first time. "So you got a new boyfriend."

I wanted to run, but he and Buzzer were blocking me. "He doesn't like me talking to other guys."

"That so." Nug stepped closer. "What does he like?"

I stepped back from him, hitting the table behind me. "Don't."

"Don't," he mimicked in a falsetto. He shoved the gun into the pocket of his jacket, then grabbed me by the upper arms and shook me. "This what he wants, *chiquitita*?"

"Stop it!" I lurched away from him and thudded into Buzzer, my back against his front. He put his arm around my waist and held me in place.

"Sweet Tina." Nug sounded as if he was gritting his teeth. "We can't have her, can we? She's too fucking pure." Sarcasm edged his voice like a blade. "You think I don't know, don't you?"

I stared at him. "Know what?"

"You never gave me the time." His anger cut around him like black and red streaks. "But I gave you slack. I thought, 'She's different. Special. You got to try harder.' Well, I tried, and you didn't even look at me, like you thought you was too good. Even then I gave you slack. Thought maybe that cousin of yours had told you shit about me. I gave you more slack than I've ever given anyone." He stabbed his finger at my face. "I seen you this morning, slut. I seen you come out of your building with that guy. He there all night, Tina? You fuck him all night?"

"Nug, don't," I said.

"What's wrong?" Nug said. "I got everything he has. Better, I'm sure."

What had they done to Althor? Nug must have sent his men to take care of him. When they were done with him, he would be finished period. Sure, Althor could fight off Nug, but against three or four of them, he didn't have a chance. And Nug wasn't stupid. Even though we were in a library with big windows, Buzzer's body hid me from view. Anyone outside would see nothing more than what looked like two guys talking.

Nug glanced toward the counter where String had gone after Martinelli. I couldn't turn around to look with Buzzer holding me in place, but I heard a thud, the sound of metal hitting muscle, followed by a grunt and the bigger thud of a body hitting the ground.

"Come on," Nug said. "We're outta here."

"No." I tried to pull away from Buzzer.

"Shut up," Nug said.

He and Buzzer dragged me to a side door while I struggled to pull away. It happened so fast, I barely had a chance to breathe, but I kept fighting them anyway. String jogged up to join us, his knife still drawn. When he snapped the blade against my hair, cutting off a few strands less than an inch from my cheek, I stopped hitting Nug. I hadn't planned on dying today.

We came out into an alley between the library and the cleaners. No windows showed the walls on either side, no place where someone might look out and see I needed help. Another of Nug's guys was posted out there, a skinny guy named Pits.

"Get the damn car," Nug yelled at him. "I told you!"

Pits blanched and took off, running toward the parking lot in back of the library. If they took me in their car, that was the end. I'd never get away. Half panicked, knowing they might kill both Althor and me, I jerked up my foot and stabbed my spike heel into Buzzer's leg. As he yelled, his hold loosened and I twisted out of his arms. I ran for the street in front of the library. If only I could get out of the alley. San Carlos was a busy street. If I made it that far, someone *had* to see me. I could run into the road even, make a car stop.

Another of Nug's men stepped out at the end of the alley, blocking the way, a huge guy with black hair.

With a cry, I skidded to a stop in front of him. Footsteps sounded behind me, and I spun around to see Nug right behind us. Buzzer came up on his left and String on his right, their chests heaving as they gulped in air.

"I'm getting real tired of this shit," Nug told me.

"No!" I said. "People will see—"

"Shut up, bitch." He grabbed my arm and threw me into Buzzer. I tried to scream, but Buzzer clamped his hand over my mouth. An engine rumbled as a turned into the alley from the back lot, an old Buick with Pits driving. He came up the alley and stopped a few feet away.

Nug stepped closer to me. "We're going to my place, baby. For a party. All of us." He looked around, then scowled at the big guy with dark hair. "Where are the others? Go find them."

As the guy took off, Buzzer dragged me to the car and opened the back door. He pushed me down on the seat inside, on my back, pressing one hand over my mouth while I fought. The other door opened behind me, bringing the greasy auto shop smell Nug carried around with him. I could just see him hovering above my head.

String opened the front door and tossed Nug a rope. "That's all we got."

Nug caught the rope. "It'll do." Leaning over me, he grabbed my wrists and pulled off my bracelet.

No! I struggled to yank away my hands. My mother had given me that bracelet, and her mother to her, and on back for more generations than anyone in our family knew. It could never be replaced.

Buzzer motioned at the bracelet. "Think it's worth anything?"

Nug watched me struggle. "She thinks it is. Maybe we can

hock it." He laughed, shaking the bracelet. "Hey, it's a prize. Whoever does her the longest gets it."

I yelled *Stop it!* and all that came out was a muffled grunt. Nug dropped the bracelet on the floor, but when they tried to flip me over, I jerked up my knees and jammed them into Buzzer's crotch.

"*Fuck!*" Buzzer jumped back, hitting his head on the top of the car, bent over in pain.

A blur whipped past my field of view so fast, I didn't realize it was a man kicking his leg until the heel of his boot smashed into Buzzer's chest and threw him away from the car. Then a blurred figure crashed into Buzzer and both men spun out of sight faster than I could follow. Behind me, Nug swore as he jumped out of the car. As soon as he moved away, I scrambled out, just in time to see Althor and Buzzer slam into the wall of the cleaner's store. String ran up behind them, his switchblade drawn, but before he could do anything, Althor whirled around, swinging Buzzer with him.

It all happened so *fast*. Althor kicked his leg with a deadly grace and unnatural speed, hitting String's wrist. The knife spun out of String's hand in the same instant that Althor drove his heel into String's chest. As String flew backward, crashing into the hood of the car, Althor threw Buzzer after him. Buzzer slammed into String and both men crumpled to the asphalt like rag dolls. They were still alive; I could see them breathing. But neither moved.

Somewhere, far away but coming closer, sirens wailed.

An explosion suddenly cracked, and Althor lurched back into the wall of the cleaners as if someone had shoved him in the torso. Nug stood facing him across the hood of the car, his Luger clenched in both hands, out and aimed at Althor. The first shot had hit Althor in the waist, just above the hip, his bullet going between the edges where Althor's vest met the waistband of his trousers.

Nug fired again, point blank, his face hard and cold. Incredibly, his shot missed—because as he pulled the trigger, sparks of light flashed across his face, making him squeeze shut his eyes. It took me an instant to realize Althor had drawn his knife even as he dodged with that eerily blurred speed. In the dim light of my apartment, his blade had glinted; out here, it dazzled, fracturing the sunlight into a blinding display of light and colors like a prism on steroids.

Althor snapped his wrist and his knife streaked through the air. Nug was already moving, so the blade missed his heart, but it stabbed him in the arm. He shouted and dropped his gun, his face contorting with rage. Althor was already running around the car, straight at him. If he even felt his own gunshot wound, he gave no clue. He slammed Nug against the hood of the car, but Nug was smarter than his men. Instead of trying to overcome Althor's strength and speed, he grabbed Althor's vest and used his weight against him, turning Althor's momentum into a throw that hurled Althor onto the hood. Althor rolled across the car and came down in front of its grill, landing on his feet.

The sound of the police sirens was closer, the wail going up and down, changing to a faster beat, then back to a drawn-out cry. Althor and Nug ignored everything else as they grappled with each other, both moving so fast, it was impossible to see who had Althor's knife. The blade flashed around their bodies, stabbing in glitters of light.

The sirens swelled as police cars pulled into the plaza in front of the library. Pits was still in his Buick, trying to back away from Althor and Nug. He smashed the car into the wall of the library and I could see his mouth open as he yelled *Fuck this* inside the car. He jerked open the door jumped out, then took off in a sprint, headed toward the back of the library as fast as fire on oil. I wasn't sure if he was running from the cops or from Althor.

Suddenly Althor stopped moving—and Nug collapsed to the ground. I stared in disbelief at the crumpled heap of the man I had believed was an unstoppable evil, the devil who had terrorized my life for years, killed the only family I had left in the world, and who had tried today to make his destruction of my life complete.

Nug wasn't breathing.

"Drop the knife," a voice commanded, like honed steel cutting the air.

I looked up slowly, as if the world had turned to molasses. A cop was standing at the end of the alley, his gun out and aimed. Althor just stared at him. He stood over Nug's body, his boots on either side of Nug's hips, the knife in his hand. Blood dripped off its diamond-bright edge and splattered on Nug's closed eyelids.

"Drop it," the officer repeated. "*Now.*"

Althor just kept staring at him. The cop visibly tensed, his gaze hardening even more. The sun beat down on the tableau they formed, dominated by the giant form of a man with an iron-cold face standing over what I knew, without doubt, was Nug's dead body. Althor didn't move, and for a terrible instant I knew he was about to die, shot by the police instead of Nug's gang because Althor couldn't switch off whatever had turned him into a killing machine.

Then Althor let go of his knife. It hit the asphalt with a clatter that sounded bizarrely loud in the silence of the alleyway. Even the rumble of traffic out on San Carlos seemed muted here.

Footsteps sounded behind me. I spun around, afraid Pits had returned with the rest of Nug's gang. But it was a second officer coming up the alley. The door of the library opened, revealing

Martinelli with a third cop, a policewoman. Martinelli's clothes were a mess, wrinkled and torn, and an ugly bruise showed on his forehead, purpling in the center and red with blood. Another siren was wailing somewhere distant, faint but rapidly growing louder.

The woman came over to me. "Are you all right?"

Somehow I managed to say, "I'm fine," even though it wasn't true. I wasn't fine. I wouldn't be fine for a long, long time. Althor was going to prison, and all the dreams he had spurred in my mind, all those thoughts about loyalty and honor—they were crushed under the reality of what had just happened.

"It was self-defense," I told the lady cop. "Althor was protecting me. Nug attacked us. He tried to kill Althor. To take me away. He was going to—to—" My voice cracked.

"You can give your statement at the station." She tilted her head toward Martinelli. "It's best if you go back inside with him. You'll be safer inside." Then she headed toward the other cops.

I couldn't leave Althor out here alone. I went back into the car and grabbed my bracelet off the floor, then backed out.

As I straightened up, one of the policemen told Althor, "Stand up against the wall." All three cops were watching Althor. He stared back at them, his head turning from one to the other like a well-oiled machine.

"Move it," the first cop said.

It scared me, the way the police looked, as if they believed they would have to shoot. I didn't know how to warn Althor, what to do, if it was even possible for him to turn off whatever had changed him during the fight. He was watching the police as if they were new enemies to be neutralized. The tension stretched out tighter and deadlier—

Althor! I thought, desperate. *You have to do what they say!* I made a vivid image in my mind of him facing the wall, ready to be searched.

I didn't know what I expected, but his reaction was immediate. He shot me a startled look as if I had yelled in his ear instead of in my own head.

A thought brushed my mind, cold and impersonal: Combat mode toggled off.

Althor's face changed, still impassive, but like a man now instead of an inhuman machine. He backed up slowly, facing the cops, until he hit the wall of the library.

"Turn around," the first man ordered.

Althor turned and put his palms against the wall the way I had shown him in my mental image. The police wasted no time. One went over and picked up Althor's knife, squinting as it flashed in his eyes. The second strode over to Althor and pulled Althor's arms behind his back, pushing up his wrist guards. A loud click broke the silence as he handcuffed Althor's wrists. None of the cops seemed to realize Althor was injured. His vest hid the wound where Nug had shot him and he didn't even flinch when the cop searched him. In fact, he gave no sign that he felt anything at all. The blood on his clothes could easily have come from Nug, who was covered in it, and the dark color of Althor's vest made it impossible for me to tell if he was also bleeding.

I took a step forward, intending to tell the cops he was injured, but the instant I moved, Althor turned his head and looked straight at me.

Tina, no. His thought came into my mind. Stay back.

The sound of his "voice" stopped me cold. *Madre de Dios,* he really could speak in my mind. That had been him this time, Althor the man, not the metallic thought of a computer.

The siren that had been distant was growing louder. It

swelled into an ear-splintering wail as an ambulance pulled into the alley. Two people jumped out of it, one of them striding to where Nug, String, and Buzzer lay on the ground and the other running into the library. God only knew what Althor had done to the guys who jumped him in there.

The officer who had searched Althor never took his attention away from his prisoner, even with paramedics hurrying around them. He spoke to Althor in a cold voice. "Walk out front. No fast moves."

Althor turned and met the man's hard stare with his own. But he did what the cop told him and walked toward the end of the alley, his hands cuffed behind his back. The cop kept pace with him.

The second policeman spoke to me in a kinder voice. "You'd best come with us, Miss." The tag on his uniform glinted in the sunlight. Officer Stevens. He had a name. It made him more human, despite his impassive face and his blue-black revolver. But nothing would fix any of this. I felt queasy. We were in trouble, deep trouble, and I had no idea what to do.

We walked in silence, with Stevens at my side and Althor and the other cop a few steps ahead of us. The traffic on San Carlos sounded far away, as if we were all trapped in a bubble, waiting for it to explode. We came out into the plaza in front of the library, where two police cars waited. As we headed toward the closest car, Stevens pulled out his keys—.

And Althor whirled around, kicked his leg at Stevens, moving in a swirl of motion. In the same instant, he threw his body at the other cop so that he was stretched out in two directions as if he were doing a street dance, but fast faster than anything possible. The gold shield had come down over his eyes, making him look inhuman.

The bark of Stevens' gun cracked like an explosion even as

Althor's boot heel rammed into his chest. Stevens flew backward, knocking me over as he crashed to the ground. I fell to my knees and caught myself with my palms flat on the asphalt. At the same time, Althor slammed into Stevens' partner. The other man lost his balance and crashed against the car, his head thunking its roof when he collapsed down the vehicle and hit the ground. It all happened in seconds.

"Tina!" Althor's word came out in a rasp. "Get in the car." With a grunt, he half fell, half dropped to one knee.

I scrambled to my feet, staring in disbelief at the officers. They lay still, breathing but unmoving. In barely two seconds, Althor had knocked both of them out.

I ran toward Althor. No! Steven's gunshot had hit him and blood was pumping out of his shoulder. Something looked wrong about the blood, but I couldn't see it well enough against the black vest. With his hands still locked behind his back, Althor scrabbled for the gun one of the policemen had dropped. He closed his hand around its handgrip and then lurched back to his feet. As he moved, he pulled his cuffed wrists around his body, straining to hold the gun at his side.

"Can you drive this vehicle?" he asked me.

"Steal a cop car?" Everything was out of control. "Are you nuts? Althor, you need a doctor."

A woman shouted from the alley. "You don't need to take her."

I spun around. The policewoman stood half-hidden at the corner of the library by the alley. She had her gun up and trained on Althor. Another cop was behind the front door of the library, mostly hidden, but I saw the glint of his revolver. Neither of them fired, probably because I was so close to Althor, they could easily hit me instead.

"Let her go now and you won't make this any worse," the woman said. "If you take her, you'll have a lot more trouble."

Althor stared at the policewoman, holding the gun he had taken at his waist aimed at her. I didn't think most people could shoot from that position, but I had no doubt Althor could manage with deadly accuracy.

"Tina, hurry," he said in a low voice. "We have to go. And get my knife."

What to do? I had to make a choice. If I did what he wanted, nothing would ever be the same. I'd be in trouble, on the run, my dreams of school ruined. If I didn't help, he would be tried for murder. He said a lot of crazy things, but this much I knew: he had protected me from Nug, probably even saved my life, and he had almost lost his own life because of that. He was one of my clan now, and we looked after our own.

I scooped up Althor's knife and Stevens' keys, then yanked open the passenger's door of the car. As I slid inside, to the driver's side, Althor hauled himself after me and slammed the door with his hands still cuffed behind his back. I dumped the knife in his lap, then shoved the keys in the lock and started the car. I had no plan except to stop the other police from following us. I shoved the transmission into drive and jammed the accelerator to the floor. The car careened across the asphalt, its tires screeching in protest—and plowed into the other police car with a shriek of crumpling metal.

The crash threw me against the steering wheel, and Althor grunted, slouched in the passenger's seat. I shoved the stick into reverse and backed up *fast*, tires screaming, and then we were off, tearing into the street. I was scared shitless, but I kept going, because I didn't know what else to do. In the rear view mirror, I saw cops running after us, their mouths open in shouts.

At the next intersection, I swerved into a side street, taking us out of view of the library. As we sped away, I glanced at

Althor. Up close, I could see him better. He was bleeding bad, both from the bullet wound in his shoulder and the one that had hit him at his waist.

"We have to get you to a hospital," I said. I didn't even have anything to use as a bandage.

"No."

"Althor, you need help!"

"They will see I am not human." His voice scraped like sandpaper. "Tina, if they catch us, you go with them. Stay safe. Tell them I force you to come."

"No."

"Tina—"

"*No!*" I felt as if I were on a too fast ride at a carnival, but I wouldn't desert Althor. I owed him. Even if Nug and his men hadn't killed me after they were done, I wouldn't have felt like living. And that wasn't the only reason. I had something with Althor. It reached deep into me, into a place like the sand dunes of a desert sculpted by memories of my mother and Manuel, an arid landscape that had known only loneliness for too long.

I drove past the back lots of the neighborhood, past torn fences, abandoned buildings, and a derelict playground. The streets baked under the Southern California sun. At the end of a lane lined by weed-covered lots, I swerved into a boarded up gas station. Behind its main building, out of sight of the street, I pulled into a parking space where the white lines were mostly worn off the cracked asphalt. That put us at the top of a grassy slope that rolled down to the freeway several hundred yards below the gas station.

"Where. . . ?" Althor coughed, his words ending in a rasp.

"We have to get out of this car," I said. "It's too easy to spot."

He held up his hand with the bloodied knife clenched in his fist. "Put back. In—my boot."

I didn't want to touch the knife that had killed Nug, but

Althor could barely move. I had to pry it out of his fist. As I slid the blade into its sheath inside his boot, blood ran over my hand. Straightening up, I stared at my fingers. What the hell?

"What's wrong with your blood?" I asked.

He grimaced, his face contorting. "It is coming out of me."

"Althor, the color isn't right. It's practically purple."

"Is fine."

"Is *not* fine." I looked around for something to use as a bandage, but we had nothing. The back seat was separated from the front by the usual screen. I wished now I had on my waitress uniform; I could have torn off a layer of the skirt. It wouldn't be enough to stop the bleeding, but it would help.

I turned back and grabbed the wheel, smearing red-purple blood across its surface. "I'm taking you to the emergency room."

"No. I am fine."

I started the car. "It's better they arrest you than you die."

"Tina, stop!"

I kept going. As I put the car into drive, words flashed in my mind: Prepare to download.

And the flood hit.

Althor dumped what he wanted me to know straight into my brain, and all that data struck my mind like water blasting from a fire hose. He had a blood disorder similar to sickle-cell anemia. It came from a genetic mutation in his hemoglobin, the molecule that carried oxygen in the blood. Each of his hemoglobin molecules had two incorrect amino acid residues that distorted it into the wrong shape, like mismatched pieces in a jigsaw puzzle. Forcing the pieces together deformed the blood cells. His spleen took the bad cells out of his blood like the cops taking bad money out of circulation, leaving him with terrible anemia.

My brain soaked up the data so fast, my head felt like it would burst. I couldn't see, couldn't move. To fix the problem, his doctors had extracted something from his bone marrow. *Erythropoietic stem cells.* They inserted a corrected gene into those stem cells and put the cells back inside of him. The altered cells prodded his body to make the right amino acids. But his doctors couldn't fix all of his bad genes, because some did more than affect his hemoglobin—they also affected his ability to sense moods. If the doctors fixed his genes completely, it would take away what made him an empath.

Empath. *Empath.* That's what we were called. I suddenly had a word for a condition I had lived with my entire life, convinced something was wrong with me. Althor's people considered it a gift. To preserve his empathic ability, his doctors injected him with molecules that were like tiny laboratories. *Nanomeds.* The meds were controlled by pico-computers that ran on quantum transitions. They locked onto Althor's hemoglobin and finished pushing the molecules into the right shape. The process had a side effect: when exposed to ultraviolet radiation and nitrogen gas, the meds turned blue. Inside his body, they stayed colorless, but in sunlight and air, they converted, giving his blood a purple tinge. With all that going on inside of him, it would be obvious to anyone who knew anything about blood that he wasn't human.

"Okay!" My mind was reeling from the deluge. "I won't take you to the hospital. But don't do that again, Althor! You'll tear apart my mind."

"Sorry." His voice rattled. "No . . . time to explain."

I clenched the wheel. "Your blood is all over this car. If anyone analyzes it, they'll know you aren't like us."

"What you—suggest we do?"

That shook me. Really shook me. Althor had seemed

invincible. He had defeated Nug and his gang with terrifying ease. Cracks were showing in his armor now, and whatever his body had been doing to mute his pain, it wasn't working anymore. The agony saturated his mind. He needed help, serious help, far more than I knew how to give.

I shoved open the door and ran around to his side. He was already opening his own door. As he dragged out his legs, using both his hands, he rasped, "Bring gun."

I stared past him to where Steven's gun lay on the passenger's seat. "I can't do that."

He rose to his feet outside the car, gripping the top of the door to stay upright. "Bring it."

"I hate guns. They killed my cousin and they almost killed you. I won't bring it."

"We need defense."

"I'll get us protection."

"Tina—"

"No." I didn't want him to die, shot by the cops or someone else because he pulled a gun on them. It didn't matter how fast he could move; he was too badly injured to use that speed now. If he drew on anyone, they would shoot him the moment they saw the weapon.

"Trust me," I said. "Please. No gun."

I felt his reaction. He was in trouble, losing strength fast, and he had no leeway to take chances, not if he wanted to survive. And yet, incredibly, he would trust me. I wasn't the only one sensing moods, and whatever Althor was picking up from me, it convinced him that I would keep my word.

I slid my arm around his waist, behind his handcuffed wrists. When he leaned on me, I almost fell over; he was more than a foot taller and twice my weight.

I nodded toward the freeway. "We're going down there."

"Why?"

"I'll show you."

I helped him down the grassy slope that separated us from the freeway. We stumbled together, Althor lurching and my heels sinking into the sod on every step. The smell of new grass rose around us. It was only a few hundred yards, but it felt like miles. Mercifully, we finally reached the tunnel for pedestrians that ran under the rumbling freeway. It was dark inside, with names spray-painted on the walls. No more fresh, healthy scent; in here it smelled like concrete that had baked in the hot sun too long, with hints of smoke, piss, and dust.

I took Althor halfway through the tunnel, far enough from both ends so that no one could see us. Then I said, "If you turn around, I'll get those cuffs off you."

He nodded, silent as he sagged against the wall, half-turned with his back to me. I tried out Stevens' keys on the handcuffs until I found one that worked. A quick turn of the key snapped open the cuffs. They fell off Althor's wrists and dropped to the ground with a clank.

"Good," Althor whispered. He clamped his hand over the wound in his left shoulder as if that could stop the blood from pumping out.

Please, God, I thought. *Don't let him die.* I dropped Stevens' keys on the ground by the cuffs and then put my arm back around Althor's waist to help support him. "I know a place we can go."

He didn't answer, he just draped his good arm over my shoulders. So we went the rest of the way through the tunnel, Althor limping along the cracked pavement. I didn't know how he stayed on his feet; anyone else I knew would have been out by now. But he kept going, dogged and silent. We passed tags painted on the concrete walls, some garish in vivid new colors, others fading and worn, an aged shrine to the lost boys and girls who came down here in the night, bringing their guns and their desperation, looking for answers where they had none. The entire time, I waited to hear sirens wailing outside, the screech of police cars, the harsh shouts of the cops as they trapped us in the tunnel.

Instead we came out into an empty lot surrounded by a chain-link fence. A clutter of junk filled the area: old tires, twists of wire, broken bottles, the remains of a rusted carburetor. We picked our way across the uneven ground, taking it slow. A yellowed bag that had once held fries blew across our path and caught on Althor's leg, then fell to the ground as the puny breeze died.

Althor started to turn toward the exit from the lot to our left, but I tugged him forward instead. We finally reached the fence on the other side of the lot. I took him to the place where the chain links were ripped apart in a hole that stretched from the ground up to about my height. As I pulled the opening wider, Althor bent his head and squeezed through. His clothes caught on the broken links, but the material didn't rip. He eased out on the other side and stood up, holding the fence to stay upright, his big fingers clenching the links so hard, his knuckles turned white.

I stepped through the opening. "Can you keep going?"

His voice scraped. "How far?"

"Not much. A few houses."

Althor managed a jerky nod. He spoke in another language, one different from anything I had heard him use before. And yet—I almost recognized the words. I shivered, unsettled by their eerily familiar sound. If I hadn't known better, I'd have thought he was speaking Tzotzil Mayan, words from the healing ceremony of a Zinacanteco shaman: *Ta htsoyan hutuk 'un:* I shall entrust my soul to you a little.

"I'll take care of it," I murmured as I put my arm around him, keeping my hand away from the wound in his waist. I only realized after I spoke that I had said the words in Tzotzil.

We made our way along the alley that stretched away from the empty lot, an uneven walk over hot pavement. The narrow street ran behind houses with their back doors all closed. The sun had bleached the frayed paint on their walls to the hue of old adobe. The air was clearer out here, but it had a parched smell, as if God had baked it in a kiln. The sky stretched above us, a pale expanse the color of blue stones that had faded in the relentless desert heat. This was the Los Angeles hidden under all those glossy images people knew, the modern skyscrapers of Century City gleaming against a fresh sky, the glamour of Hollywood, the beautiful people. This world, my world, lay beneath all of that, unspoken and unseen.

We soon reached the house I wanted. Its screen door was closed but the inner door hung open, drooping on its hinges, suspended between the decision to stay attached or clatter to the floor. I helped Althor inside, out of the glassy sunlight. The living room inside drowsed in the heat, a well lived-in place with a worn couch, a scratched wooden table, a bookshelf with a clutter of paperbacks, and a rug woven from red and white wool.

"Where. . . ?" Althor whispered.

"Mario's family lives here." I took him to the sofa and helped him ease out of my hold. He sank into the soft cushions, then closed his eyes and let his head fall back against the faded top of the couch.

"You wait here," I said. "I'll be right back."

Althor barely nodded. Despite his closed eyes, however, I had no doubt he was aware of everything around us.

Although the house was quiet, I knew Mario might be

around if he hadn't found a job. I called his name, but no one answered. I didn't find anyone in the dining room where he usually spent his time, either watching TV or reading. Mario liked books, contrary to what people thought, that he was barely literate. In prison, he hadn't had anything to do but read. They had a lot of red tape about what you could bring prisoners, but I had worked my way through it until they would let me bring him paperbacks. He mostly liked action adventure stories and thrillers, but he asked for nonfiction, too, especially history and auto mechanics.

Mario wasn't in the den, he wasn't in the bedroom he shared with his younger brother, and he wasn't in the attached garage where he worked on the old car he was trying to restore. Someone must have been here, though; I smelled the crispy sweet *sopapillas* his mother cooked and soaked in honey. She didn't make them often, though, because of her long hours at work. Mario's father had passed years ago in a car accident. Maybe if he had lived, things would have been different, but he had died and Mario's mother did her best. She loved Mario with the fierce intensity of a cat looking after her kittens, though he had grown into a lion that terrified most people.

I went to the kitchen—and froze.

Jake, my old boyfriend, was sitting at the table, as calm as you please, reading the newspaper and eating a peanut butter and jelly sandwich. Jake. Joaquin Rojas, actually. Years ago an Anglo teacher had stumbled over his name, saying 'Jaken.' The other guys had razzed him about it, calling him Jake, and the name stuck.

He looked up, his sandwich halfway to his mouth, and stared as if I were a ghost. Then he grinned, his teeth flashing in his handsome face. "Where did you come from, *querida*?"

That hurt with a bitter sweetness. Jake was the only guy I

knew who called his girl *querida*. Darling. No one around here talked that way, using a word that formal and old-fashioned, which was why I had always liked it. He let only me see that side of him, so out of character with the hard-edged fighter he showed the rest of the world. Lean, mean, and simmering with suppressed violence; that was the Jake most people knew.

I thought of Althor in the next room. Not good. I said only, "*Hola, Joaquin.*"

His gaze shifted to my blouse and his smile vanished like a doused candle. "Tina, is that *blood*?"

A heavy footstep sounded behind me. Jake jumped out of his chair and lunged behind the kitchen counter on his right. When he straightened up, he was holding a 12-gauge shotgun, his face clenched. For one insane instant, I thought he was going to blast me. Then I realized he was looking at something—or someone—behind me.

I spun around. Althor was standing in the kitchen doorway, one hand clamped over his wounded shoulder, his biceps covered with blood. It was partially dried, which made the strange color less obvious. He stared down the bore of the gun, his face unreadable, showing no sign of the pain and exhaustion in his mind.

"Tina, get back," Jake said in a hard voice.

"No, it's okay." I went over and stood next to Althor. "He's with me."

Jake's expression turned ugly, a look he had never given me before. "Since when did you hook up with Nug's garbage?"

"This is Althor. He isn't one of them." That shotgun scared me. "Jake, he killed Nug. He saved my life."

"He *what*?" Jake stared as if I were speaking some language he didn't understand. His hostility filled the room like smoke.

A deep voice came from across the kitchen, rumbling in Spanish. "Who saved your life?"

I turned with a start. Mario stood towering in the doorway of an inner room, the cubbyhole where his mother had her sewing machine. He walked toward us, seeming to shrink the kitchen with the massive build that, when he had played football in high school, had earned him the name *Destruidor.* Destroyer.

Mario considered Althor with a long, cold stare. Then he spoke to me. "Why is he here?"

"We need your help," I said. "Please, Mario."

He didn't say a word, just motioned for me to come into the other room. I shook my head, afraid to leave Althor alone with Jake and the shotgun.

Mario turned to Althor and pointed at a chair. He spoke in English. "Sit down."

Althor sat. His gaze flicked between Mario and Jake, and then he gave me a look that plainly said: *I hope you know what you're doing.*

Mario spoke to me using his no-arguments voice. "I need to talk to you. Private."

I nodded, knowing if I wanted his help I shouldn't refuse him in front of a stranger. So I followed him into his mother's sewing room.

When we were alone, Mario regarded me with his protective look, the one that made me feel as if I were his little sister. "What did Nug and them do to you?"

"Nothing," I said. "Althor stopped them."

"Stopped them from doing what?"

"It was nothing, Mario."

His gaze never wavered. "Don't tell me 'nothing.' What happened?"

I had no answer for it but to tell him. "Nug and his gang grabbed me. They dragged me out of the library and put me in their car. They meant to take me to Nug's place. Althor stopped them."

Mario's face took on a terrible look, ice and granite. It was the same look he had worn the day we buried my cousin Manuel. Two days later the police found one of Nug's men beaten and unconscious in the sewer, the guy we knew had helped Nug kill my cousin. They never found enough evidence to convict anyone of the attack, but I had no doubts about who had left that *cabrón* stewing in a cesspool. I had seen Mario's face at the funeral.

He spoke with a dangerously quiet voice. "We'll take care of it."

"Mario, no!" I took a breath. "No more fighting. Please." When he didn't answer, just kept looking at me, I said, "Promise me."

"I can't do that."

"Mario, listen! Nug is *dead*. Finished. So who dies next?" My voice cracked. "You? Jake? Me? I've already lost Manuel. It would kill me if they took you, too."

He looked as if he didn't know what to do with me. He stood there, huge and fierce, and I had the oddest feeling, as if he were breaking inside. He was so *angry,* at Nug, at the police who had never convicted Manuel's killer, at the guy Mario had left in the sewer, the bastard he could've so easily killed but *hadn't,* at all the people who wouldn't give him a job, at the prison and the system and this uncaring city that lived its glittering life while we struggled in the darkness.

When Mario finally spoke, he said only, "We'll see."

I knew that was the closest to a promise I would get. "I came to ask you to help me and my boyfriend. He's in a lot of trouble."

"Your boyfriend?" Mario scowled. "Who is this guy?"

"His name is Althor." I plunged ahead before he could tell me just exactly what he thought we should do with Althor. "The police arrested him. He had a fight with them. I stole a police car."

He stared at me with disbelief. "You *what*?"

"I stole a police car."

Mario crossed his arms, his muscles bulging. "I thought you were smarter than that."

"We didn't have no choice."

"Why not?"

"Just believe me. We had to."

"Tina, this is one of the first places the cops will come asking questions." He lowered his arms and lifted his palms as if to show me his house. "I hide you here, they'll catch you."

"I know. I wouldn't ask to stay here. I just need a car and your sister's blond wig. And a blanket."

"Why?"

"Don't ask." I silently willed him to say *yes*. "Then if people come with questions you won't be lying if you say you don't know. Someone robbed your house."

He scowled at me. "For what? To steal all those valuable blankets of mine?"

I could tell he was softening. "To steal your car."

"This Althor isn't one of us."

"Please, Mario. For me."

"Ah, Tina." He made a frustrated noise. "Don't look at me that way."

I didn't know what he meant by my look, but I could hear the give in his voice. So I waited.

As he watched me, his face gentled. Finally he said, "There's keys to my car on the shelf out front. If my wheels get ripped off, I don't know nothing about it." Then he added, "My gym bag is in the car. It has a cloth he can use for the gunshot wounds. And give him the water bottle."

I reached up and pulled down his head so I could kiss his cheek. "You're a prince."

He gave me a half smile as he straightened up, which for Mario was a lot of emotion. "If my car gets boosted, where do you think I can find it again?"

"You remember that party we went to in Pasadena? Look on the street outside the apartment house there."

"Pasadena?" His forehead creased. "What's in Pasadena?"

I hurried to the door. "I'll never forget you helped us, *mijo*." Then I sped back into the kitchen.

I found Jake with his shotgun still out and aimed, but at least he had given Althor a dishtowel to soak up the blood from his shoulder. The white cloth had turned purple-red.

"Althor and I have to go," I said.

Jake didn't move. He wouldn't look at me, he just kept watching Althor, his face cold.

"Let them leave," Mario said from the doorway behind me.

Jake was clenching the shotgun so hard, I wondered if he would ever be able to let go. But he lowered the weapon.

"Thank you," I said softly. Althor rose to his feet, his face strained, and walked with me out of the kitchen. He made no attempt to lean on me with Mario and Jake watching, though I felt what that took out of him. Men. It made no difference if they came from the barrio or outer space, they were alike. But I understood. It wasn't just pride; he couldn't show weakness in front of potential enemies, not even those I claimed as friends.

Back in the living room, I grabbed Mario's keys off the shelf where he always left them. "Here." I pushed the keys in Althor's hand. "Go wait in the old blue car at the end of the alley. There's an athletic bag in the trunk with water and more towels. You can use them."

"Aren't you coming?" He glanced toward the kitchen. "It's not safe for you here."

"I'll be fine. I just have to get some things." I didn't like sending him out alone, but he was the one in danger if he stayed in the house. Neither Mario nor Jake had followed us, but either of them might change his mind at any moment.

Althor kept frowning, but he went. It was odd in a way I had never thought about before, that he trusted my judgment. Mario trusted my belief in Althor, it was true, but Mario had known me for years, besides which, Althor had killed the person that Mario hated most in the world. Jake "trusted" Althor only because Mario told him to. But Althor accepted what I said with none of that to go on, and he also trusted my judgment about my own ability to take care of myself in Mario's house. Until this moment, I hadn't realized no one else had ever viewed me that way, at least not in a crisis.

I checked the couch, but it was clean, no blood from Althor's wounds. Then I ran into Rosa's bedroom. Her blond wig was on a Styrofoam bust on her dressing table, the long curls spilling everywhere. I grabbed it and some wig tape, and then I pulled a blanket off her bed. As I turned to leave, Jake appeared in the doorway, holding the shotgun down at his side.

"Tina, wait," he said.

I stood there, the wig and blanket clutched in my hands. "I can't."

"Are you all right?" His gaze flicked to my bloodstained blouse and he brought the shotgun to his shoulder, the bore pointing at the ceiling. "If that guy hurt you—"

"It's his blood, not mine." If he noticed the purple tinge, he gave no hint. I went over to him. "Jake, he saved my life."

I wanted to push the gun away, but I wanted to touch it even less. That was why I had stopped seeing Jake; I couldn't bear the thought of losing anyone else I loved to violence. Now everything was out of control.

"If this guy could finish Nug, you shouldn't be near him." Jake brushed his fingertips over my cheek. "We should help you."

"I have to do this myself."

His voice softened. "Tina . . ."

Even just standing near him was tearing me apart. It brought back all the memories, that bond he and I shared, what had drawn us together. People thought it was physical with me and Jake, and sure, he was handsome, or at least I thought so. But this link had nothing to do with sex. I felt the same bond with Joshua and it had been even stronger with my mother. Althor had finally given me a word for that magic. Empath.

"Jake, I'm sorry. I really am." A tear slid down my face. "But I have to go."

He watched me with his dark eyes, his tangle of emotions hidden. He wanted to tell me something. Something important. It hung around him in blue mist, barely visible. The words remained unspoken, indistinct even within his mind, as if he were struggling himself to face them.

Finally he spoke, his voice tender in that way he never showed anyone but me. "If you need us, we're here, Tina. Always. Just say the word."

"I know." I pressed my palm against his chest. "*Muchas gracias, Joaquin.*"

I left then, slipping past him, leaving Jake and the life I had known with him behind. I ran through the living room, painfully aware of him watching me go.

Outside, I found Althor lying in the backseat of Mario's car, an old blue Camaro with big wheels parked in the alley. He lifted his head as I opened the back door. His face had gone so pale, he barely looked alive. He was still holding the blood-soaked towel over his shoulder, plus he had pressed a clean one from Mario's bag against his side. After I spread the blanket over him, I closed the door. We could use the cloth from Mario's gym bag for bandages, but we didn't have time now. I got into the front and scooted the seat way forward so I could reach the pedals. Piling my hair up on my head, I tugged on the wig. It had enough room because Rosa's hair was almost as long as mine.

"Hot—" Althor muttered in the back.

"I'm sorry about that," I said. "But the cops are looking for a man and a Latina girl with black hair. So you got to stay hidden under the blanket. Do you think you can?"

"I'll be all . . . right." His voice was barely audible.

I feared nothing was going to be all right. I started the car and backed out of the alley, into the afternoon's fading sunlight.

4

STORM HARBOR

It was early evening when I parked on the shoulder of the road. We were on a mountain far above the city, well away from the noise, smog, and bustle. In the back seat, Althor sat up with painstaking slowness, letting the blanket slide down around his waist.

"Where?" he asked.

"This is Mount Wilson," I said. "We're above Pasadena." I opened my door, bringing in the dry wind and a piney scent from the trees that rustled all around the car. "I know a place here you can hide while I get help," I told him as I got out. "I won't be long. I'm going to a friend, but I can't bring you to him in this car. If anyone saw, the police might trace you to Mario, and I can't take that risk."

Althor opened his door and pulled himself out of the car, clenching the doorframe, moving slow and careful as if he had to ration his movements because he had so few left. I slid my arm around his waist and he put his arm over my shoulders, more willing to accept help here in the solitude of the forest. The dying sunlight leaked past the branches and made his eyes look sunken in hollows.

"Where we go?" he asked.

"Josh showed me a cave here. No one else knows about it."

"Josh?"

"Joshua James. He's a friend of mine."

"I don't think I want to meet any more of your friends," Althor muttered.

"You'll like Josh fine."

Althor just grunted. He fell silent as we picked our way through the pine trees and underbrush, but after a while he said, "What is wrong with this world, that its children arm themselves and kill each other?"

I spoke softly. "Nug was a grown man. He made his choices." My memories cut like shards of glass. "If he could have killed you, he'd have done it in a second and enjoyed watching you die. He doesn't deserve your remorse."

"That doesn't make what I did right." His voice scraped like gravel. "And that boy at the house—why the gun?"

"You mean Jake?"

"Yes."

I walked in silence for a while, thinking about my answer. Then I said, "Mario, Jake, my cousin, they're all fighting a war, too. Except their enemy is one you never see or hear, a silence that says you're nothing, nobody, you got nowhere to go, no place in the world."

"Your friend Jake isn't like the others."

I tensed against whatever condemnation he had of a man I had once loved, who would always have a part of my heart. "He's a good person."

"Empath."

I blinked, caught off guard. No one else had ever realized that about Jake before. "You felt it?"

"Like a furnace."

"Yes," I said. "He feels everything too much. But it doesn't stop the anger. It only makes it hurt more."

"Nothing stops the anger." Bitterness edged his words.

I spoke unevenly. "Seems to me that people have to stop killing each other. There must be a better way."

It was a moment before he answered. "I hope we find it."

I felt what he left unsaid. He believed none of us would ever find that peace, neither his people nor mine.

We kept walking, struggling through the underbrush. Althor's pain from the two bullet wounds flooded my mind. How he kept going, I had no idea.

After a while, he spoke in a rasp. "Tell me a story."

"A story?"

"About your life. A good story."

I understood. He wanted a distraction from the pain. "I'll tell you about my best day. My *quinceañera*."

"*Quince. . . ?* Fifteen?"

"It's the celebration of a girl's fifteenth birthday, a church ceremony and a dance." I smiled at the memory even though it hurt in so many ways. "Jake was my escort, what we call the *chambelán de honor*. I don't have a father, so Manuel walked me and my mother down the aisle, in church, for Mass. They were all there, my *corte de honor*. My *damas* and *chambelánes*."

"Ladies and lords?"

"That's right. Twenty-eight of them, my girlfriends and the guys in VSC. We all drove low and slow to the church." I laughed softly. "And Joshua! He stood out so much, with his yellow hair and blue eyes, but no one cared. My mother sewed a beautiful dress for me. The guys wore tuxedos. Can you see it! *Los Vatos de la Calle San Carlos* in tuxedos with blue sashes, or whatever you call those things. Cummerbunds. They pooled their money so they could rent the outfits. I made them promise no weapons." My voice caught. "It was such a wonderful day. It seemed like Jake and I danced forever."

His voice gentled. "Why does your happiest day make you cry?"

"It's all gone. Everything."

His arm tightened around my shoulder.

I thought of my mother, of the tears on her face that day. I had felt her joy, tasted its sweetness. While she helped me dress for the party, her body so thin from her cancer, she had told me ancient tales to describe the bond she and I shared. Her words had painted luminous pictures of the *ceiba*, the axis that existed everywhere, a tree with its roots anchored in Olontik, the Underworld, its trunk rising through the Middleworld where humans live, and its branches stretching through all levels of the heavens. She believed our two minds coexisted the same way the spiritual and material universes coexisted through the tree that spanned them.

My mother had been a *h'ilol*, a holy woman. She prayed for those whose sickness came from a loss of their inner soul or from a witch practicing his craft against them. Few women held the title, yet no one had doubted her claim. Her ability to heal had been legendary. She taught me prayers, verses to Christ and the *kalvario*, the sacred mountain. She told me about the girl from Chamula who became the Morning Star in the sky, where she swept a path for the sun, just as here on Earth my mother's assistants had swept the earthen path for their *h'ilol* during a curing ceremony. I can still hear her voice murmuring in the slumbering heat of a Chiapas night. It wasn't until years later that I realized those curing ceremonies were actually ancient

Maya rituals blended with the Christianity brought to us by Spanish missionaries.

A rocky hill loomed on our left, half hidden by shadows and trees. With relief, I recognized the place. I had begun to wonder if I had forgotten how to find this cave. We walked along the base of the hill until I located a pile of rocks we needed. Behind them, two huge slabs stood leaning against each other in an arch, creating a narrow entrance into the hill.

"Through here," I said.

Althor was so far gone, he didn't even question my telling him to squeeze between two rocks on a mountain in the middle of nowhere. He just turned sideways and pushed through. Inside, a trickle of the fading light seeped through the entrance, barely enough to show that we were in a small cave a few paces across. He sank to the rocky floor and sat there holding the blood-soaked towel against his shoulder, his gaze hollow.

I knelt next to him. "You rest here. Don't try to move anymore."

He just nodded. "I will be fine."

I knew he wasn't anywhere near fine. "I won't be long." I hoped.

"Tina—" His ragged voice could have belonged to a skeleton.

"Yes?" I asked.

"You will come back?"

It hit me then just how much he had to believe from me. This was different from leaving him alone in my rooms for a few minutes while I ran down to Bonita's apartment, or in Mario's house while I looked for help. He was *dying*, and I was stranding him alone in the mountains. He knew almost nothing about me except that I had violent friends.

I took his hand. "I'll come back. I swear to you that I will."

He nodded, the motion short and jerky. I squeezed his hand.

I left the cave then and ran through the forest, stumbling in my stupid heels, back to the car.

It took forever to drive to Pasadena. I parked where I had promised Mario that I would leave his car, just a street in a residential area. I stowed the blanket Althor had left behind in the trunk and locked up the car. Then I looked around. I had only been to Pasadena twice before, once at a party and once last summer to help Joshua move into his dorm. I knew nothing about the city except that we had parked here. This had to be the right street because I could see a tower in the distance rising above the houses, modern and angular, reflecting the sunset in its glassy surfaces. That was the building Joshua had called Milikan Library at Caltech.

I pulled off my shoes and ran in my stocking feet down the street, through the dry California evening. Within a few blocks, I came out in front of the college. I was pretty sure I had reached Caltech, but nothing looked familiar. Across the street, I could see the lawns of a campus. Low buildings bordered them, Spanish architecture, pale yellow walls with rounded archways and red tile roofs. Milikan library stood in the center of the lawns, a gleaming monolith rising into the sky.

Wait! I remembered. Joshua's dorm, Blacker House, was beyond the library. That's why nothing looked right; I had come in on the wrong side. I crossed the street and ran across the lawns, speeding past a guy with long hair and glasses who stared at me as if I had come from outer space. Warm evening air streamed past my cheeks and prickly grass tickled my feet through my stockings.

The dorms were a cluster of Spanish-style buildings. I slowed down and walked under an archway for Blacker House. It opened into a small courtyard paved in bricks with a tree growing in the center. I ran to the stairs on the other side of the courtyard and sped up the steps. What if Joshua wasn't here? I had no idea where else to look. The library? I didn't even know if people who weren't students or teachers could go into the library.

The second floor of Blacker House was painted black with flames on the walls. Joshua had told me that "flaming" meant flunking out of Caltech, and reasons why people flamed were hidden in the wall paintings. I ran to room fifty-two and pounded on the door. Then I stood, heaving in breaths, my pulse hammering.

No answer.

"*No.*" I groaned the word. If Joshua wasn't here, I didn't know what to do—

The door opened and Joshua stood there, dressed in a T-shirt and jeans, tousled yellow curls falling across the top of his glasses. *Dios Mio,* I wanted to kiss him.

For an instant he looked confused. Then a grin spread across his face. "Tina! You went blond!" With a laugh, he added, "What are you doing here?"

I heaved in a breath. "Josh, I need your help."

His smile vanished. "Good Lord, what's wrong?" He pulled me inside and closed the door. "You look like you've been in a war."

"A friend of mine is hurt." I was so out of breath, the words came in gulps. "I was hoping he could stay here."

He stared at me, his face paling as he took in everything, the dried blood on my clothes, my wild hair the wrong color, my shoes clenched in my hand. No one in their right mind would agree to help someone who arrived at their door looking like that.

"All right," Joshua said. "For you."

I closed my eyes. After everything that had happened to him,

Joshua didn't trust easily. He chose his friends with care, but once you were one of them, he was fiercely loyal.

"Tina?"

I opened my eyes. "*Gracias, mi amigo.*"

"Are you all right?"

"I'm fine." I exhaled slowly, trying to calm down. "My friend needs help."

He nodded. "Do you have a car?"

Just like that. No questions asked. It was Joshua's way, once he decided you were his friend. He would do whatever he could for you no matter what. To me, that seemed far more like courage than the way Nug's gang strutted around and threatened people. What they would do now, after his death, I had no idea. Without their leader, they might fall apart. Or they'd come looking for Althor, seeking revenge.

"I have Mario's car," I said. "But we can't use it. I'll explain later."

His gaze flicked over my clothes. "You can borrow my tennis shoes. And you better wear a sweater." Uneasily, he added, "It'll cover up the blood."

My voice shook. "Thanks." I thought of all the hours I had spent weaving and embroidering my blouse, and I wanted to weep for its ruin. I was losing one of the last pieces from my life in Chiapas. But I had no time for tears.

Joshua went to his desk and switched off his lamp. A book there lay open to a page with pictures of pulleys and ramps. Papers covered with equations were scattered everywhere. He ignored his homework and brought me clothes from his closet. His sweater hung to my hips. At first his shoes slipped off my feet, but when I crumpled one of my stockings into each heel, it filled the extra space.

We left his room, and he took me down the hall, past

dismantled pieces of electronic equipment stacked against the wall. We stopped at another room with the initials DEI on the door designed from old computer chips. I didn't know what DEI meant, but seeing it reminded me of the way that VSC carved their initials in places, marking their territory. Joshua knocked and I hung back in the shadows.

A guy opened the door. He was holding a half-eaten Milky Way bar and wearing a T-shirt that said *Confederation, 44th World Science Fiction Convention.* "Hey," he told Joshua. "What's up?"

"Daniel, I was wondering if I could borrow your Jeep," Joshua said.

"What for?" Daniel's gaze shifted past Joshua and stopped on me. He looked until he realized he was staring, then he reddened and turned back to Joshua. "Uh, yeah, sure. Just a second." He vanished into his room and reappeared with his keys. "Keep it as late as you want."

"Thanks," Joshua said. Then we took off.

The Jeep was open, and the wind threw my fake yellow hair around my body as we drove. I told Joshua everything, except for letting him believe Althor came from Fresno. I hoped I hadn't made a mistake, hiding Althor on the mountain. Thinking of him alone and injured made the minutes seem endless.

By the time Joshua pulled off the road up on Mount Wilson, the evening had turned into night, dark except for the starlight. I jumped out of the jeep while Joshua was turning off the motor and took off into the woods, running awkwardly in my over-sized tennis shoes, crunching on dead leaves and needles.

"Tina, wait!" Joshua called.

I couldn't stop. Leaves crackled as he ran, and a light appeared behind me, the glow of his flashlight. With his long legs, he caught up in a few strides, and together we ran past scraggly trees that threw shadows across our path, pools of darker black in the night. Wind whispered in my hair, heavy with the smell of rich, crumbly dirt that lingers in the air after a hot day in the San Gabriel Mountains. Where was the cave? We would never find Althor in time, he would bleed to death—

Wait. There, on the hill—yes, that was the two stones leaning together.

"Here," I gulped in a breath as we came up to the stones. "Do you remember this place?"

Joshua slowed down with me. "Just barely."

I eased my way between the stones with Joshua right behind. The cone of light from his hand lamp played over the ceiling of the hidden cavity, along the walls, on the floor—and across Althor's body. He lay on his back, still and silent.

I ran over and knelt next to him. "Althor?"

When he didn't answer, my heart felt as if it jumped a mile. I laid my fingers on his neck, and when I felt his pulse, relief rushed over me like a wind. But he was burning with fever.

"Althor, can you hear me?" I asked.

No answer.

"Althor, please," I said. "You can't die."

His lips moved, but he words were too low to hear. His eyes were still closed.

"¿Que, cariño?" I asked. "What did you say?"

"Took out bullet," he whispered.

Surely he couldn't mean what that sounded like. "You took a bullet out of yourself?"

His voice was barely audible. "With knife."

I saw it then in the glow of Joshua's flashlight, the bloodied knife and the remains of a bullet lying on the ground by Althor's arm. Bile rose in my throat. He had cut that out of his own body?

I didn't see how he could have even stayed conscious, let alone forced himself to take out the bullet. He had lost so much blood. Even if we could have gone to a hospital, I doubted any blood type on 1987 Earth would work for him.

"We need to clean it," I said. Even if his knife was clean, his wounds could so easily become infected.

Joshua crouched next to me. "We have to get him to an emergency room. No matter what he's done, it's better the police catch him now than he bleed to death."

"No hospital," Althor whispered.

I laid my hand on Joshua's arm. "We can't take him to the hospital."

"Tina, this is serious." He regarded me steadily. "This man could die."

My voice cracked. "Going to a hospital will make things worse. Please. Trust me." I prayed I was right. "Josh, help us. I can't turn to anyone else."

He didn't answer, just kept watching my face, until I wondered if I had pushed our friendship further than even a bond as strong as ours could stretch.

Then Joshua exhaled. "Moving him to my room will be hard. He's so big."

I squeezed his arm. "Thank you."

"I can—walk." Althor slowly opened his eyes. His inner lids shimmered gold in the dim light, glinting like metal.

Joshua squinted at Althor's face. "What happened to your eyes?"

"Eyes fine," Althor rasped. "But I need—clean wound. Can you?"

"We brought first aid supplies." Joshua pulled off his backpack. "We'll do what we can."

I touched Althor's forehead, brushing my palm over the heated skin. Images flashed in my mind. They were—what?

Coming from Althor. His thoughts. It was as if I were seeing a video of little thought packets flowing along the pathways of his augmented brain.

Connection established. The strange metallic thought formed in my mind, the words in English. *Large coupling constant.*

I stiffened. *What was that?* My startled response came in Tzotzil Mayan.

New words flooded my mind, this time in Mayan, except when no Mayan words existed for the concept. Then it was in English. Although it wasn't all clear, I picked up the general ideas. Althor and I were Kyle operators. Empaths. The quantum wavefunctions of our brains interacted, oscillating like chaotic breakers on the shores of our minds. His brain stimulated thousands of molecular sites in my brain, millions, even billions. Had he been a less powerful psion, the link we were making could have crippled both of our minds, creating massive neural discharges that led to convulsions, like epileptic seizures. But his mind was strong, stronger than anyone I had ever met, and I was there with him, a witness to his struggle for life.

I understood then. Althor was battling his injured body, fighting to heal his heart, lungs, intestines, glands, muscles, blood, all of it. His "troops" were nanomeds, tiny molecular laboratories that circulated in his blood, some specifically designed to do repairs, others assigned to maintain his health. They regulated his blood flow, rushed nutrients where they were needed, changed chemical concentrations, knit together rips in his tissues, all in a race to outrun his death. But he couldn't keep up that battle. He was losing consciousness. Even if we took him to a hospital, he would die without help they didn't know how to give. His physiology was too different from ours. He needed my help *now* and I had no idea what to do.

I couldn't think of anything except to submerge my thoughts

into his. I imagined letting our thoughts blend—and his mind suddenly swelled to alertness like a dry sponge expanding with water, as if my mind came to his like rain saturating the air. Data poured through me: *Mitosis. Cells divide; prophase, metaphase, anaphase, telophase. Cells split: 1, 2, 4, 8. Tissue growth. Blood vessels form. Blood flow increases. 64, 128, 256. White blood cells; antibodies; infection. Send lymphocytes. Build fibrin. Clot blood. Parenchymal cells: prophase, metaphase, anaphase, telophase. 16384, 32768, 65536. Bleeding, stroma, bleeding, fibrosis, bleeding, bleeding, bleeding . . .*

"Tina?" The voice came from far away. So far away . . .

"Tina, what's wrong?"

I ignored the intrusive words, swimming in the sea of Althor's mind.

"*Tina!*"

The voice pulled until I couldn't resist. I rose back to conscious thought like a dolphin surfacing in the ocean. I opened my eyes to find Joshua kneeling in front of me, his hands on my shoulders.

"My God," he said. "What *happened* to you?"

"Happened?" I looked around, confused. Why hadn't Joshua opened his pack? It still lay closed on the cave floor. "We have to clean Althor up and bandage him. Josh, we can't wait."

He spoke quietly. "I already did that. I worked for almost an hour. The two of you have been in a trance."

An hour? It had felt like a moment. I looked at Althor. He was still lying on his back, but his eyes were open and full of awareness. A clean white bandage covered his shoulder. He silently mouthed two words: *Thank you.*

On the drive back to Caltech, Althor sat slumped in the backseat of the Jeep, leaning against me, his head resting against the top of my mind. When we reached the campus, Joshua pulled into the parking lot outside the Athenaeum, behind Blacker House. The lot was empty except for a few cars. In the dark, they looked like chromed beasts sleeping in the shadows, quiet now, waiting for a driver to bring them growling into life.

It took both Joshua and me to support Althor as he climbed out of the Jeep. We helped him across the lawn to the dorms, what Joshua called the south house complex, and into the Blacker House courtyard. In the far corner, we climbed the stairs to the second floor. I kept straining to hear voices, footsteps, any warning that someone might happen onto us out of the night.

We managed to reach the second floor without being discovered. A few more steps and we were at Joshua's room. Althor slumped against the wall, standing with his eyes closed while Joshua worked the combination lock on his door. Joshua's relief was like misty tangerine light, translucent in the air. As he opened his door, I let out a breath. We were safe—

A door down the hall creaked opened and Daniel stepped out, staring straight at us.

Damn! I froze, standing next to Althor.

Joshua cleared his throat. "Uh, hey, Daniel."

Daniel spoke in a neutral voice. Too neutral. I couldn't sense his mood. Emotions came to me from someone else if that person's mood was strong or they were standing close to me. But people could shield their minds without even realizing it, especially it they weren't empaths. Right now, Daniel's mind was shuttered. Unreadable.

"Josh, can I talk to you?" Daniel asked.

"Yeah, sure." Joshua spoke to me in a low voice. "Take Althor inside." Then he headed down the hall.

Althor watched Joshua and Daniel like a soldier analyzing the enemy. He pushed away from the wall, keeping one hand against it for support, his gaze never wavering. His look reminded me of when he and Nug had faced off outside my apartment, poised to tear each other apart. But I felt the truth. Althor was ready to fight, yes, whatever it took to survive, because he was designed that way, but he was also drained, ready to collapse. I also had no doubt that in this condition, dying and backed into a corner, he was just as dangerous as before—if not more.

Taking his arm, I nudged him into the room. Although he gripped the doorframe, he showed no other sign of his bone-deep exhaustion. As soon as I closed the door, though, he collapsed against the wall, his face grey under its gold tinge. Yet even now, he was taking in his surroundings. His scrutiny made me hyper-aware of the small place. Across the room, a bed stood against the wall under a window with blue curtains. Shelves were on the left, crammed with books, and a sink and cabinets on the right took up most of that wall. Joshua's desk stood right here, next to the door, with his computer, books, and papers. A Def Leopard poster and a picture of Marie Curie hung on the wall above the desk. That made me smile. Joshua had once told me, with great enthusiasm, how Madam Curie was the first person ever to win two Nobel prizes, one in chemistry and the other in physics. He had always liked brainy women.

I helped Althor limp to the bed. He lay down on his back as if he were moving by remote control. Sleep dropped over him like a heavy blanket cut from the night sky. I sat on the edge of the bed next to him and watched the door, wondering what Joshua was doing.

It didn't take long to find out. Within moments, Joshua came back. Daniel was with him and they both looked grim.

I sat up straighter, my gaze shifting between the two of them. "What's wrong?"

Daniel closed the door and stayed there, holding the knob like he wanted to make sure he could make a fast exit.

Joshua pulled a chair over to the bed and sat down. He motioned at Althor. "Is he asleep?"

"Out cold." In truth, I wasn't sure. Although I had no doubt Althor had dropped off, it wouldn't surprise me if his augmented mind could monitor us even while he slept. That was better left unsaid, though, given the way Daniel looked ready to take off and warn someone.

Joshua didn't waste any time. "Daniel saw police sketches of you and Althor in an article in this evening's paper, down in the lounge. The police are saying Althor's name is Ray Kolvich, that he broke out of San Quentin yesterday, and that he's a PCP addict."

"The hell with that," I said. "They're lying."

Joshua's face was ashen. "The article also says he killed Matt Kugelmann."

I met his gaze. "It was self-defense."

"You mean he *did* kill Nug?"

"Only after Nug tried to kill him." I had no trouble feeling Joshua's mood right now. He was scared to holy hell. It didn't stop him from helping us, though. He was a lot braver than people knew.

"Althor saved my life, Josh." I shuddered, wishing I could forget those moments. "He kept Nug and them from doing their worst to me."

"Do the police know that?"

"The police don't know anything. We ran."

"Tina, why?" He pushed back his unruly bangs. "If it was self-defense, why not say so? The police already know what Nug inflicts on the world." In a subdued voice, he added, "Inflicted."

"You wouldn't believe me if I told you why," I said.

Daniel spoke, his voice deep and curt. "Yeah, well, you better start telling if you don't want us to call the police."

I kept my gaze on Joshua. "Trust me. Please."

"You know I always have. But this—" Joshua shook his head. "I don't know what to say."

I had to tell them something, so I might as well go all the way. Nothing I said was going to sound credible anyway. "You know that test plane they found this morning? The drone?"

"I heard about it," Joshua said.

"It's not a drone. It's Althor's space ship."

Daniel gave a disgusted snort. "You think this is a joke?"

I regarded him coldly. "Do you see me laughing?"

"He told you it was a ship?" Joshua asked, incredulous. "His ship?"

"Yes," I said.

"And you *believed* him?" Daniel asked. He looked ready to laugh, but he didn't. He probably would have, though, if I hadn't been sitting next to a man who had just killed someone.

I ignored Daniel. To Joshua, I said, "You saw his eyes. And his blood."

"I saw something," Joshua said. "But it was too dark to tell what."

I didn't want to wake up Althor, but our choices were limited and this was going nowhere. So I leaned over and shook his shoulder. "Althor."

No response.

I shook him again, harder this time. "Wake up."

His lashes raised—leaving a gold shimmer over his eyes. No pupil, no iris, no nothing. Just gold.

"Whoa," Joshua said.

Daniel came over to the bed. "What the hell?"

Althor's face was unreadable. His gold inner lids retracted like a receding wave on a beach.

"Cool," Daniel said. Then he straightened up as if he were coming to his senses. "But that proves zilch, except that he has strange contact lenses." Underneath that dismissal, though, his mood included something else. He was . . . what? His mix of emotions was hard to read. Fear, yes. Anger, too, because he thought I was jerking around Joshua, his friend. But he was also curious. Insatiably, audaciously *curious.*

Joshua glanced at Daniel. "You know people who can do that with contacts?"

Daniel shrugged. "I'd believe contacts before I'd believe he's an alien."

"He's not wearing contacts," I told them. "And I never said he was an alien."

"You have to admit," Joshua said. "His eyes are more likely a birth defect."

Althor sat up, his large size dominating the space around us. His voice rumbled. "Not a defect."

Both Daniel and Joshua jumped back. Joshua spoke quickly. "Hey, sorry. I'm sorry. I didn't mean any offense."

For a moment, everyone stayed frozen, Althor staring at Daniel and Joshua, and the two of them staring at him. Then Althor exhaled and relaxed, not a lot, but enough so that he didn't look as if he were about to explode. Both Daniel and Joshua responded, probably without even realizing it, their posture easing just the slightest. Although I had never really understood why guys fought so much, at least the ones I knew, I'd learned to read their body language. The threat from Althor had passed.

I also came to another realization. Regardless of what Daniel and Joshua claimed, they had to have their doubts about that news article saying Althor was an escaped convict; otherwise, they would never have given me a chance to explain or have talked this way in front of Althor.

"Think about it," I said. "How could any normal man go through what's happened to Althor and still be in such good shape?"

"I don't know," Joshua said. "But some rational explanation must exist."

An idea came to me. "I need a pair of scissors."

"For what?" Daniel asked. "You plan on cutting someone?"

I scowled at him. "No."

Joshua went to his desk and came back with scissors. "What are you going to do?"

"Watch." I turned to Althor, holding the scissors, and he raised his eyebrows at me.

Trust me, I thought. I didn't know if I could reach him, but I was willing to try anything at this point.

All right, he thought.

I blinked at him. I had almost convinced myself that I had imagined hearing his words in my mind earlier today. That moment with the cops outside the library had been so intense. But it was true. I could hear him in my mind, not much, but a few thoughts when we put in enough effort.

Althor's face changed as he watched me, his expression becoming less hard, and I had an odd sensation, as if he smiled at me in his mind.

"Can you lie down again?" I asked him.

He nodded and lay on his back. Although he stared at the ceiling, I had no doubt he was aware of every move from both Joshua and Daniel. For all I knew, he could even keep track of their breathing and heartbeats.

Althor didn't protest when I tugged up his vest, uncovering his bandaged torso. Joshua had wrapped the gauze all the way around his waist. We'd have to change the bandage soon; blood had already soaked through on the left side where the bullet had hit him, leaving a purple-tinged stain. I felt under the gauze on the other side, just above his hip. When I found the dent that marked his transcom socket, I cut away a square of the bandage, uncovering his skin. The socket looked intact. If I hadn't known what it covered, I wouldn't have thought it was too unusual. It looked like a birthmark or scar tissue.

I prodded at the square of skin. Nothing happened.

Althor lifted his head to watch me, then laid it down again. He pressed his hand against his side, massaging the square of skin, moving his fingertips in a circle. In response, a membrane pulled back in his body—and the transcom slid into his hand, leaving behind a small cavity in his body lined with metallic gold skin.

Joshua gaped at him. "What *is* that?"

Daniel came back over to the bed. "Hey."

"Is similar to what you call computer." Althor held out his hand with the transcom sitting on his palm. The box was transforming from a soft gold cube to the hard-edged device with glowing squares I recognized. Joshua and Daniel watched, their eyes as big as the proverbial saucers. Althor said nothing, just let them look.

After a moment, Althor closed his hand over the transcom. He returned it to his body, pushing it inside his socket. The box molded itself to fit and changed color to blend with his skin. When it finished, the membrane of his skin slid into place, hiding all trace of the transcom.

"Holy shit," Joshua said.

"That thing must have some kind of nanotech!" Daniel said. "Something that alters its composition on a molecular level." He snapped his fingers. "It responds to a change in its environment, right? When you remove it from your body, that's what signals it to change."

Althor slowly sat up, favoring his injured side. "That is right."

Joshua squinted at him. "To fit that into your body, wouldn't you have to move your internal organs? And that membrane looks like it's alive."

"Yes," Althor said.

For a moment, Daniel was silent. Then he said, "That kind of nanotech doesn't exist. Neither does the medical knowledge needed to put a system like that into your body. Not that I've heard of."

Hah! "Now do you see what I mean?" I said. Althor sat watching us, his gaze intent. He wasn't one to talk much, but I could feel him concentrating, taking in everything we said. Listening. Smart man. They weren't likely to talk to him.

Daniel frowned at Joshua. "I still don't believe them."

"You have a better explanation?" Joshua asked.

"My mother says the military retrieved something called the F-29," Daniel told him. "It's a hypersonic test plane that malfunctioned."

"How would she know anything besides the story they're telling everyone?" Joshua said. "Thousands of people work at Yeager. Probably only a handful saw what the shuttle brought down, and I doubt that includes your mom. Besides, I don't believe a test plane would fit into a space shuttle."

My hope leapt. "Daniel, your *mother* works at Yeager?"

He spoke coolly. "A lot of people work at Yeager."

"Could you get us onto the base?" I asked.

"No." He scowled at me. "Even if I believed your story, which I don't, and even if I could get you badges, which I can't, no way would I sneak you into a secured military base."

I wasn't surprised. But I knew they hadn't found an F-29, whatever that was. I rubbed my eyes, trying to clear my mind. It felt as if taffy filled my thoughts.

"Tina, you look worn out," Joshua said.

No kidding. "Can we finish this tomorrow? Althor and I need to sleep."

Joshua nodded his agreement. "I have an extra blanket in the closet you can use."

Daniel made an incredulous noise. "You're going to let them stay here?"

"We can't move Althor," Joshua said. "He'll start bleeding again."

"Do you know what aiding and abetting means?" Daniel said. "You let them stay, you're committing a crime. If I don't say anything, that makes me an accessory."

Damn. I had to do something. But what? I concentrated on Daniel, trying to sense what made him tick, what would convince him to help us. He was a complicated guy, no doubt about that, but some of his emotions stood out more than others. One especially, though he would never admit it to us.

I got up and went over to him. "Suppose, just for a minute, that Althor is telling the truth. Think about it. *You're* the one who has him to yourself, an astronaut from the stars, a man who could answer all those questions you have about space, maybe even make your dreams about the stars come true."

Daniel crossed his arms. "Don't lay that crap on me."

"You won't ever have this chance again," I told him.

"You're nuts if you believe his story."

"You're afraid."

"That's right," Daniel said. "Of being thrown in jail."

"If you don't tell, how will anyone know he's here?"

"I found out."

"You can always say we forced your help by holding Joshua hostage."

"For God's sake." Daniel glowered at Joshua. "Are you listening to her?"

"She has a point," Joshua said. "Saying he used force could protect us if someone finds out he was here."

Daniel shifted his gaze to Althor, who was watching us with that intent look of his that seemed to take in everyone and everything around him.

"*Are* we hostages?" Daniel asked.

"If you need to say so," Althor said.

Daniel shifted his weight. I doubted any of us missed the fact that Althor hadn't said we weren't hostages.

I spoke to Daniel. "Just give us a few days. Please. That's all we're asking."

He considered me, then glanced at Joshua. "You trust her?"

"Always," Joshua said. "I have with my life."

With his life? Where had that come from?

A sudden image came into my mind, a memory that wasn't my own. And yet I saw it; Nug and his men stood in a line facing me. All eight of them held semi-automatic rifles, the metal glinting in the harsh sunlight, their faces ugly with derision. Nug shouted orders like a mock general, making his men twirl their guns and aim them at me. The hot sun beat on my head, the dry air parched my skin, the tight cords bit into my bound wrists behind my back. More than anything, I felt the terror—

Joshua drew in a sharp breath and the image cut off in my mind. For a second I reeled with the intensity. Then a new image formed. It took me a moment to recognize the memory. Yes, I knew this one. But the view was wrong. I was seeing it as if I was standing by the door of the room instead of in front of the couch. We were in Mario's house, in the living room. All of VSC was there, even Manuel. They lounged against the walls or sat in chairs, some of them cleaning weapons, big Magnums or Uzis.

I understood then. These were Joshua's memories, vivid memories, ones so intense that I picked them up from his thoughts. And yes, I even saw myself. I was standing in front of the couch and talking to Mario with an ease that astonished Joshua, as if Mario were a beloved older brother instead of a notorious gang leader. Protection. I wanted them to protect Joshua. And in the end, incredibly, VSC agreed to do just that, so that no one ever again terrorized Joshua.

As the image faded, Joshua let out a barely audible breath. If I hadn't been so attuned to him, I wouldn't have even noticed. But nothing was subtle about his mood. Although I had sensed he was uneasy that day I took him to Mario's, I had never realized he felt as if he were trusting his life to me. Being an empath wasn't enough; I only picked up pieces of what people felt, rarely all of it, unless their moods were intense and I was concentrating on them. And sensing someone's mood wasn't the same as knowing the reason they felt that way. Before this moment, I had never truly understood the fear that VSC inspired or how much it had shocked Joshua that they agreed to help a math nerd they called *güero* or *blanquito,* the little blond boy.

Daniel was also watching Joshua. "You okay?" he asked.

Joshua met his gaze. "I trust Tina. If she says we should trust Althor, I believe her."

Daniel didn't answer him. He didn't answer anyone. He was silent for much too long, his face unreadable.

And then Daniel said, "You have two days. *Two* days. After that, if you haven't convinced me that this isn't all some scam, we go to the police."

Gracias a Dios. "Two days," I said. "Deal."

5

JAGERNAUT MODES

. . . build new tissue cells. Increase blood flow. New blood vessels—

"Tina, what's wrong?" The voice came from far away. I ignored the interruption.

Repair cells. Slow pulse. Fix gashes . . .

"Tina, wake up."

The voice wouldn't stop calling. Something was shaking me, too. Distracted, I eased out of Althor's mind. He let go, and I felt him sink into a true sleep.

I opened my eyes. I was lying next to Althor on top of the bed covers, but we were no longer the only people in the room. Joshua was standing next to the bed, leaning over, shaking my shoulders, his face creased with concern.

"Josh, don't." My voice vibrated with his motion.

"Thank God." He let go of me and sat with a thump on the edge of the bed. Late afternoon sunshine slanted through the window, laying rectangles of buttery light across the bed.

I sat up, squinting in the brightness. "What time is it?"

"Almost five in the afternoon," Joshua said. "I was getting worried. I couldn't wake up either of you." He waved his hand at the desk on the other side of the room. "I brought you lunch hours ago."

As soon as I saw the loaded cafeteria tray on his desk, my mouth watered. "You're a prince." Turning, I nudged Althor's shoulder. If someone my size, with no injuries to heal, was so hungry, he must be starving.

"*¿Puedes oírme, león dormido?*" I asked.

No reaction. My sleeping lion, it seemed, intended to stay asleep.

I tried again. "Althor, can you hear me?"

Nothing.

"Maybe it would help if we sat him up," Joshua suggested.

"It's worth a try." I climbed over Althor and knelt next to him while Joshua stood by the bed. Together, we pulled Althor into a sitting position.

"Thor, wake up," I said.

No response.

Joshua shook his shoulders, but it didn't help. He tried harder, still with no success. He shook even harder—

Althor's hand shot out in a blur and he grabbed Joshua's wrist. As his outer eyelids snapped open, he shoved Joshua away, sending him flying into the chair by the bed. It skittered out backward and Joshua thumped to the floor, sitting down hard.

"*¡Hola!*" I grabbed Althor's arm. "Hey, it's okay! We just wanted you to wake up."

His head swiveled to me. Gold shields covered his eyes. Machine man. Just as abruptly as he had sat up, he slumped in my arms. He was too heavy to hold upright and we both fell on the bed, Althor landing on his back.

Joshua picked himself up off the floor. "Uh—is he awake?"

"I'm not sure." I sat up on my haunches and leaned over Althor. "Can you hear me?"

His inner lids lifted halfway, making him look like a stoned turtle. Whatever trance he and I had been in before Joshua woke me up, Althor was still there, healing his body.

"I think this is the best we're going to get," I said.

Joshua rubbed his chin. "Maybe we should feed him ourselves."

It was worth a try. "Okay."

When Joshua brought the tray over to the bed, I had to struggle not to grab the food all for myself. Watching me, he said, "I brought plenty. You eat. I'll take care of Althor."

I could have kissed him. "Thanks."

He set the tray on the bed and sat next to Althor. I took a so-called tortilla off the tray and held it between my thumb and index finger, letting it dangle. "What is this?"

Joshua smiled as he picked up a glass of orange juice. "You know what that is."

"A big corn chip?"

He leaned over and tilted the glass to Althor's lips. "What, you don't approve of our tortillas?"

"Calling this a tortilla is like calling costume jewelry a diamond necklace." Waving the imposter tortilla at Joshua, I added, "No one makes them like my mother did." Hers had been big and soft, cooked just right on her *comal*, a round metal plate she propped up over the fire on two old pots and a rock. I could still see her patting the maize dough back and forth, around and around. I had loved that sound. For the first eight years of my life, I had heard it in the early morning every day of my life.

Now it was gone.

I put down the tortilla and took a sandwich instead.

Joshua kept coaxing Althor to drink the orange juice, with no success. Finally he held Althor's mouth open and dribbled juice between his lips. At first nothing happened. Then Althor sputtered, splattering drops everywhere. He lifted his head and gulped down the juice, never slowing even as Joshua wiped his chin clean with a napkin. Althor's inner lids slid down as he drank, turning his face into a mask.

After Althor finished the juice, Joshua set the empty glass on the tray—and froze.

I stopped eating. "What's wrong?"

"Look at him."

I couldn't figure out what Joshua meant. Althor wasn't doing anything except lying on his back with his eyes closed. His arm was bent at the elbow and his hand stuck up in the air. I supposed it did look a little odd, a man asleep with his hand up that way. Then I realized what had startled Joshua. Althor's hand had hinged in half, from his knuckles to his wrist, like a closed book, so that his middle and index fingers lay flat against his ring finger and little finger. Actually, "little" was the wrong word; all four of his fingers were about the same size. His thumb was left on its own, pointing toward the wall as if he were hitchhiking.

"That is seriously weird," Joshua said.

"It is different," I allowed.

Althor unfolded his hand like a robot opening its grip. He reached out, hinged his hand around an apple on the tray, raised it to his mouth, and ate the fruit bite by mechanical bite. When he finished, he set the apple core on the tray. Then he rested his elbow on the bed again with his hand up. He opened his hand halfway, making a V-shape, and waited.

Joshua blinked, first at Althor, then at me. "Is he awake?"

"I'm not sure," I said. "Maybe he's on autopilot."

"What should we do?"

"I think he's still hungry." I put another apple into his waiting palm.

Althor's hand closed around the apple, and he raised the fruit to his mouth for a bite. So it went. He ate four apples and finished off a bowl of squash and some corn. He wouldn't touch the hamburger. Except for his moving arm and his chewing, or us holding him up when we spoon-fed him, he was otherwise still. After he downed the last kernels of corn, he lay on his back with his arm relaxed on the bed by his side. His outer eyelids rolled down over the gold shimmer that covered his eyes, and his breath deepened into the slow, steady rhythm of sleep.

"That was bizarrely amazing," Joshua said. "Does he always act like that?"

"I don't think so." I hesitated. "At least, he never did before with me."

"What if our food makes him sick?"

"He's never mentioned it as a problem." Not so far, anyway.

Joshua tilted his head, watching me. "You sound different lately."

"Different how?"

"I'm not sure. Your vocabulary is bigger, I think. And your English is better."

I had no illusions about my English. No one would ever mistake me for a native speaker. But I was learning more words. "I practice all the time."

"I guess that's it," Joshua said.

We left it at that. If something else was happening to my brain, I had no idea what.

. . . water cup. Beads of moisture cling to its outer surface, poised to slide down the smooth sides, surfaces swirling with clouds,

blue, gray, white, swirling. A hollow cup shaped like a woman riding a centaur with six legs, four to stand on, two that paw the air . . . Instead of a head, a spout where water pours out, cool and sweet, running in a glistening stream, sparkling . . .

I woke up gradually, comfortably, wrapped in a blanket with a hard surface under my body. The floor. Yes, I remembered, I was on the floor. The cup image remained vivid in my mind instead of fading the way my dreams usually did after I woke up. I wasn't thirsty, but I could see an afterimage in my mind of that cool, delicious water pouring out of a spout. How odd. I felt an urge to find a glass of water, and yet I didn't feel at all thirsty.

Early morning sunshine lightened the room. I had slept on the floor because the bed was too cramped with Althor taking up most of the room. Joshua had given me a T-shirt to wear so I could wash my blood-soaked clothes, and they were hanging above his sink now, fresh and dry in the sunlight.

I rubbed my eyes as I rolled onto my side. A paper crinkled, and I found a note on the floor by my pillow. It was penned in Joshua's sloppy handwriting: *Hey, Tina. I'm at class. I'll be gone all day, to lecture and then the library. Back this evening around 5. See you—Josh.*

Now I felt guilty. Joshua hated getting up in the morning. High school had been pain for him, but since coming to college, he was in heaven. He could sleep until noon and study until the sun came up. He never signed up for morning classes unless he had no choice. If he had left early today, he was doing it to give Althor and me privacy, bless his drowsy heart. I looked to where Althor was asleep on the bed—

And he was wide awake, lying on his side, staring straight at me.

Althor didn't need to say a word. I knew what he wanted. I climbed to my feet, letting the blanket drop into a pile at my feet.

The t-shirt I had on was so big, it came halfway to my knees. A quick search of the cabinets over the sink turned up a battered cup made from orange plastic. It was nowhere near as beautiful as the one in my dream, but it would do. I filled it with water and brought it to the bed. As Althor pushed up on his elbow, I sat next to him and gave him the glass. He gulped it down so fast, he practically inhaled the water. Then he dropped onto his back and let out a relieved breath while the empty glass fell out of his hand, onto the bed.

"How do you feel?" I asked.

"Better." He lifted his head and glanced around the room. "Where are your friends?"

"Studying. Josh'll be back this evening."

He nodded and lay back, closing his eyes. The blue blanket covered him from the waist down like a stretch of sky. His torso was bare above the bandage around his waist, showing the sculpted muscles of his chest. Sunlight filtered past the blue curtains, drawing glints of gold from his skin and the dusting of hair that curled on his torso. An old scar showed on his arm and another slashed across his upper chest. I shifted uneasily, wondering what had caused such ugly marks. If he came from a people advanced enough to have star travel and cybernetic warriors, surely they could remove the scars. Then again, Althor didn't strike me as someone who would care. Regardless, he looked beautiful to me, scars and all. Sexy man, all sleepy and warm in bed.

I leaned over with my hands on either side of his shoulders and kissed him. His lids lifted halfway, both the inner and outer—and he pushed me away.

Ouch. Had I broken some taboo? Maybe he just didn't feel like being kissed. He had barely made it back from the edge of death and here I was, coming on to him. For all I knew, he wasn't interested anymore. After everything that had happened with my friends, I wouldn't blame him.

His voice rumbled. "The soldier from Troy. We need it, yes?"

A startled flush heated my face. "I don't have them. I left the box in my apartment."

Althor gave me a slow, drowsy smile. "I brought them."

Well, so. Apparently he was thinking about a lot more than just kissing. I smiled. "My, aren't you optimistic?"

He hinged his hand around my T-shirt and tugged. "Beautiful woman," he murmured.

I liked that he called me a woman instead of a girl, but I felt too self-conscious to try kissing him again.

"Don't be embarrassed," he said. "You're a Raylican goddess." When I looked up, he spoke softly. "My ancestors were an ancient race, one that is almost extinct among my people now. You look like images I have seen of their fire goddess." He spoke in another language, the same one he had used before we reached Mario's house, words that had sounded achingly familiar, so much like the Tzotzil Mayan of my childhood.

"What language is that?" I asked.

"It is Iotic. Ancient Iotic." He drew me down on the bed. "Almost no one speaks it anymore."

"How do you know it?"

"My grandmother descended from the Raylicans." Althor wrapped his arms around me as I stretched out against his side. He lifted the blanket and slid me on top of him. He felt warm. Solid. I could smell the sexy Althor scent of his body. I'd been so lonely before, but no more, not with him. I lifted my head to kiss him—

And saw his face.

He was staring at the ceiling with his inner lids down, leaving his eyes as metallic shields. It wasn't the face of a living man. I was making love to a machine.

I rolled off him and sat up so fast, it felt like wind gusted past my skin. Pulling the blanket around my body, I held it there as if it were protection.

Althor's head turned to watch me like a metal part swiveling on ball bearings. "We have not completed the call." His voice was flat, a dry plain with tumbleweed blowing across the barren ground. Reaching out, he curved his arm around my waist.

"No!" I pushed him away. "Don't touch me."

His arm returned to his side. His face remained impassive. "Why not?"

"Where is Althor?"

"I am Althor."

"I mean the real Althor. The man."

"I am not a man. I never was."

I pulled the blanket tighter around my body. "You aren't. But *he* is. Bring him back."

"I am him."

"But why do you sound different? You're like a—a machine."

"I am a machine."

I shivered even though the room was warm. "Please let Althor come back."

"I am Althor. How do I make it clear?" His voice had almost no inflection. "This is a mode, an incomplete representation of my emotive-mechanical interface. What you call the 'real' Althor is another mode, one currently inoperative." With a voice as flat as a desert plain, he added, "This is what I am. If you don't want this part of me, don't ask for anything else."

Just like that. Take all of me or nothing. In some ways, it was easier to deal with his killing Nug than with this. As much as his violence shook me, I understood that part of him. This was too alien.

And yet . . .

I had asked him to accept me exactly as I was: a nobody. A man like him could have so much more, yet I was asking him to want me *for* me, to accept me even though I was no one. Why should I expect anything less from myself than I did from him?

"If we do this," I said, "would I be making love to your other mode too? I mean, the Althor one."

"A mode is not a different personality." Although he seemed to be looking at me as he spoke, I couldn't be certain with the gold covering his eyes.

"So if I'm here with you," I asked. "I'm with the Althor I know better?"

"Yes. We are the same."

I placed my hand against his chest. He felt human. Alive. *You can at least try,* I told myself. I lay down and pressed my lips against his chest in a kiss.

Althor moved his hands along my back in measured strokes. Then he pulled off my t-shirt and dropped it on the floor by the bed.

"Resume," he said.

Resume? I had no chance to ask what that meant. Instead of brushing his lips over my face, like he had done before, this time he pulled me up and kissed me straight on, too hard, as if he hadn't calibrated the force. He rolled over on top of me, bringing us to the edge of the bed. His uniform pants lay in a heap on the floor. He reached down without pause and pulled a condom out of a pocket I hadn't even realized was there. Sitting up, he knelt on his haunches, straddling my hips with his knees while he examined the foil packet. I couldn't stop watching him. It was mesmerizing, like seeing someone move by remote control.

"Althor?" I said.

He looked up. "Yes?"

"When you're like this, will you still feel—" I tried not to stutter. "You know."

"I do not know." He continued to regard me, or at least his shielded eyes were turned in my direction.

My face felt as if it was on fire. "Making love."

"Yes." He opened the packet and pulled out the Trojan. "No reason exists for my physical sensations to cease because my emotive-mechanical interface is degraded."

Well, wasn't that romantic. Of all the things I'd imagined about my first lover, I would have never come up with a machine that discussed emotive-mechanical interfaces while putting on a condom.

In any case, he and his interface were clearly glad to see me. He rolled on the condom, smooth and slow, latex on gold. Who could have guessed he could make it look so erotic? I cupped my hand around his balls, wondering if he would feel the way he looked, like flexible meal. He didn't. He felt warm and human.

He lay down on me, and it still felt suffocating, not only because he was heavy, but also because my mind created metallic sensations out of whatever had happened to his thoughts. As soon as that thought formed in my mind, though, he pushed up on his elbows.

"I am too heavy." He spoke as if that fact were a datum he had added to his memory storage.

"Can you feel my emotions even when you're like this?" I asked.

"Yes." He kissed me, once, twice, a third time, as if he were sampling a data set. "I cannot make myself weigh less, however."

"It's okay." I didn't know whether to laugh or be flustered. "You don't have to."

He let himself down more carefully, his hands gripped around my upper arms. Although this time he held his body slightly off mine, so I didn't feel smothered, now he was holding my arms too hard. Before I could say anything, though, he loosened his grip. I had the oddest thought, that his damaged mind was assigning incorrect values to that data that specified how tightly he should hold someone my size, but that when his systems detected my tension, they recalibrated the numbers and made him loosen his hold. I shook my head, trying to clear away the strange impression.

I expected him to do what he wanted then, fast and efficient, like a machine, but he was actually gentler than before. It didn't hurt. Who knew, maybe he could calibrate his lovemaking to any level of tenderness he wanted. Whatever the reason, it was lovely. I hugged him, savoring the way his muscles flexed as his body moved.

Upload, he thought.

Upload? What did that mean? Metallic sensations were flowing from his mind into my mine.

He touched my cheek. Download?

I don't know what you mean. I didn't realize I had thought the words until they formed in my mind. The last time we had made love, the "download" thing had just happened. I put my lips against his ear. "Kiss me more. The way you do it, good and hard, like you can't get enough."

And so he did, his tongue taking data to fill a new array. I felt how this mode interpreted pleasure, with a hard, metallic edge, urgent and strong. Knowing a man wants you that much may be the greatest aphrodisiac to exist, far better than any chemical love potion.

His words flashed in my thoughts. Link opened.

That was when my brain went into overdrive. It was as if Althor flooded me with his metallic sensations, smothering my perceptions. Suffocating, *I was suffocating—*

Wait! My fingers dug into his back. *It's too much!*

Carrier attenuated, he thought.

The sensations receded to a bearable level and he slowed down as well, moving strong and evenly on my body. Closing my eyes, I tried to sense only Althor the living man.

Waiting. His word entered my mind like a prompt.

Waiting? I asked.

Waiting. He continued his slow, measured strokes.

Waiting for what? I thought, flustered.

To authorize release. His tension built like pressure in an airlock, bowing out the doors.

What do you mean? I asked.

He exhaled in a small explosion of air. Overriding. His movements surged, much faster now. I hung on as his river of sensation flooded me. He pushed his arm under my waist and lifted me off the bed, pressing us together as we moved. His sweat dripped down and moisture slicked between our bodies. When his peak broke, his muscles spasmed and we both went rigid with the intensity of our release.

Gradually the river receded. His grip loosened and we sank back into the bed, Althor lying with his cheek against the top of my head. Eventually, when our breathing quieted, he slid off and lay against my side. His body felt human. As long as I didn't see his face, I could believe a man lay next to me rather than a machine.

"Wow," I said. That had been amazing.

"Return," he said.

I opened my eyes. "What?"

He didn't answer.

My lion had fallen asleep. I closed my eyes and lay curled against his side. My mind soon wandered into the drowsy haze that hangs over my thoughts just before I fell asleep.

Fragments of Althor's earlier words drifted in my mind, words from an ancient tongue of his ancestors: *Shibalank, Shibalan* . . .

I awoke into a room aged by sunlight that had lost its morning quality. The distant sounds of people talking came from outside the window. With my eyes half open, I peered at the clock on the wall over the desk. We had slept several hours, and we had a few more before Joshua was due back.

I stretched next to Althor, warm and sleepy. As I moved, his head turned toward me and his outer lids opened. I propped myself up on my elbow, watching his face. "Are you all right now?" I asked.

"I am discontinuing."

He sounded even more like a machine than before. "What's wrong?"

"My functions are degrading."

"You mean you can't heal yourself any more?"

His eyes closed. "Access denied."

"No, wait. Don't do that." I didn't like this mode at all.

Althor opened his eyes, this time both the inner and outer lids. His face relaxed and his voice rumbled with his familiar accent. "Access denied means you ask question I cannot answer."

Relief swept over me. "You're back!"

"I never went away."

"It seemed like you did." I hesitated. "Does that bother you, that we, uh—you know."

He laughed amiably. "That we what, Tina? Woke up?"

"No." I cleared my throat. "Made love while you were him."

"Him is me. So no, this doesn't bother me."

"Do you remember it all?"

"Every second." He grinned. "I can play it back in my memory as often as I want."

My face heated up. "You're kidding."

"Not at all." His voice softened. "My sorry if this is strange for you. Usually my interface with humans is not so obvious."

"When you're the way you are now, you seem human."

He ran his hand along my side. "I feel like any man. The biomech doesn't take that away."

"Were you born this way?" His caress was pleasantly distracting. "I mean with biomech."

His hand stilled and his mood shuttered like a light switching off. "No."

Was this yet another mode? I didn't think so. He was pulling back on purpose. "Did I say something wrong?"

It was a moment before he answered, but he did finally speak. "I was not born with the biomech web. But some of my modifications, they are at the germ level."

"Germ?" I hadn't expected that. "You don't look sick."

"Not germ in that sense. Germ as in genetics. It means that if I have children, I will pass on to them the medical fixes that the doctors have made to me. They won't inherit most of my physical problems." He was trying to act as if it didn't matter to him, but I wasn't fooled. "My doctors do not know if it will work, however. I am one of first they try with these particular procedures."

"That's horrible! How could they experiment on you?"

He shrugged. "Someone had to be first. I am a good test case."

"No one has a right to make you a 'test case.'"

He stopped trying to look as if he didn't care. "Doesn't it occur to you that I *want* this? That it fixes problems I don't want to inflict on my children?"

Ah, I was an idiot. His anemia. His hands. Maybe other problems too, ones I didn't know about. "I'm sorry. I didn't realize."

He relaxed. "I am maybe too sensitive about it. Or so Ragnar tells me."

"Ragnar." I tried to recall the name. "You mean the admiral? Your mentor?"

"Yes. Ragnar is brilliant biomech surgeon. When I was young, he was my doctor, head of the team that made my biomech web." His expression gentled. "He used to walk with me while I was learning to use my legs. We talked about so much."

Learning to use his legs? Something here didn't fit. I touched the socket in his wrist. "I thought these linked you to your ship. The Jag."

"They do."

"But you said the Jag was a starfighter."

"It is."

"Your military wires *children* into warships?"

His expression turned impassive. "Of course not." He cut me off from his mind as if a shield had slammed down over his thoughts. "Jagernauts receive their biomech as adults, just before they are commissioned."

Than why did he have his as a child? I could almost feel him warning me not to push. I would alienate him if I didn't let it go. So as much as I wanted to know more, instead I asked, "What did you mean before, when you said you were discontinuing?"

His voice lost its edge. "My internal web is part of the Jag's onboard mesh systems."

"Mesh? That means computer, doesn't it?"

"Essentially. But it has a problem. It is—how to say?" He paused. "The Jag's mesh system is coming apart. Because your military tampers with it. The Jag is in automatic shutdown, but the tampering still makes damage. And my mind is part of that mesh. If the Jag fails, I don't know what will happen to me." He shook his head. "I keep switching in and out of different modes, probably more than you realize. The last was more obvious, but others have happened too. It disorients me."

It sounded a lot worse than disorienting. "Will you be all right?"

"I don't know. I need my ship."

I thought about our love-making. "What did you mean earlier, when you said we hadn't 'completed the call'?"

"I meant the mod call."

"The what?"

He thought for a moment. "You know what is a subroutine call in a software code?"

"Sort of." I didn't really, but I recognized the words. "We studied computers in school. A little." A very little.

"A mod call is more sophisticated, but the basic idea is the same."

I stared at him. "Are you saying that when you make love, you're running a computer program that tells your body what to do?"

"That is a simplification, but yes, essentially."

"Althor, do you have any idea how kinky that sounds?"

"Kinky?" He regarded me with a curious smile. "This means bent?"

"This means weird." Seriously weird.

"It is me, Tina." He spoke carefully. "I think the Jag recognizes you as part of my systems now, which makes you part of the ship, too. It may even be augmenting your mind, expanding your knowledge base and vocabulary."

An image of myself with a machine face jarred my thoughts. I looked down at my hands. They looked human. They *were* human. If anything, being with him made me feel more human, not less.

Althor pulled me closer. My body responded immediately, wanting him, but I held back. I kept seeing him staring at the ceiling with half-open eyes, a computer having sex.

He spoke in a low voice against my ear. "Am I really so repugnant to you?"

"Althor, no." I couldn't understand how he could be so empathic and yet also be a machine.

"Then come here," he murmured.

So I did. Yet even as we made love, the memory of his metallic eyes stayed in my mind. For these few moments, he was human, but how long would that last?

6

HEATHER ROSE

The only sound in Joshua's room came from his television muttering in the background: *This is a test, this is only a test, this is a test of the Emergency Broadcast System.* I had changed into my cleaned clothes, and Althor sat next to me on the edge of the bed, dressed in his black leathers. He kept bending and relaxing his arm, the one with the injured shoulder, as if he were testing the limb.

A grating noise scraped through the air, warning that someone outside was working the combination lock of the door. As I jumped to my feet, the door swung open.

"Hey." Joshua stood there, framed in the doorway, and it was just him, thank goodness, no one else. He came inside and locked the door, then turned around. "You don't have to jump up for me."

I smiled. "Always, Josh."

He laughed, but he smile faded as he looked at Althor. Well, so. It was one thing to have Althor passed out and injured; it was another to have him wide-awake and restless. Even sitting on the edge of the bed, he seemed to fill the room, not only with his size but also with the force of his presence.

"Where is your friend Daniel?" Althor asked.

Joshua stayed by his desk. "He'll be here soon. He's checking some things."

"Checking what?" Althor asked.

"Yeager Test Cen—"

Althor stood up, looming, and the room shrunk even more. "You *contacted* the base?"

Joshua stepped backward, flat against the door, staring up at him, his face pale.

Althor, don't, I thought. *Take it easy.* I created an image in my mind of Nug and his gang, all of them dressed like Althor, terrorizing Joshua behind the school. Then I showed him a different image, how Joshua had tended Althor's wounds with such care up in the cave.

Althor let out a breath and sat on the bed. He spoke in a quieter voice. "Why did Daniel contact the base?"

The color came back into Joshua's face. "He called his mother."

"Won't that make her suspicious?"

Joshua actually smiled. "You mean, suspicious that her son and his buddies have an alien stashed in their dorm?"

Althor's forehead furrowed as he stared at Joshua.

After a moment, Joshua flushed. "I was kidding." When Althor didn't respond, Joshua said, "I just meant she wouldn't think anything of it. Daniel always talks the business with his parents. They're systems engineers and he's majoring in computer science. If he bugs his mom about what's the deal at her work, she'll only think he's being his usual self."

Althor spoke slowly. "His parents work with mesh systems?"

I realized what was wrong. "Josh, don't talk so fast. And don't use so much slang. He doesn't understand you."

"Oh. Yeah, sure, sorry." Before Joshua had a chance to say more, the TV started droning with another emergency broadcast. He stalked over to the set and switched it off. "If I hear 'This is only a test' one more time, I swear, I'm going to break something. You'd think we're about to have a war."

"Maybe we are," I said. "Haven't you heard? Russia is claiming we sent a spy plane to invade their air space. It's no wonder everyone is scared."

"Of course I heard," Joshua growled. "It makes no sense!" He frowned at me as if I had single-handedly managed to start World War III. "Why would we do that with a freaking spy plane? It's stupid to suddenly ramp up the Cold War again when we've come so far in winding it down."

Althor spoke. "I don't know what you mean by Cold War, but I can say this. If other nations have any idea about what your military is hiding—my Jag—then they have good reason to go on alert. The technology on my ship could obliterate any balance of power on this world." He paused. "Or maybe your governments are working together, pretending to this chilly war so your countries can go on alert without starting a world-wide panic. If your militaries understand even a small amount about my fighter, they have good reason to think they are facing much worse than a planetary war."

Joshua stared at him. "*Are* we facing much worse than that?"

Althor met his gaze. "No."

"Tina said you bled purple blood all over that police car."

"Is true," Althor said. "They must know by now that I am not human."

A knock sounded on the door.

"Hey!" Joshua jumped. "Who is it?" he called.

"Daniel," a voice answered from the other side of the door.

Joshua exhaled. He went over and let Daniel in, then locked up the door again.

"Did you talk to your mother?" Joshua asked him.

Daniel glanced at Althor, then turned to Joshua. "Yeah. She says it's just a plane."

"You found out nothing?" Althor asked.

"Look, I can't help you," Daniel told him. "Maybe I do dream about the stars, like Tina said, but what's happening in this country right now is nobody's fairy tale."

"I'm not here in any military capacity," Althor said. "I just want to get my ship and leave with Tina."

I jerked. "Do what with me?"

Someone outside started doing the combination lock.

We all stared at each other. Given that everyone who knew about Althor was already inside this room, we had one second to panic before the door swung open.

A girl stood there. She was a few years older than Joshua, slender and tall, dressed in blue jeans and a pullover, with green eyes and a gorgeous mane of curly red hair. She blinked as we all gaped at her.

The girl turned to Joshua. "Do I have the wrong day?"

"Damn! I forgot." Joshua strode over, pulled her inside, and shoved the door closed. "Some, uh—some friends came to visit."

She considered us all. "Yeah. I see."

Joshua turned to us and lifted his hand, indicating the girl. "This is Heather, everyone. Heather Rose MacDane. She helps me with calculus."

Hah! In different circumstances, I would have grinned. Joshua never needed help with his homework. That was like me needing help being female. He was so shy he had never had a girlfriend, but someday he was going to make some girl a wonderful boyfriend. Whether or not this Heather person deserved him remained to be seen.

Heather glanced at Joshua. "We can study later if you want."

"Yeah. Okay." He looked like a cat jumping from a firecracker.

"Would you mind helping me carry some boxes up the stairs?" she asked. "I left them in the courtyard."

"Oh. Yeah, I can do that." Joshua shot me a warning look. "I'll be right back. You stay here."

"Sure," I said, doing my best not to look like a criminal on the run from the cops.

Both Joshua and Daniel left with Heather. When they were gone, I sat on the bed next to Althor. "I hope we aren't in trouble."

"I think it is time for us to leave," he said.

"You can't," I said. "You shouldn't even be up." He had lost so much blood, I was surprised he could sit up straight for more than a few moments.

"I'm all right," he said.

I hesitated. "What did you mean before, that thing about me leaving with you?"

He spoke quietly. "I want you to come home with me."

"Why?" I couldn't imagine how he thought I would fit into wherever he came from.

"I—enjoy your company."

"You enjoy my company?" Mister Romance he wasn't. "You want me to leave everything I know, everything I've ever loved, everything in my life, and go with you to some universe that's so different I can't even imagine it, all because you 'enjoy my company'?"

"Yes."

"That's nuts." He was hiding something, but at the moment, I couldn't pick up squat from his mind. That was the problem being with someone who knew he was like me. He also knew how to shield his moods. "What happens when you get tired of me? You'll strand me someplace I don't know, someplace I've never heard of, where everyone and everything is strange to me. I'll be lost. Centuries lost."

His gaze never wavered. "I wouldn't strand you."

"You say that now."

"I say it now. I say it a century from now."

I shook my head. I couldn't even absorb his words, let alone consider such a choice.

"That boy," he said. "The one with the gun. He is why you can't leave?"

That caught me even more off guard. "You mean Jake?"

"Yes."

"Why do you think that?"

"Because he loves you."

"Stop it." I was breaking inside. "How can you know that?"

He touched my cheek. "His mind was practically shouting how he felt."

I didn't want to say anything. It hurt too much. But Althor had been straight with me, and he deserved a real answer. "Jake and I used to be together. But something is missing with him and me. I don't know how to explain."

"It's like starving inside."

"Yes." He understood. "With you it's different."

"We're full psions, Tina. Telepaths, empaths." He took hold of my shoulders, his huge grip engulfing them. "Do you know how rare that is? Probably we'll never find it again, not like we have with each other. Don't throw that away. Come with me."

"I can't." I had already changed universes once in my life, when I left Nabenchauk and came to Los Angeles. Both my mother and Manuel had died, leaving me alone to grapple with a universe I didn't understand, a place where I was alien. Now

Althor wanted me literally to leave my universe. He expected me to trust him, a man I hardly knew, one who I was beginning to suspect was years older than he looked and who, as far as I could see, had no reason to stay once he got tired of me.

And yet . . . we couldn't hide from each other. Yes, he could barrier his mind, and I understood now that I had learned long ago how to raise rudimentary mental shields without knowing it. But our connection was strong enough that I sensed his mind anyway, despite our shields. He wanted to force me to go with him. His impulse lasted only a moment, but it was so intense, I stiffened in his hold. Then his mood changed to anger at himself. His code of honor wouldn't let him take me against my will. He would accept my choice even though that decision hurt him in a way I didn't understand, leaving a sense of loss deep inside of him. Even if I had known how to ask why it affected him so strongly, I couldn't talk about leaving my home, even my world. It was too much.

Althor's slid his hands down my arms as if he were holding a wild bird that would fly away when he let go. When he bent his head to kiss me, I felt his sense of loss in the place where I hid my own loneliness.

When Joshua came back into the room, his agitation hung around him like a gritty haze. "It's a mess," he said as he locked up the door.

I sat up and swung my legs off the bed where I had been resting with Althor. Next to me, Althor continued to sleep. To heal.

"What did Heather say?" I asked.

"She recognized both you and Althor as soon as she opened the door."

"Josh, no! Is she going to turn us in?"

"I don't know." He came over to the bed. "She's coming back in a few minutes."

"Why?"

"It's hard to tell with her." His voice warmed. "She's brilliant, Tina. She doesn't think like the rest of us. She's up there where no one else can follow."

I couldn't help but smile. "It sounds like she means a lot to you."

His cheeks turned red. "She's a senior. She doesn't have time for a frosh like me."

Behind me, Althor said, "This is why she has the combination to open your door?"

Joshua practically jumped. "I thought you were sleeping."

I glanced back to see Althor sitting up. He gave Joshua a skeptical look.

"She watered my plants last time I went home," Joshua said. "That's all."

A knock sounded on the door. "It's us," Daniel called.

Joshua escaped Althor's scrutiny by going to open the door. The mysterious Heather came in, followed by Daniel, who was doing his best to look noncommittal. He didn't fool me. He was just as fascinated as he was skeptical about this whole business. Heather was harder to read; she instinctively protected her moods better than most people. She took one of Joshua's chairs to the bed, turned it around backward, and straddled the seat, folding her arms across the top while she considered Althor. She had a sheaf of papers in one hand.

Althor sat on the edge of the bed with his boots planted on the floor, regarding Heather. She met his gaze, and he squinted as if he had no idea what to make of her. Joshua stood next to Heather's chair, close enough to show support, but not so close that he intruded on her personal space. He glanced at her, then blushed and looked out the window. Daniel was standing by the door, a grin tugging his mouth as he watched Joshua pretend not to notice Heather. Then he glanced at Althor and stopped smiling.

I concentrated on Heather, trying to sense her mood. She had an outer toughness, no doubt about that, probably the defenses of someone used to making her way in places like Caltech where she was so outnumbered by the guys. Beneath that I detected the gentler emotions that she kept hidden. More than anything else, she exuded an insatiable curiosity.

At the moment, however, she was scowling at Althor as if she were fed up with him even though they had just met. "Josh tells me you claim to have a ship that goes faster than the speed of light."

"I don't have it," Althor said. "Your air force does." His deep voice chimed on the last word.

Heather's eyebrows went up in an elegant arch. I hadn't known people could really do that with their eyebrows, but she managed quite well. Then she handed Althor her papers.

"I'm learning complex variable theory this semester," she said. "Can you help with this problem?"

I glanced at Joshua, making my "what's going on?" face. He lifted his hands and shrugged.

Althor took the papers. "I don't know why you think I can help."

"Just wondering," she said, as if asking for help on your homework was a perfectly reasonable approach to your first contact with an alien race.

Althor glanced through the papers. "This is inversion theory."

"Inversion?" she asked. "What is that?"

"It is what happens when you go faster than light." Althor lifted the papers. "This is—I don't know the English word. Treatment with no acceleration. No tensors."

"I've never heard it called inversion," Heather said. "But yes, that's what I get when I put faster-than-light speeds into the equations of special relativity."

So. This was a test. Good. Althor would show them.

"I'm an engineer," Althor said. "Not a theorist. It is almost thirty years since I study this and I never do that well with it even back then."

Heather didn't look surprised. "I figured you'd say something like that."

Althor stiffened. "I didn't say I couldn't do it."

She just did that thing with her eyebrows again.

Althor scowled at her. He scowled at Joshua. He scowled at Daniel. If I hadn't been next to him, he probably would have scowled at me. Then he peered at the top paper, his forehead creased as he read her equations. I was about to protest that he didn't know English that well, but then he spoke, asking Heather what some symbols meant. After she answered, he went back to reading. Eventually he put the first paper on the bed and went on to the next page.

Althor pointed at a line of squiggles. "This has a mistake."

Heather leaned forward to look. "Where?"

He indicated a term in one of the equations. "It's upside-down."

The spicy scent of Heather's surprise drifted through the air. Her reaction didn't come because of the mistake; I was sure she had put it there on purpose. She reacted that way because she hadn't expected Althor to find the error. Hah! Good for him.

She said only, "You're right."

He continued to study the papers. As he found other mistakes, the fragrance of her astonishment filled the room. Finally he indicated the last page. "A factor is missing here."

"No, that one is all right," she said.

"Is not all right," he insisted. "You left out a two."

She took the page from him. "Oh! You're right. I did."

"You see?" I told her. "He knows what he's talking about."

Daniel shrugged. "All it shows is that he can do Heather's math."

I glared at him. "Along with all those other millions of people who can do complex variable whatever?"

"Tina has a point," Joshua said.

Heather ignored us as she studied Althor. "So you claim your alleged ship does what those equations predict."

"Essentially," he said. "My ship is a Jag. Not an alleged."

"And your Jag does all this by starting from sublight speeds?"

"Of course," Althor said. "How else would it work?"

Heather pounced with her words. "That's impossible. To reach faster-than-light speeds, you would have to go through the speed of light. You can't. Mass becomes infinite compared to anything slower. Energy becomes infinite. Time stops. Length shrinks to zilch, zip, nada. Even if you could go through light speed, faster-than-light travel has so many problems, it could fill a book."

"You don't go through light speed," Althor said. "You go around it."

Heather blinked. "Say what?"

"You circumvent light speed," Althor said. "You never actually go through it."

"Yeah, right," Daniel said. "The hyperspace bypass from Cannes to Hell."

Althor looked bewildered. "That what?"

"It's just a saying," Joshua told him. "He means he doesn't believe you."

"Why not?" Althor seemed genuinely puzzled. "Light speed is just a pole in the complex plane. To go around it, you leave the real axis."

"Of course," Daniel said. "A pole. How about a vaulting horse, too?"

"He means a singularity in the complex plane," Heather said.

Daniel looked exasperated. "And that's not mumbo-jumbo?"

"Actually, no." Heather considered Althor. "Mathematically, if you could go around light speed instead of through it, you're right, you would bypass the singularity. But physically, that makes no sense."

"It make perfect sense," Althor told her. "You just add a **** term to your speed."

"A what term?" Joshua asked.

"It means—" Althor let out a breath. "I don't know the English word. Ortho-real."

"Oh!" Heather snapped her fingers. "I know what you mean! An imaginary number."

"Yes," Althor said. "You add an imaginary part to your speed."

"Imaginary?" I asked. "That's the square root of a negative number." I had always liked that part of math. It was so delightfully weird.

"That's right," Althor said.

"Oh, come on," Daniel told him. "You can't add an 'imaginary part' to your speed."

Althor glared at him. "Tell this to the millions of starships doing it."

Heather spoke dryly. "And just exactly how are they accomplishing this feat?"

"You rotate your ship through complex space," Althor said.

"Of course," Daniel muttered. "The ol' complex space rotation."

"It still won't work," Heather said. "If you could go faster than light, you'd have all sorts trouble. For one thing, you could go back in time."

"This is not a problem," Althor said. "Your ship just looks like it is antimatter traveling from its destination to its departure point."

"Oh come on," Daniel said. "That's lame."

With no warning, Althor rose to his full height, towering over Daniel with his fists clenched at his sides. "Are you saying I am crippled?"

Daniel stepped back. "Well, no. I didn't mean that."

Althor stood there, his fists knotted, while we all gaped at him. It was the first time he had displayed any hint of anger despite all the verbal jabs they had taken at him. No one said a word. I could almost hear the others thinking *This man committed murder.*

Althor? I asked. *Are you all right?*

I had the oddest sense, as if he *reset* himself. Drawing in a breath, he sat on the bed and unclenched his fists, letting them relax on his knees. He spoke to Daniel in a quieter voice. "My sorry."

"Uh—yeah," Daniel said. "Me, too."

Heather spoke. "Althor, what you describe about going into the past—that was written about in some early papers on tachyons in places like *The American Journal of Physics*. It's called reinterpretation. Bilaniuk, Deshpande, and Sudarshan had articles on it, also Asaro. Feinberg too."

"Then why you act so surprised at what I say?" Althor asked.

"Because no experiments have ever supported those theories." Her curiosity filled the room with the scent of spices. "And the theory has problems. For one thing, if you could go into the past, you'd have paradoxes. Like you could go stop yourself from being born."

Althor just shrugged. "It doesn't work that way. What happens in one reference frame must happen in all of them, as specified in the Lorentz transformations."

"I don't know what that means," Joshua said.

Althor considered us, and I could almost feel him straining to translate his ideas into English. Finally he said, "I'm at rest compared to myself. So relative to myself, my speed is zero. That means I always observe myself going into the future no matter how fast I'm traveling relative to anyone else. If I could have stopped my own birth, I would have already seen it happen. Obviously I didn't."

"That's my point," Heather said. "It's a paradox."

"There is no paradox," Althor told her. "You can't do something in one reference frame and *not* do it in another. It may happen differently, but it happens. If I didn't experience it, neither can anyone else."

"I still don't understand," Joshua said. "Especially not the reference frames." He spoke carefully, and I didn't miss that he avoided any slang Althor might misinterpret.

Althor thought for a moment. "Suppose I am driving from Los Angeles to CalTech. I am going at sixty miles per hour. A car passes me at ninety miles per hour. They see me falling farther and farther behind them. In other words, in their frame of reference, I am traveling backward."

Heather laughed. "Until a cop stops them for a speeding ticket."

"Oh, I get it," Joshua said. "They see you going backward, but someone who's driving slower than you would see you moving forward. That's what you mean by different reference frames."

"That's right," Althor said. "Those two drivers don't see me doing the same thing, but their observations have to be consistent. They both see me drive from Los Angeles and CalTech."

"And you're saying that works for time, too?" I asked. I couldn't get my head around the idea. It made sense to say that

CalTech and Los Angeles existed at the same moment in time, but I didn't see how every moment in time could exist at the same place.

"Essentially," Althor said. "What everyone observes has to be consistent, even if they don't see events in the same way or even the same order."

Heather spoke thoughtfully. "Okay. You're alive, so you've already 'observed' your birth. Even if I saw you go back to that time, I couldn't observe you doing anything that didn't already happen because it would be inconsistent with what you observed."

"That's the general idea," Althor said.

Daniel was so intrigued, he forgot to pretend this didn't all fascinate him. "It's cool, sure," he told Althor. "In theory. But I don't see how that stops you from offing your younger self."

Althor leaned forward. "Faster than light travel isn't some magic time machine. In order for me to go back in time relative to the place of my birth, I must go *fast*. Faster-than-light. By the time I reach the day I am born, I am far away. When I turn around to come back, my speed changes sign in the equation. It means I go into the future as I return home. So how do I get to my birth? Is not so easy."

"That may be," I said. "But Althor, you're here with us before you were born."

Everyone stared at me.

"She has a point," Heather said.

Althor rubbed his chin. "I am here before the Althor of this universe was born. But he is not me."

"That is truly weird," Daniel said. He looked quite gratified with that statement.

"I suppose." Althor sounded tired. "All I know is that something went wrong. But what? I can't fix my ship if I don't know what made the problem." None of us needed telepathy to know what bothered him. If he couldn't undo whatever had sent him here, he couldn't go home.

"Maybe you're on the wrong Riemann sheet," Heather said.

We all looked at her.

"The wrong what?" Joshua asked.

Althor spoke slowly, his gaze intent on Heather. "My people use different words than yours. I am not sure what you mean by Riemann."

I had a feeling it wasn't only the word that puzzled him. Heather seemed like a math type, into abstract ideas, and Althor was more of a hands-on, practical guy. Still, he would understand better than the rest of us. Maybe her ideas could help him.

"Try comparing it to some non-math thing we'd all know," I suggested.

Heather sat thinking. Then she said, "Okay. Think of a Riemann sheet as a clock, the kind with hands that go around in a circle. The clock face is cut from, say, its center to the number twelve. The hour hand goes around from midnight to noon and then slides through the cut to a second clock underneath. It's the same as the first clock, except the hours go from noon to midnight. At midnight you slide through the cut back to the first clock."

"Okay," Daniel said. "So what?"

"Those two clocks together form a simple Riemann sheet," Heather said. "The more complicated the function, the more clocks you stack up."

"Ah. Yes." Althor nodded. "We call them phase maps. But these sheets, they are only math concepts. They don't really exist."

"How do you know?" Daniel asked. "You claim imaginary speeds exist."

Joshua spoke. "Althor, I think Heather is saying that maybe

when you did this inversion thing, you came out on the wrong sheet. Like you ended up on the wrong clock. Same time, different phase."

Althor went silent, staring at them. Finally he said, "That would explain a lot."

"You should check a history book," I suggested. "See if everything here is the same as where you came from."

Joshua pulled a green book off his bookcase and gave it to Althor. We all waited while Althor flipped through pages, stopping often to read. Several times, his face blanked into its computer mode.

"Find anything?" Heather asked.

He looked up at her. "I am trying to match this book with the history files in my spinal node. Much is similar, but the files aren't identical. Like here—" He indicated a map on the page he was reading. "The Greeks migrated south later on this Earth. I can't find any record in my files about this Egyptian 'Desert Conquest.' And Zoroaster was born later here."

"Who?" Joshua asked.

Althor peered at the text. "Zoroaster. He founded an ancient Persian religious system. It looks like the development of Messianic religions was also delayed." He glanced at Joshua. "You date your years from the birth of Jesus Christ, yes?" When Joshua nodded, Althor said, "He was born later here than in my universe. That's why the celestial time is the same in both our universes, but your history is shifted relative to mine." After a pause, he said, "On the scale of a planet's history, those few years are nothing." He didn't add the obvious, that on the scale of his life, those "few" hundred years made a huge difference.

Heather motioned at her papers, which he had set on the bed. "Those equations require two Riemann sheets. Maybe your universe is one sheet and ours is the other."

"Actually, the real equations are more complicated," Althor said. "They need an infinite number of sheets." He lifted the papers. "Your theory is incomplete."

Heather straightened up. "You can't be claiming that what I've written there is actual physics."

"It's not," Althor said. "It's missing the corrections derived by James."

"Never heard of him," she said.

I grinned at Joshua. "Maybe you're going to be famous." When Althor gave me a questioning look I said, "Joshua's last name is James."

"Maybe," Althor said. "I don't have the full name in my files. But I don't think his name was Joshua."

"Oh." Joshua looked disappointed.

"You're asking a lot for us to believe this is more than a game," Heather told Althor.

Joshua laid his hand on her shoulder. "I think we should help Althor."

The moment he touched her, I knew he was wrong about Heather not having any interest in him. The sensual fragrances of her mood curled around him, accompanied by the pulse of a drum, the song of an oboe. For the first time I noticed the way his T-shirt hugged his torso *just so,* the way his jeans clung to his long legs—

Ay! I broke away from Heather's mind, mortified. Joshua was like a brother to me, totally different from the hot guy she saw. Neither she nor Joshua noticed my twitch. She was smiling at him, her look far softer than anything she had for the rest of us. Joshua stood waiting for her answer, oblivious to his effect on her, but just as hypnotized by her existence. On the surface, neither of them seemed aware of the other's response; people could block all sorts of obvious things when they were self-conscious. But on a deeper level, I thought they already had a bond. Joshua deserved someone to love. A girl like Heather could be good for him. She had better treat him right, though, or she would answer to me.

"Okay, Josh," Heather said. "Let's see what we can do."

7

THE HUMMINGBIRD

"*Tina?*" The voice called in the dark, low and urgent, coming from far away. "*¿Eres tu aquí?*"

I lifted my head. Althor lay asleep beside me and Joshua was snoring on the floor. I had been dozing next to Althor, fully dressed, for hours. It was probably past midnight.

"*¡Tina! ¿Puedes oírme?*"

Puzzled, I got up on my knees and looked out the window above the bed. Outside, the moon laid its silvered light across the yard two stories below, enough for me to see who stood there, calling up to the window. Jake Rojas.

I answered in a low voice. "Jake! How did you know I was here?"

"Why else would you come to Pasadena, except to see Josh?" He spoke softly, but it was so quiet outside, I easily heard him.

Behind me, Althor sat up and slid his arms around my waist, his front against my back. A rustle came from back in the room, and I looked around to see Joshua standing up near the door, where he had been sleeping on the floor, all tousled in his t-shirt and gym pants. He came around to the end of the bed and leaned over so he could see out the window.

"Jake, is that you?" Joshua asked. "Wait just a second. I'll bring you up."

Jake nodded to him. "*Gracias, vato.*"

Joshua threw on a jacket and left the room. A few moments later he appeared in the courtyard below us. He and Jake shook hands, and they both took off, striding out of our view and into the night's shadows.

It wasn't long before the door to the room opened and they came inside. Jake glanced around as if he didn't know what to make of the place. I doubted he had ever seen a dorm room before.

"Jake, is everything all right?" I asked. Althor had turned toward the door, staying in front of me, and I had to move around him to see Jake.

"We've been worried about you," Jake said. "First the cops came asking questions. Then the FBI. Then some dudes who wouldn't say nothing about who they were. It took me this long to sneak past the guys they got watching us."

"You know that test plane they found?" I said. "The one that's been on the news so much?"

"What about it?" Jake asked.

"It's Althor's."

Jake snorted. "What, he told you that?"

"It's the truth," I said.

"Yeah, right. He a spy or something?"

"Or something," I said.

Jake considered Althor with a long, cold stare, and Althor met his gaze with an impassive stare. Turning back to me, Jake spoke in a quiet voice. "Nug's funeral was yesterday."

So they had buried Nug and his twisted dreams. I tried to feel regret for his death, but I kept remembering my cousin Manuel, how he used to laugh and swing me around when I was a little girl, his face lit with joy, backlit by the deep blue sky above the Chiapas highlands, the last traces of the dawn's fog burning off in the sunlight. Now he was dead. I felt Jake's grudging respect for Althor, who had done what they all wanted to do, what VSC would have done someday if Nug and his men hadn't finished them all first. From Althor, I felt a remorse Nug didn't deserve. With Nug driving so much hatred, the violence he thrived on would never have ended until he was either dead or the only one left standing.

I felt as if I were breaking inside. "Jake, you guys have to stop killing each other."

Jake glanced at Althor and Joshua, then spoke to me. "I need to talk to you private."

"We can go out in the hall."

Althor grasped my wrist. "No."

I laid my hand on top of his. "I need to do this."

"I'll go with you," he said.

"Like hell," Jake told him. His look could have burned rubber off a tire. "She told you she's going, *cabrón*. So let her go."

If Althor knew what Jake had just called him, he showed no sign. He must have understood, though; I had no doubt his spinal node could translate *bastard* into plenty of languages. I wished more of the guys I knew had his self-control. I could tell he was pissed off, though.

"Althor, I'll be all right," I said.

The cords in his neck tensed and Jake's anger simmered around us. Just when I thought Jake would go into his own version of combat mode, Althor let go of my wrist. Once again, he was going to trust my judgment and my honesty. I wondered if he had any idea how much that meant to me.

I slid off the bed and padded over to Jake. We left the room in silence, keeping enough space between us to keep Althor from exploding. When we were outside in the empty hallway, I pulled the door shut, giving us privacy. I didn't know what Joshua had told the other students on this hall, but I had no doubt they knew he was hiding people in his room. Joshua and Daniel were two of their own; as long as we were here on their approval, this unseen community accepted us. But if we did wrong by either of them, the other students would deal with us in their own way. I had no doubt their response would be far more subtle than what VSC would do to anyone who intruded in their barrio territory—but it would disrupt our lives just as much, if not more.

I felt the world shifting. Mario and his men had been the powers at our high school, lords of the land, and Joshua had been the vulnerable kid who needed their protection. But someday Joshua would be the one with power and riches, not because he planned it that way, but because his genius would bring him wealth without his even thinking about it. And he would never forget what VSC had done for him. Mario hadn't acted with any ulterior motives. I was sure it hadn't even occurred to him that Joshua could ever do anything for them. But I had no doubt; someday Joshua would return what he considered the great gift Mario had given him.

Jake raised his arms to pull me close, as we had done so many times, and I almost stepped toward him. We both stopped ourselves before we touched.

He spoke in a low voice. "Tina, I've been crazy trying to find you."

"I'm all right." I was far more shaken at seeing him than I wanted to admit.

"I had to warn you," he said. "About those FBI guys. They

keep asking questions. They'll find out about you and Josh being friends, and they'll come here."

I wanted to kick myself. I had believed a dorm room at Caltech was the last place cops would look, and that false sense of security could have ruined us. "Thanks, Jake."

"Tina."

"Yes?"

"I came to say good-bye, too."

The hall suddenly seemed too quiet. "You're leaving?"

"I meant to tell you at Mario's." His voice tightened. "But you were with that guy."

"Jake, he—" I stopped when he raised his hands, not against me, but as if he were defending himself against my words.

So instead I asked, "Where are you going?"

"Arizona." He lowered his arms. "My stepfather says there's a job in his garage if I want it."

"That's a good thing." His mother lived in a small town with hardly any people at all, let alone gangs. As much as I didn't want him to go, I wanted even less for him to die fighting over streets full of broken asphalt and pain. "What made you decide to leave?"

He pushed his hand through his tousled hair. "I'm tired, Tina. Tired of coming closer and closer to—I don't know what." His eyes were dark in the shadows of the hallway. "I went to Nug's funeral."

It was the last thing I expected him to say. "Why?"

"I don't know. Maybe because I'm glad it wasn't me."

"I am, too." A tear was gathering in my eye.

He touched my cheek. "No more guns, baby. If that's what it takes to bring you back, I'll do it. Whatever you want, I'll do."

I was caught on an edge, poised to jump. But which way? Jake offered everything I wanted: a predictable world, stability, someone like me. Althor offered chaos.

"Are you asking me to go with you to Arizona?" I said.

"Would you?"

The hall seemed muted, as if we were caught in a pause of the universe. "I don't know what will happen with Althor."

"We haven't said nothing to those FBI guys," he said. "But trust me, they won't give up."

I nodded to him. "We owe you."

"I didn't come here to help him. Just you."

"Jake, I won't forget." I had loved him for so long, I couldn't imagine living without him. But for now, I had made a commitment to someone else. "I have to see this through with Althor."

"I know." He spoke as if the words hurt. "You always stand with your man. But when this is over—if he—if you—" He stumbled to a stop. Then he said, "You know my mom's number in Arizona."

"I'll call, Jake. If I'm still—" Still what? Free? *Alive?* I had no idea how this would end.

"If you can," he said.

"Yes. If I can."

He made an odd sound then, as if he were losing a battle he had been fighting since we stepped into the hall. He pulled me into his arms and I held him close, memories of our times together flooding over me.

"*Adios, mi hija,*" he whispered.

"*Adios, Joaquin.*"

Then he was gone, running down the steps and into the night.

"Breaking into military networks is illegal," Heather said flatly. We were standing in Joshua's room: Althor, me, Joshua, Heather, Daniel. Heather and Althor were facing off like fighters in the ring.

179

"But you can do it." Althor made it a statement rather than a question. He motioned at Daniel. "He has the password."

Daniel stiffened. "I told you I don't have it."

"You're lying," Althor said.

"What, you know what's in my brain?" Daniel demanded. "I already said I don't know the password to my mom's account." The lie of that surrounded him in an orange haze.

"It doesn't matter what he does or doesn't have," Heather said. "I'm not fooling with any system at Yeager Flight Test Center."

Althor answered in a too-quiet voice. "I need your help."

Damn. He was getting that look. I had already seen, with Nug, what happened when Althor felt backed into a corner.

Heather paled, but she didn't back down. "You claim you're some futuristic fighter pilot. You told Tina you brought a warship here that could blow California to smithereens. Then you expect me to break into a military network and falsify records so you can get onto a secured base? At the very least, you want me to compromise the security of this country by letting an escaped killer loose in Yeager. If your story is true, you're asking me to risk the safety of our world."

"I'm asking you to help me keep my freedom," Althor said. "Would you want to be locked up, maybe killed, when you had done nothing wrong?"

Heather lifted her hands, then let them drop. She walked away from us, to a window near the bed, and stood there staring out at the courtyard. When I glanced at Daniel, he averted his eyes. Even Joshua wouldn't look at me.

Finally Heather spoke. "If I did help you—and I'm not saying I will—but if I did, the best I could do is get you onto the base." She turned to him. "And that's only with Daniel's help, if he's willing."

Hope jumped in Althor's voice. "Just get me there. I do the rest."

Heather regarded him steadily. "Do what?"

"Leave," Althor said. "And never come back, if I have a choice."

"Why wouldn't you have a choice?" Joshua asked.

"My ship may be too damaged. Or what brought me here maybe can't be reversed." Althor lifted his hands, then dropped them again. "If this is true, my only real choice is to die in space or come back to Earth. *This* Earth."

For an instant, as he spoke, his mental armor slipped and I saw what he truly felt. He clamped down his barriers, but he was too late. I knew. To him, this Earth was primitive. He feared he would die a long, ugly death far from home. The process had already begun. The longer the military worked on his ship, the more they were hurting him.

In that instant, when Althor's shields slipped, Joshua jerked as if a bullet had hit him—and Heather also stiffened.

No wonder she and Joshua liked each other. It was the same thing that made Joshua and me friends, that drew me to Jake, and especially to Althor. Empath. Like sought like. Neither she nor Joshua seemed to have any clue about it, but that made no difference. The bond existed.

"If I help you," Heather told Althor, "it comes with a price."

He regarded her warily. "What price?"

"A ride in your starship."

Daniel grinned. "Yes! All of us."

"This isn't a game," Althor told them. "If you get killed, no magic potion will make you alive again."

"And if you're telling the truth," Heather said, "this is a chance we'll never have again."

"The inversion drives have a malfunction," Althor said. "If I get home, I have no intention of returning here. I might not get home a second time."

"Just take us somewhere in the solar system," Daniel said.

Althor scowled at him. "No."

"No ride," Heather said, "no security pass."

Althor muttered in his own language, but I didn't need to recognize the words to know he was cussing. I also felt Heather and Daniel's doubts hovering behind their bravado. If he didn't agree soon, they were going to withdraw their offer.

I laid my hand on Althor's arm. "This may be our only chance."

He turned with a start. For a moment he just looked at me. Then he turned back to Heather. "If we reach the ship, I'll take you in orbit around Earth. That's it. Nothing more."

Heather glanced at Daniel and Joshua, and they both nodded.

"You've got a deal," Heather told Althor.

Moonlight sifted through the curtains, silver and pale. Outside, crickets sawed in the night, reminding me of when my mother had taken Manuel and me to New Mexico, near Las Cruces, before we moved to Los Angeles. I remembered lying in bed with the window open while the crickets outside in the desert sang and hopped, filling the air with their endless rasping trills. I sat now with Althor on the bed, unable to sleep, listening to those tiny jumpers whistle their love songs. The desert air smelled sweeter now, clearing up after the sun had set and the smog receded.

Joshua and the others had gone to prepare for our trip to Yeager, and Althor and I couldn't turn on the light when the room was supposed to be empty. Althor was silent, sitting against the wall by the window, lost in thought.

After a while Althor spoke. "Tell me a story."

"What would you like to hear?" I asked.

"I don't know." He lay on the bed and put his head in my lap. "Anything to make me forget I might die tomorrow."

I brushed his hair back from his forehead. "You won't die. You'll get your ship and find your way home."

"I hope so." His voice was low.

I slipped into the lilting style of speech I had learned from the best storyteller I had ever known. "This tale was told to me by my mother, Manuela Santis Pulivok, told to her by her brother, Lukarto Santis Pulivok, who heard it from a traveler in Santo Tomás Chichicastenango. It is the story of the Ancestral Hero Twins." I paused for effect. "Before the birth of the twins, their father and uncle offended the Lords of Death. The two men made a great commotion while playing a ball game in a court above Xibalba, the Underworld where the Lords of Death lived. So the Lords killed them, sacrificing both of the ball players for their offenses. They buried the uncle under the court, and they hung the skull of the father in a gourd tree, a warning to humans that they should beware of provoking the gods."

Althor smiled. "The gods could have tried wearing earplugs."

I held back my laugh. That would have interfered with my storyteller's dignity. "Perhaps. This all happened before the birth of the dead men's sons, Xbalanque and Hunahpu—"

"What?" He sat up. "Where did you hear those words?"

Startled, I blinked at him. "What words?"

"Shibalank. Quanahpah."

"It's pronounced Xbalanque. And Hunahpu."

Althor took hold of my arms. "Where did you hear them?"

He was certainly getting all het up. "This story comes from the *Popol Vuh*. It's an ancient holy book of the Quiche Maya."

"What made you think of it tonight?"

"You asked me to tell you a story."

"But why *this* one in particular?"

I hesitated. "I don't know. Why are you upset?"

"Just before we made love yesterday, I told you a quote from

183

the Iotic language." Moonlight sifted through the curtains and cast his face in planes of shadow and light. "It was about the great beauty of a woman called Shibalank."

"In the stories I know, Xbalanque was a man," I said. "But I remember now. Some of the words you said sounded familiar. That's probably why I thought of this story."

He let go of my arms. "Tell me more."

Pleased with the effect of my tale, I resumed. "The daughter of a Death Lord found the skull of one of the ball players hanging in the gourd tree. It got her pregnant by spitting into her hand."

Althor gave a dry laugh. "I can think of far more pleasant routes to fatherhood."

I smiled and traced my finger over his knuckles. "Is that like your story of Shibalank?"

"Not exactly." He had a far away look. "Shibalank and Quanahpah were twin sisters. They founded the first two houses of the ancient Raylican dynasties."

Huh. This had too many coincidences. "Xbalanque and Hunahpu were twin brothers."

Shadows played across his face. "These legends of my people are over six thousand years old, by Earth reckoning."

"Maya civilization is nowhere near that old."

"This is what you are? Maya?"

"My mother was." I should have left it at that, but then I added, "I never knew my father."

His face had turned pensive. "Our scholars believe my ancestors came from Earth. Our DNA is almost identical to humans here."

"You seem human to me." Dangerous, too, but so were most men I knew.

"Tell me more of your story," he said.

"The Xbalban god was enraged by his daughter's pregnancy."

No surprise there. I had seen what my mother endured from many people in our village as an unwed mother. "She escaped to the Middleworld, where the grandmother of the dead brothers took her in. She gave birth to the twins, Hunahpu and Xbalanque. They became great ball players." I lowered my voice as if to confide a great secret. "One day they played in the court where their father and uncle had disturbed the gods. They too angered the Lords of Death. But they survived *every* trial the Lords put before them, even returning to life again after letting themselves be killed." I let my voice rise. "The Lords of Death were so angered when the twins overcame death that they demanded the brothers kill them and bring them back to life, so they too would learn how it was done. So the twins killed them." With satisfaction, I said, "But they didn't bring the angry lords back to life."

Althor smiled. "That was not so smart of Death, insisting to die."

I laughed. "I guess not."

"Can you tell me other stories?"

"I always like the hummingbird song." I concentrated on the words, translating them from Tzotzil into English in my mind. Then I sang in a low voice.

> The hummingbird is good and big.
> So that's the way it is;
> There were workers in hot country;
> They were burning bean pods,
> The fire could be seen well, it was so tall.
> The hummingbird came,
> It came out,
> It came flying in the sky.
> Well, it saw the fire;

Its eyes were snuffed out by the smoke.

It came down,

It came down,

It came down so that they saw that it was big.

Don't you believe that it is little, it is big.

Just like a dove, its wings are white,

All of it is white.

I say they tell lies when they say that the hummingbird was little,

The men said it was very big.

Then they recognized how it was,

For none of us had seen it.

We didn't know what it was like.

Yes, it says "Ts'un ts'un" in the evening,

But we didn't know what size it was.

But they, they saw how big it was,

They saw that it was the same as, the same size as a hawk,

Having to do with the father-mother,

"One leg" as we call it.

Remembering the words made me miss my mother even more than usual. I could see her in my mind, her face rapt as she recited the lines. She loved telling stories, even acting them out with her hands.

Althor, however, was staring as if I had grown a second head. "How old is that story?"

"I don't know. It's a Zinacanteco myth."

"What is father-mother?"

"It was the best translation I could think of for the word *Totilme'il.*" He certainly seemed upset all of the sudden. "It means the ancestral gods."

"The hummingbird is a god?"

"No. A messenger for the gods."

"This story is not about bird."

"It's not?"

"It's about a starship."

I couldn't help but laugh. "Oh, Althor."

He didn't smile. "It came flying out of the sky? It was big and white? This is how a hummingbird looks?"

"Actually, no. Hummingbirds are tiny and dark."

"They make this sound 'ts'un ts'un'? They stand on one leg?"

He had a point. "Well, no. Nothing like that."

"A civilization must grow from roots." He was watching me closely. "What came before the Maya, six thousand years ago?"

"Stone-Age Indians, I think."

"Could this hummingbird story be six thousands years old?"

I shook my head. "I don't see how. Maya civilization is nowhere near that old."

Althor considered me. "Yet the stories of your people and mine are so alike. It is far too much for coincidence." He motioned toward the night sky outside the window. "In the tales of my people, the twin sisters travel away from Earth on the Star Path. It is a black fissure in the stars."

He was right, this was beyond coincidence. "The Maya have a legend like that."

"We call it the legend of the Star Path," Althor said. "Our historians believe it describes the trip my ancestors took when they were moved from Earth to the planet Raylicon."

"But who moved them?"

"We have no idea." The moonlight caught glimmers from his skin. "The kidnappers disappeared. We've never found any trace of them."

It made no sense. "I can't imagine why anyone would take a bunch of Mesoamerican Indians to another planet."

He was quiet for a moment. Then he said, "The ancestors of

my people, the ancient Raylicans, carried a pure strain of the Kyle genes."

"You mean they were empaths."

"Empaths. Telepaths." He sat thinking. "Maybe whoever took them wanted to concentrate their DNA. My ancestors carried a form of the Kyle genes that is almost extinct now. It shows up only in rare descendants of the original Raylicans."

"You think the Maya are your ancestors?"

"Maybe."

"Althor, you're about as Indian as a cotton swab."

He blinked. "Cotton?"

"I meant you don't look Indian." Though it was hard to tell with the metallic tint to his skin.

He tilted his head, his expression turning inward. "India doesn't—wait, I see. Indian also refers to native peoples of the Americas. This is you, yes?"

"Partly." Most people called me Hispanic, but that meant Spanish speaking, and my first language was Mayan. I wasn't comfortable with Latina because it sounded too much like *Ladino,* which referred to the mixed blood descendants of the Spaniards who had conquered the Maya. Among my friends back home it also meant those of our own people we felt had betrayed our ways to make themselves wealthier. I supposed I could say *Mejicana.* On forms that asked for ethnicity, I checked off Chicana if that was my only option, but that wasn't really right, either.

"I'm mestiza," I said.

"Mestiza." His face blanked into computer mode. "Mixed blood."

"That's right. Indian, Mexican, maybe some Spanish."

He came back to normal. "Why maybe?"

I shrugged, pretending I didn't care. "Because I've no idea

who was the *pendejo* who fathered me and then walked out on my mother."

I didn't fool him anymore than he fooled me. "Tina." He took my hand. "He could have left for any number of reasons."

I couldn't talk about my father. So I said, "How about your family? Do they all look like you?"

"Actually, my grandmother looked like you." He smiled wryly. "They say she was formidable."

I liked that. I was about as formidable as a kitten, but I would have loved to be a bad ass. "How about you?"

"I look like my father, some. More like my maternal grandfather."

He said it with such ease. His father. I'd always wondered if I looked like mine. Did we sound alike, laugh alike, think alike? Had he asked my mother to come with him when he left Chiapas? She had never told me. Maybe she refused him the way I refused Althor, too afraid to chance the unknown. It would make the loss so much easier to bear if she had chosen to let him go without her. I couldn't imagine her deciding to stay by herself, though. She had been so lonely.

"It's all dreams anyway." I took off my bracelet and handed him the metal ring. "This is the only truth I have. My family has passed this from mother to daughter for generations, from mother to son if there was no daughter to inherit it, and from father to daughter, for longer than we can remember, back until forever in the past." My voice caught as I thought of the family I had lost. "Someday I'll give it to my daughter."

Althor pulled me into his arms. "Come with me, Tina. Don't stay here. The loneliness will kill you."

I laid my head against his chest. "I can't."

He pushed me back, gripping my shoulder with one hand while he held up my bracelet clenched in his other fist. "Why is this so important? It's just a damn ring of metal. Come with me. Find new memories."

"It's all that's left of my clan," I said. "Everyone and everything I knew when I was a child is gone, all except for that bracelet." As long as I believed my father existed somewhere, I could hope to find him someday, to have family again, a heritage. Althor was asking me to give up that dream. For what? An uncertainty so complete it seemed like a nightmare.

Except Althor wasn't looking at me anymore. He was staring at my bracelet as if it had sprouted horns.

"It's not *that* surprising," I said.

His face became unreadable and he shuttered his mind. "I need a light."

"Joshua has one on his desk."

Without a word, Althor got off the bed and crossed the room. He took the desk lamp and sat on the floor with it in front of him. When he switched on the light, gold radiance appeared around him like a leak in the darkness, making his skin shimmer. I went over and sat in front of him. He was holding my bracelet under the lamp, turning the circlet over and over, running his fingers along the hieroglyphs engraved inside the ring.

"What are these symbols?" he asked.

"Ancient Mayan glyphs." I wondered why he cared. Most people didn't even notice. "They're just a copy, though. My bracelet couldn't be old enough for those symbols to be authentic."

"Why do you have it?" he asked. "And your mother and her mother? Inheritance in your cultures here usually goes through the male line, doesn't it?"

"Mostly. I don't know why we pass it from mother to daughter. That's just what we've done."

He looked up at me. "Raylicon was a matriarchy."

"What does that have to do with my bracelet?"

Althor showed me the glyphs engraved on the metal. "This inscription is Iotic."

"Your language?" That was nuts. "It can't be."

"Maybe Iotic was your language before it was mine." He lifted the ring. "This isn't a bracelet."

Could have fooled me. "Then what is it?"

"Part of the fitting for the tubes on the exhaust of a Raylican transport shuttle."

I smiled. "Sure it is."

"Is not a joke."

"Althor, I have no idea what Raylican transport shuttle even means."

His eyes were dark in the lamp's glow. "I know them as ruins on the shore of the Vanished Sea in the Sleeping Desert. They are the oldest artifacts on Raylicon, dating from six thousand years ago. These shuttles, they are not built for humans. The proportions are wrong." He turned the bracelet in his hand. "I have seen others of these on the transports. We think the Iotic inscriptions were made by the first human settlers to Raylicon, to help them identify different parts of the alien ships. Some of them were almost surely engraved before they left Earth. That's how you could have one."

He was being loco again. "A bronze bracelet in as good of condition as mine couldn't be six thousand years old."

"It is not bronze."

"It's not?" It certainly looked like bronze.

He held the bracelet in front of me. "It is an alloy called cordonum, made atom by atom using nano-bots. It endures much better than bronze. A ring like this *could* last for ages if it were treated well." Softly he added, "If, say, a family revered it as an heirloom, passing it from generation to generation."

Generations I could believe. But thousands of years? "Mayan glyphs didn't exist that long ago."

"I don't know how you have this ring," he said. "But these glyphs *are* Iotic. Our scholars say the ancestors of my people brought Iotic with them from Earth, that the language is a remnant of our lost home." He spoke quietly. "Before tonight, my ancestors had no past. Do you know what that means? The history of my people ends six thousand years ago. We know nothing of ourselves from before that time. Now, when I may never again see my home, you offer me a history. I have this incredible gift of knowledge and no one to tell."

I took his hands, folding my fingers around his fist and the ring of metal. "You'll find your way home."

"I hope so." He didn't sound like he believed it.

Althor pulled me close and switched off the light. We sat in the dark holding each other, silent in the silver night, grieving for what neither of us might ever have again, a history and a clan.

8

THREE HANGARS

The Mojave Desert rolled by as Daniel drove his jeep along Highway 14. The engine hummed and wind rushed by us, the only sounds in the otherwise deep silence of the land. The desert stretched out in gray-green rolls of land splotched by yellow dust, prickly ocotillo plants jutted their spindly stems up from the ground, topped with sparse red flowers. Tumbleweeds blew across the road. Although it was only eight in the morning, heat already shimmered on the asphalt, giving the highway an unreal look in the distance, as if it were separating into flat layers of mirrored water. The sky was a pale blue expanse arching over a parched day that smelled like grit.

I sat in the back of the jeep, scrunched between Althor and Joshua. I had on Rosa's wig and I also wore a cap, but the wind still whipped my hair around. I still didn't believe myself as a blond, but I could deal with that better than the wire-rimmed glasses Daniel had given me. They weren't any kind of prescription, just glass with no effect on my eyes, but they felt wrong. I pushed at them, trying to settle them on my nose. And I felt silly wearing the grey business suit Heather had lent me. Anyone who saw me would surely know I was a fake.

For Althor, Joshua had dug up a yellow stage beard with grey streaks from a play put on by the chemistry graduate students, and he found a boring blue suit big enough to fit Althor's large frame. I dyed Althor's hair blond. So now he sat next to me with his suit jacket across his knees, his tie loosened and his collar open. He kept squinting. A few times he raised his hand to his eyes, but he always stopped himself before he rubbed them.

"Are the contacts bothering you?" I asked. When he cupped his hand to his ear, I raised my voice so he could hear me over the wind. "Heather's eye lenses. Are they bothering you?" The tinted contacts turned his distinctive purple irises into an ordinary blue.

"Everything blurs," he said.

Heather had turned around to watch him from the passenger seat in the front. "Can you see enough to walk?"

Althor squeezed his eyes shut, then opened them again. "Yes, I should be fine."

"Try not to smudge your face," I said. "It makes the gold show." I took a bottle of foundation out of my purse and touched up a streak under his eye. I had to be careful: if I used too much foundation, it would show, making people wonder why this macho dude in a conservative suit was wearing make-up, but if I used too little, it wouldn't hide that faint but telltale shimmer of his skin. I couldn't make the hinge in his hand go away, but as he didn't fold his hand in two, it probably wouldn't show.

"There we are," Daniel called.

I glanced up to see a sign on our side of the highway:

ROSAMOND BLVD. YEAGER MILITARY FLIGHT TEST
CENTER.
NASA-AMES-DRYDEN RESEARCH FACILITY.

Under it, an older sign in faded letters said: EDWARDS AIR FORCE
BASE.

"Edwards." Althor snapped his fingers. "Now I recognize this.
It is called Edwards Air Force Base in my universe."

"It used to be that here," Daniel said. "They changed the name
in honor of Chuck Yeager, after he died."

"In my universe," Althor said, "General Yeager lived well past
the 1980s."

Daniel turned onto the exit beyond the sign. It was early
enough in the morning that we were part of the day's commute.
Cars hummed along the road ahead and other cars followed us
from the highway onto the exit. We all drove through a land
dotted with blue and yellow flowers, and the vivid orange
glow of California poppies. After we crossed a dry lakebed, we
entered a wrinkled-blanket terrain covered with yellow flowers
that spilled everywhere like paint.

Six miles in, we hit a security checkpoint. Cars filled both
lanes, backed up with the morning rush hour traffic. As we
waited in line, the engine of the jeep idling, Daniel glanced back
at us. "This is the West Gate."

Althor looked past him to the small booth up ahead. "Does
this gate always have so many security police?"

"Security police?" Daniel asked.

Althor motioned toward the booth, where harried guys in
uniforms were trying to deal with all the traffic. "The guards. I
count six."

"We call them milcops," Daniel said.

"Whatever you call them," Althor said, "this gate has too many."

"The other times I've been here, I've only seen a couple," Daniel said. "Most days, they wave you past as long as they see the base sticker on your vehicle." He eased the Jeep forward as the guards let another car through.

"A sticker," Althor said, more to himself than us. "That's not much security."

Joshua was looking around with unabashed curiosity. "How many people work here?"

"About 5000 military," Daniel said. "I'm not sure about the rest. Maybe 6000 civilian and 8000 contractors."

Heather whistled. "I had no idea it was so big. Sounds more like a city than a base."

"Do you think the milcops know why the base upped their security?" I asked. It was yet more evidence that Althor was telling the truth about his Jag.

"I doubt it." Daniel regarded us uneasily. "It's not like they have a need to know." He turned back around to the front. "They probably have some good guesses, though, given the news about that plane the military found in orbit."

We moved forward in spurts, inching closer to the gate, until finally it was our turn. Daniel pulled alongside the milcop at the booth and held up a phony badge for a place called JPL, which he said stood for Jet Propulsion Laboratory. I watched like a deer caught in the headlights until Joshua elbowed me in the ribs. Startled, I opened my purse and took out the MIT badge he and Daniel had mocked up for me. Then I waited, stiff in my seat, certain the milcop would know we were fakes.

Heather had found a file in the Yeager computer system about a group expected at the base today, specialists brought in to study the "test plane." We came early because the real specialists weren't scheduled to arrive for several hours. The previous night, during our planning, Daniel had said that if we pulled this off, it would be even more impressive than three years ago, when two CalTech students, Dan Kegel and Ted Williams, took over the scoreboard computer for the Rose Bowl. They changed the team names on the scoreboard from UCLA and Illinois to Caltech and MIT, with Caltech beating MIT by 38 to 9. I had pretended to scowl, but I didn't fool him. He knew I thought it was funny. Today, however, nothing was funny. The stakes were much higher, deadly even, and so much could go wrong.

Daniel and the others put on a good show of nonchalance as the guards looked over their badges: another morning, another job. But underneath they were tense and eager.

Althor was harder to read, enough so that I wondered if he had switched into another of his modes. When I concentrated, I picked up more. The lack of security amazed him. The thought of something called "9/11" jumped into his mind, an event that would someday tighten security all over this country. It hadn't surprised him that Heather managed to hack the Yeager system; apparently this Earth was at such an early stage of computer development, he expected students on the cutting edge of the technology to know more about the burgeoning networks than most of the people using them. But her simple methods startled him. I wondered if any of us could even understand the level of sophistication for security in his universe.

After the milcops looked over our badges, a dark-haired guard asked for our on-site contact. As Daniel gave him the phone number, I held my breath. The guard went into his booth and picked up a phone. I watched him through the tinted glass, reminding myself to stay calm while he spoke to whoever was on the other end.

The guy came out and I froze. But he said only, "They're waiting for you up at North Base," and waved us through the gate.

And that was that.

As we drove away from the guards, Joshua exhaled and Heather closed her eyes. My relief felt big enough to cover the base.

We rode with a line of other cars through the crinkled hills. It took only minutes to reach the base. It was the size of a small city, but with a practical look, too functional for a college, too boring for suburbs. As we drove along, the other cars pulled off into the parking lots for various buildings. We kept going until we were headed back into the desert on the other side of the base.

Althor made a strange sound, a small explosion of breath. Following his stare, I saw a silver aircraft in the distance. Mounted on a pedestal, it looked like a fat rocket with short wings and a needle nose.

"I've seen that plane somewhere," I said. I didn't remember where, though.

"It's an X-1," Althor said.

Heather glanced back at us. "A what?"

He pointed at the silver aircraft. "That. It's an X-1. A *real* one."

"Yeah, it's an X-1," Daniel said. He sounded far less impressed.

Althor grinned at him. "I never thought I would see a real one. Does it fly?"

"I don't think so," Daniel said.

Althor motioned at a distant structure that rose above the desert like the giant scaffold of an unfinished skyrise. "What about that lift? What does it launch?"

Daniel peered at the lift. "I think it's for the space shuttle."

"That's NASA's Dryden Research Facility," Heather said.

I snapped my fingers. "I remember! The Six Million Dollar Man."

"Say what?" Joshua asked.

"It's an old TV show." I motioned at the X-1. "It starts with the crash of a plane like that."

"I'm pretty sure it was an M2-F2," Daniel said. "Not an X-1. They used actual NASA footage. Bruce Peterson, the real pilot, survived even though he hit the ground at, like, 250 freaking miles per hour."

Heather was watching Althor. "This must all seem prosaic compared to what you've seen."

His laugh rumbled. "Aircraft are never dull. I've liked them since I was old enough to build a rocket and shoot it into the air."

Heather gave a startled smile and Joshua's surprise made yellow loops in the air. I realized it was the first time any of them had seen Althor laugh.

Daniel didn't react, intent on his driving as he turned onto a street called North Base Road. Another security checkpoint lay ahead on the left. It stood near a big white and black trailer that looked temporary, as if someone had just dropped it onto the desert. We stopped at the checkpoint and a milcop there looked over our IDs, comparing them to whatever documents he had on his clipboard.

The guard indicated a lot by the road. "You can pull in there." Then he motioned toward the trailer. "While we inspect your Jeep, you can get your site badges."

My pulse jumped. Two other cars were parked in the lot, with guards going over them like cops searching for crack.

Daniel just said, "Sure thing." He sounded perfectly relaxed, as if he did this all the time.

After Daniel parked, we climbed out of the Jeep, smoothing down our wind-blown clothes. The heat blazed. Neither Daniel nor Althor put on their jackets, but Althor let me fix his tie. As I pushed up the knot, he muttered something about "bizarre barbaric custom, tying a rope around your neck." I couldn't help but smile. I knew a lot of twentieth-century guys who agreed with him.

Inside the trailer, a man behind a makeshift counter checked our IDs. Althor stood at the back of our group, tall and silent, dressed in his mundane suit, blending with the scenery. To fit our parts, the rest of us had needed to look older. Heather and I managed with business suits and makeup, and Daniel had a snappy coat and tie, but nothing we did helped Joshua. Heather finally changed the age of the guy he was supposed to be, making it twenty-two, and we crossed our fingers that they would take him for one of those brilliant types who earned a Ph.D. practically as a kid. It wasn't that far from the truth. If he hadn't had other problems to worry about in high school, like getting his head blown off by Nug's gang, he could have easily graduated years early.

The man finished with Daniel and spoke to me in a bored voice. "ID."

Okay. This was it. I handed him my MIT card and waited for him to figure out it was fake. Amazingly, he just typed at his terminal and gave me back the card. He looked at Joshua's next. This time, he stopped and stared at the screen, his forehead furrowing.

We all tensed. I felt it, like plastic pulled tight around us. We were fried.

The man peered at Joshua. "Chakrabarti? That's an Indian name, isn't it?"

Joshua regarded him with innocent blue eyes. "Yes, sir. My mother was Swedish."

"Huh." And just like that, the guy handed the ID back to Joshua. No alarms, no shouts. He motioned toward a doorway behind the counter. "Go on in there. Marjorie will make your badges."

So we all went, pretending this was normal. Marjorie, a

plump woman with red hair piled on her head, was waiting in the "photography studio," which consisted of one bright light and a grey board for a background. I tried to relax while she snapped my picture, but I kept wondering if this was how it felt to have your mug shot taken. Except she put the photos onto cards with our names, laminated the whole business, gave us each our badge, and shooed us out of the trailer.

We walked outside into searing sunlight with the Mojave Desert all around us. The milcop was still at the checkpoint by the road. He waved us toward the Jeep. "You're all set," he called.

Daniel raised his hand in acknowledgment. Incredibly, we had made it. We were in—

Althor stopped.

He froze, standing in the middle of the street, his face contorted.

We halted next to him. "What's wrong?" Joshua asked.

When Althor didn't respond, I spoke to him in a low voice. "We have to keep moving. We don't want to draw attention."

Althor shook his head, his forehead creased with what looked like pain.

"Come *on*," Daniel said, low and fast. For the first time, his outward cool slipped. "We can't stop here."

Althor dropped his hands and said, "* * ***."

"What did you say?" Panic edged my thoughts. I tried not to notice the milcop, who was walking toward us from his guard booth.

Heather swore under her breath. "What the hell is wrong?"

Althor said something else, these words just as indecipherable as his last.

The milcop joined our group. "Is there a problem?"

Heather was pulling a tissue out of her purse. With an

apologetic look at the guard, she blew her nose loudly and messily. I thought she was nuts until I saw the milcop turn from Althor to her.

"Are you all right?" the guard asked.

Heather sniffled. "Hay fever." She even sounded stuffy. "The pollen is killing me."

The milcop actually smiled. "You and half the base. Spring is hay fever hell out here." He shook his head. "Some people do fine with over-the-counter treatments, but if it's already causing you trouble, you may want to see a doctor."

Heather gave him a wan smile. "Thanks. I'll look into it."

He nodded, seeming satisfied, and headed back to his post. We started walking again, and Althor came with us.

"How did you know about the hay fever?" Daniel asked Heather.

"I really have it." With a grimace, she added, "He wasn't kidding about hay fever hell."

Joshua was watching Althor. "Are you all right?"

"Yes," Althor said.

I exhaled with relief to hear him speak normally. "What happened?"

"The Jag." His accent was stronger. "We are close. I try to reach it. The onboard systems, they have damage. Some from before, some new." Sweat sheened on his forehead. "It affect my mind—I cannot—I am losing my ability to integrate my functions."

"What'll happen if they don't stop messing with your ship?" Daniel asked.

"I don't know." Althor picked up the pace as we strode through the parking lot. "I don't want to find out."

Within moments, we were back in the jeep and headed toward North Base. Its three hangars seemed to grow out of the desert. They were gorgeous, shaped like cylinders with rounded roofs, each painted a different color: blue, green, yellow, with bright murals, vivid scenes of aircraft soaring through the sky.

"Hey." Joshua gazed at the hangars like he was in love. "Cool."

Althor squinted at the murals. "Your military make pictures on aircraft buildings?"

"Why not?" Daniel said.

"Never seen it," Althor muttered.

We parked in a lot near the hangars. A chain link fence with another security gate separated the lot from North Base proper, staffed by two more of the ever-present milcops. As the five of us crossed the asphalt, headed for the gate, and the dry desert wind ruffled our hair. Heather sneezed.

When we reached the security gate, Daniel went first, holding up his badge. One of the milcops took it, studied the picture, looked at Daniel, gave him back the badge, and nodded for him to go past. So far so good.

I stepped up, offering my badge to the guard. After he checked it, he considered me. "How long have you worked at MIT?"

Stay calm. "Three years."

"What's a bite?" he asked.

A bite? I concentrated, trying to figure why he would ask such a weird question. All I picked up was that he didn't think I looked like a computer whiz.

I took a guess. "It's part of a computer. Inside."

His face remained impassive, but amazingly, he waved me past. He let the rest of our group by with nothing more than a badge check and a nod, even Joshua, which would have annoyed me if I hadn't been so keyed up. Then we were all through the gate and inside North Base. The place didn't look like much, just the hangars and a few other low buildings baking under the sun. Beyond the buildings, the wrinkled lakebed rolled out, parched and dry under the pale blue sky.

Daniel slanted me a look. "You're lucky that guy didn't know much about computers."

"Why?" I asked.

"A byte isn't part of a computer," he said. "It's a unit of information used by computers. Eight bits. Eight ones and zeros."

"*No one* here seems to know much about computers," Althor muttered.

"She convinced him," Joshua said. "That's what matters."

We kept walking, neither fast nor slow, nothing to draw attention. Milcops in berets and green camouflage uniforms patrolled the area with dogs. Squat vehicles rumbled by, each like a cross between a small tank and an all-terrain cockroach.

"They have a lot of security," Althor said. He sounded more normal now.

"I wouldn't be surprised if the ThreatCon is Charlie," Daniel told him.

"ThreatCon?" Althor asked.

"It's a warning system for terrorist aggression," Daniel said. "My mom talks about it. Usually it doesn't go higher than Alpha. Bravo is next, then Charlie. Delta means the situation is as bad as it gets." His grimace made him look ten years older. "If you get your plane, you can bet your ass this place will go to Delta."

Althor scowled at him. "I am not terrorist."

Daniel shrugged. "They don't know what you are."

Heather was looking through the papers they had given us in the trailer. "We're supposed to go to a security briefing—no, wait, that's this afternoon. Right now we meet our contact. Dr. Robert L. Forward."

"Hey!" Joshua said. "I've heard of him. He won the Goddard Prize in 1981." He beamed, clearly in his element. "It's a rocket science award. He got it for work on antimatter propulsion."

Althor looked far less pleased. "If your military has already discovered my Jag uses antimatter propulsion, they probably realize it has interstellar capability."

"Does that matter?" Heather asked.

He regarded her uneasily. "I think they will soon figure out that I am here alone, without a mother ship. It is much better for me if they believe someone is looking for me."

We came around the corner of a large building and walked into full view of the hangars. Up close they were even more impressive, the murals drawn in bold detail, fighters soaring in cloud-streamered skies above rural countryside or desert landscapes. The yellow and green hangars were closed. The blue one was open, but a large sheet of canvas hung in its doorway, weighted at the edges to keep the wind from lifting up the cloth. A mystery lay beyond that sheet.

A fence surrounded the structure with yet another guard booth at its gate. Inside the fence, a scaffolding towered next to the hangar, supported by cement dividers about three feet high, the kind used by construction crews. The framework looked almost ready to contain an aircraft—or a starship.

"That's odd," Heather said.

I followed her gaze. She was watching two milcops who were patrolling the hangar inside the fenced area. Large dogs stalked alongside them, lean beasts with muscles rippling under their fur.

"Those are ugly pups," I said.

"Yeah, they are," Heather said. "But I meant the guards. None of them has a gun."

"Weird," Daniel said.

"It is a sensible precaution," Althor said. "They know nothing about the defenses of my ship. They don't know what will happen if bullets hit the craft."

Heather gave him a startled glance. "Do they need that precaution?"

I expected Althor to reassure her. Instead he said, "My ship must consider them as hostiles. The less of a threat it perceives, the better."

With no warning, a man walked out of the hangar, lifting up the canvas. The gusting wind grabbed the covering and flipped it even higher into the air—revealing the beauty inside.

The Jag.

I recognized the ship, though I had never seen more than a fuzzy picture on the news. I *knew* that ship, through Althor. The Jag looked like an alabaster sculpture, its hull a blaze of white in the sunlight slanting into the hangar. Its lines were so clean, it seemed ready to leap off the ground and soar into the air.

The canvas fell back in place, hiding the ship.

Heather whistled. "That's gorgeous." Daniel and Joshua's faces mirrored her reaction.

"It is so close," Althor said. "If I could just reach it."

Close indeed. To reach the Jag, we needed to get past one more security gate, the one in the fence that surrounded the hangar. Two milcops were posted there, a man and a stocky woman, both with handguns. So. One more guard point and then we could just walk to Althor's ship.

We showed our badges yet again. The woman looked over Daniel's more carefully than anyone had at the previous stations. Then she smiled at him with that look women give hot·guys. Hah! I supposed his cocky stance and sweep of brown hair had a certain appeal.

"So you're the experts." The woman tilted her head toward the hangar. "She's a beaut."

Daniel nodded, for all the world like a tech type being taciturn about a classified operation. "So we've heard."

She motioned toward the gate. "You can go on through with your card as soon as we check everyone."

"Sure thing." He went over and stood by the gate, waiting for the rest of us. Beyond him, past the fence, the hangar waited, with the scaffolding rising high on the side closest to us.

The woman checked my badge next while Heather showed hers to the other guard, a thin man with close-cropped brown hair. I stood quietly, doing my best to look innocuous and scholarly. The glasses and business suit helped. I hoped.

The woman nodded to me. "Go on in. Good luck."

I managed a smile. "Thanks."

The other guard passed Heather on to the gate, and the female milcop passed Joshua through with barely a nod. So far our luck had held.

Althor came up to the other guard and handed over his badge. The guy studied it, peering at the picture, then at Althor, then at the badge again. I held my breath, my pulse doing a jackhammer imitation. None of the guards had spent so long on the rest of us. Althor turned out to be a lot better actor than I expected. His cool was amazing; he actually looked a little bored. Only I could see how his tension stretched in the air like the shimmer of heat.

So we waited, Joshua, Heather, Daniel, and me, trying to relax while the guard frowned. I concentrated on the guy, straining. I picked up a bit, mostly his discomfort in the hot sun. He didn't like his job, and by extension he didn't like us, either.

He finally handed back Althor's badge. With a curt wave, he motioned Althor over to us. As Althor headed over, I smiled a bit the way people might who worked together, and he nodded, casual and at ease. I was hyper-aware of the hangar beyond the gate.

Now we had to get through the security gate. A box that resembled a telephone keypad was attached at about waist height. While the milcops watched, Daniel took out the key-card they had given us at the trailer and swiped it down a slot on the box. With that done, he typed his code into the keypad. He pushed on the gate and we waited, the desert wind fluttering our hair.

Waiting.

"I must have made a mistake," Daniel muttered.

"Try again," Heather said in a low voice. "I think you get three times before an alarm goes off."

Daniel swiped his card again and re-entered the numbers. This time when he pushed, the gate opened. Yes! I had to make a conscious effort to keep from gulping in a breath. Althor's face showed no reaction, but his excitement jumped so hard, it registered on my senses like the clang of a mallet on a gong. We walked through the gate and headed toward the hangar.

We were in.

A call came from behind us. "Wait there!"

My pulse jumped. We all stopped and turned.

"Yes?" Heather asked.

Both milcops were coming over. When they reached us, the man said, "Don't forget to change into the white coveralls before you enter the craft. You'll find them in the locker inside." He was still studying Althor. "Sterile environment, you know."

Heather nodded. "Of course."

"Well, then." After a pause, the man said, "Go on ahead."

We turned back toward the ship. Just a few more moments—

"Wait," the woman said.

This time I couldn't help but jerk as we turned around. Amazingly, Daniel didn't look the least worried. In fact, he even seemed a bit annoyed, exactly as you would expect for who he was supposed to be. "Is there a problem?" he asked.

The woman was no longer paying attention to Daniel. Instead she focused on Althor. "What's on your face?"

He regarded her with what looked like mild curiosity. "My face?"

"There." Stepping closer, she indicated his sweat-sheened temples. "It looks like makeup."

"It's lotion," Heather said. "He has poison ivy."

The woman continued to watch Althor. "I don't see any rash."

"It's covered," he said. "The heat makes it worse." Whatever mode he was in right now, his accent was barely noticeable—but I did hear the slight lilt to his words.

The milcop rubbed her index finger along his temple. It came away smeared with foundation and sweat, which did actually look like calamine lotion—

Except that where she had rubbed, a gold streak of skin showed on his face.

I *felt* the milcop's explosion of recognition. She didn't know him from the sketch that had been all over the news; that leather-clad tough had no resemblance to the bearded, blue-suited scientist here. It was something else—*damn*. The guards assigned to the ship had full descriptions of Althor, everything the authorities had gleaned about him, including all the oddities, like his metallic skin.

Both milcops went for their guns—and Althor *moved*. He whipped his leg up in a blur of speed at one guard while he threw his body at the other. It happened so fast, I couldn't follow what he did; all I knew was that he knocked out both the man and the woman. As they crumpled to the ground, someone outside the fenced area shouted.

Althor grabbed Daniel's arm and ran for the hangar, yanking Daniel with him. I couldn't tell if Daniel was in shock or feared for his life, but he didn't fight, which was smart, because I had no doubt Althor would have knocked him out and dragged him. Daniel struggled to keep up with him, half running, half stumbling. I shot a glance at Joshua and Heather, who both met my look. Then we all took off after Althor. His using Daniel as a hostage hadn't been part of our deal, but unless we intended to desert them both and let the milcops take us, we had to follow his lead.

We ran alongside to the concrete dividers that supported the scaffolding on our left. Three milcops sprinted toward us, along with two monster dogs, a black Doberman and the biggest German Shepherd I had ever seen. The milcops shouted and the dogs bounded forward.

Althor threw Daniel to the side just barely in time. The dogs hit Althor full force, growling, teeth tearing, and he crashed to the ground with both of them on top of him, their furious barks exploding in the air like a rain of howls. They were going to kill him! He wrestled with them, flat on his back as they went for his neck, arms, and legs. He heaved them off his body with so much force, they flew several yards through the air before they crashed into the ground. When they hit the asphalt, I cried out, almost able to feel that impact slam through my own body. The black monster lay still, breathing raggedly. The shepherd struggled to its feet, baring its fangs, then collapsed in a heap of growling gold fur.

It happened so *fast*. Althor was already back on his feet and swinging around to us. Daniel backed away, his eyes wide, his face pale. Althor grabbed his arm, then yanked him around so they were both facing the milcops, Daniel's back against Althor's front. He slapped his knife flat against Daniel's neck, and the prismatic blade glittered in the harsh sunlight.

Everyone froze. Althor had one hand gripped around

Daniel's bicep and the knife in his other. The rest of us waited a step away, no one daring to break the stark silence of the desert. Althor was looking from the milcops by the hangar on our right to the guards at the security gate to our left. His knife splintered the sunlight into colors that refracted everywhere, spots of color flashing on the asphalt, the scaffolding, the hangar, and the guards. The red dog was on its feet again, growling, but a command from one of the milcops kept it in place. Daniel stood stiff as a board in Althor's clenched grip, sweat running down his face.

Althor let go of Daniel's arm and grabbed mine, yanking me so fast, I grunted as I thudded into his side. I knew how it looked, violent and harsh. It wasn't. With his enhanced strength, he could have crushed either Daniel or me without even trying, yet he wasn't hurting either of us. He backed up, drawing us with him, moving slow enough so that his knife didn't cut Daniel's neck.

We didn't get far. The concrete dividers that formed the base of the scaffolding blocked the way, and we backed into them. The guards were arrayed in front of us and the black dog had regained its feet, pacing and growling. The Jag was so close, only a few yards away, but it might as well have been across the planet.

On the far side of the hangar from where we stood, someone lifted the canvas and a group of people in white coveralls walked out, escorted by another milcop. Rather than take them to the gate on this side of the tarmac, which was close to us, the milcop yanked the chain-link fence away from that side of the hangar and led them out that way.

The guards in front of us were squinting in the glare created by the knife that Althor held against Daniel's neck. A man with hair the color of yellow dust spoke to Althor. "We don't want to hurt you."

"Let me by," Althor said. "Or I kill him."

Daniel's eyes widened. I didn't believe Althor intended to kill anyone, but it was obvious no one else shared my certainty.

"We don't want anyone hurt," the milcop said. He used a soothing voice, obviously trying to placate Althor, but something was wrong. Had his gaze flicked to a point behind us?

Glancing back, I saw a guard creeping through the scaffolding, moving low behind the concrete dividers. He carried a big, ugly rifle. After being around VSC for so many years, I knew guns. That guy had an M-16.

The guard gave me a reassuring nod, apparently assuming I was a hostage. Maybe he was right; I had no idea. Althor was desperate, and God only knew what would happen if he felt trapped. I nodded to the guard, just barely, like I was hiding the motion from Althor. Then I turned around, pretending I was going along with the guard, but I spoke to Althor under my breath. "A milcop is coming up on the other side of the dividers, two steps behind you—"

Althor released us and whirled around, kicking his leg over the dividers with deadly accuracy. The milcop never had a chance. Althor's boot heel rammed the man's chest, and the guard grunted as he collapsed. In barely seconds, Althor sheathed his knife, grabbed me and Daniel, and hefted us over the concrete barriers, then vaulted over the barrier after us. I fell to the ground, breaking my fall with my hands, dizzy with the shock of being thrown. The milcop Althor had knocked out lay crumpled only inches away, breathing but unconscious.

I was dimly aware of Heather and Joshua scrambling after us. As I lifted my head, disoriented, something whizzed above me, so close that it brushed my hair. With a gulp, I dropped back to the ground. Bullets slammed into the dividers, and the barrier split into a network of cracks.

"Stop shooting," someone shouted. "Take them alive! And don't hit the damn ship!"

"Holy fucking crap," Daniel muttered next to me, lying on his stomach with his palms braced against the ground. A trickle of blood ran down his arm where Althor's knife had nicked him. Joshua and Heather were on his other side, also staying low.

Someone had released three dogs, and they were bounding toward us, their fangs huge and white. Crouched behind the dividers, Althor grabbed the M-16 from the guard he had knocked out and studied it for a moment. With almost no pause, he swung it around and fired over the barrier, slamming the area in a rapid-fire rain of bullets. The milcops scattered, running for safety. Althor could have easily mowed them down, but he didn't hit a single one.

Unlike the people, though, the dogs kept coming. Althor fired and they dropped one by one. I bit my lip so I wouldn't cry out my protest. I knew they would have torn us apart if he hadn't stopped them, but I still hated to see them shot.

"Move!" Althor told us. "To the hangar. *Now.*"

None of us dared to argue. We crawled behind the dividers on our stomachs. He came with us, clenching the M-16 in one hand while he yanked up his vest. The socket for his transcom was opening. He left the transcom inside his body, tapping the edge of his hand, clenched over the box while he was still holding the gun—and a shriek burst out of the transcom. The shrill noise went higher and higher, almost too high to hear, dropped back down into ear-splitting range, and went so low that I felt rather than heard it vibrating through my body. Then it scaled up through the entire range again. I caught a metallic flash of Althor's thoughts, something about waveguides inside his body creating that horrible shriek.

The scaffolding around us began to shake, and its beams

creaked as if they were straining to burst apart. With a groaning snap, one of the supports broke free, flying away from the structure.

"Watch out!" Daniel yelled. In that instant, the scaffolding above us buckled. We lunged to our feet and sprinted toward the hangar while chunks of cracking wood fell around us.

"Damn it," a woman shouted. "What is he doing? I can't get a clear shot!"

"Don't shoot!" someone else called. "It could rebound into the hangar."

I understood then. In all this chaos Althor created, nothing was clear, no line of sight anyone's aim. They probably couldn't even tell exactly what we were doing. It was clever—

A block of wood smashed into my head. With a gasp, I stumbled and the world went dark.

"*No!*" Althor grabbed me around the waist and yanked me against his side, protecting me with his body. He tapped off the transcom siren, but with the scaffold collapsing around us, noise still thundered in the air. I struggled to run, but my head was spinning from the blow. He lifted me against his side so my feet were a few inches off the ground and then he carried me, lengthening his stride as he ran faster than I could have managed on my own.

A milcop appeared in front of us. With Althor's blurred speed and my head reeling, everything seemed to happen in a high-speed parade of snapshots: the guard raised his gun; my feet hit the ground; Althor kicked the man's arm; the weapon barked; shots went wild over Althor's head; the milcop collapsed as Althor barreled into him. Althor sprinted forward and I stumbled with him. The canvas on the hangar loomed in front of us—almost there—

And we stopped.

Four milcops stood facing us, their backs to the hangar, their uniforms dark against the white canvas. They had their M-16s trained on Althor, and the semi-automatic rifles glinted in the harsh sunlight. Althor still had his M-16, but it was pointed toward the ground. If he tried to aim, we all knew the milcops would shoot him. With his enhanced speed, he might get off one round, but not before at least some of them fired. And they were too close to miss.

We stood there while the rumble of falling debris died away. Althor stared at them, his face impossible to read, his inner lids down like metal shields. Machine man.

The guard with dust-blond hair spoke. "Drop your weapon."

Althor watched him, utterly still. I felt his frustration like steel bands. I picked up something else from him, too, an emotion less easy to define. Fear? Maybe some, yes, but this was different. *Longing.* To be this close to the Jag and be unable to reach the ship was physically painful to him. Wind blew across the canvas behind the guards, rustling the cloth, and somewhere far in the distance a car motor rumbled.

"We don't want to hurt you," the dust-blond man said. His mood scraped my skin. He felt tension, yes, but also awe. Although he would shoot if necessary, he didn't want to. It made no difference that none of the guards were supposed to know the full truth about Althor. They had guessed. This one wanted to *talk* to him, ask a hundred questions, not an interrogation, but to welcome our first visitor from beyond Earth. He wanted to understand why Althor looked human, why he was here, how his ship worked. He wanted Althor to help us fly to the stars.

Actually, two of the guards felt that way. The third was just doing his job. The fourth, a man with a clenched face, scared me. He saw Althor as a threat beyond imagining. Had he and Althor been alone, he would have shot Althor point-blank with no qualms, certain he was protecting Earth. Fear made his thoughts vivid: he disagreed with the decision to place no explosives on Althor's ship—better to lose the Mojave Desert if Althor's ship blew up rather than risk losing the entire planet.

Voices came from around us. A line of milcops had formed to the side, several yards away. One, a woman, was speaking into a walkie-talkie. Damn. She was probably calling for rein-forcements. I swayed, nauseous, my head spinning from where the chunk of debris had struck me. The dust-blond man kept talking in his soothing voice: *drop your weapon, release your hostages, come with us.*

Althor exhaled with a tired breath and his shoulders sagged. He let the M-16 slide out of his hand. As it thudded onto the asphalt, I closed my eyes. It was over. Done. Finished.

"Holy shit!" someone yelled. "*It's alive!*"

I snapped opened my eyes. Everyone was staring at the hangar. The wind had lifted the canvas, kept lifting it in fact, higher than seemed possible, given that the big drape of cloth had weights to hold it down.

Then I understood. That wasn't wind pushing up the canvas. Althor couldn't reach his Jag—

So the Jag was coming to him.

9

LIGHTNING JAG

The ship rolled straight out of the hangar. In front of us, the milcops scattered, running to keep from being crushed under the Jag's elongated wheels. As soon as the man with the clenched face was clear of the ship, he whirled around and stood with his feet planted wide while he fired, *bam, bam, bam,* ramming the Jag with bullets.

"Don't *shoot* it, you idiot!" someone shouted.

The Jag rolled out fast. Althor sprinted for the ship, dragging me with him. The ship only made it halfway out of the hangar before it failed and ground to a stop, but that was enough. We ran so close to it, my arm rubbed against the luminous white hull. The surface had a pebbly texture, like a golf ball. As a hatch sucked open, Althor hefted me up and literally threw me inside. I slid across a deck of glowing blue tiles and plowed into a pile of computer printouts that the team from the Yeager base must have left here, big white sheets of paper folded into a stack, so primitive and out of place on this sleek fighter.

Althor shoved Daniel into the ship, then lunged inside while Daniel rolled out of the way. Heather and Joshua scrambled in just before the hatch sucked closed like the shutter on a high-speed camera. As I jumped to my feet, an explosion rocked the ship and flung us across the cabin. Althor smashed into a bulkhead on his injured shoulder, and I felt agony sear through him, so intense he almost blacked out. But he never faltered. He pushed his way into the cockpit, squeezing between the bulk-head and pilot's seat. Papers, pens, and calculators left by techs from the base lay strewn over the console. He sent them flying with a sweep of his hand and shoved himself into the seat.

The ship welcomed him. It snapped a flexible framework around his body, encasing him in a silvery mesh and bringing an array of panels to his fingertips, the controls glimmering with traces of light. I sensed as much as saw the mesh clicking prongs into the sockets in his spine, connecting the Jag's systems directly to the biomech web inside his body.

The Jag touched his mind.

Althor gasped. At least, that was the audible sound. In his mind, he screamed. His link with the ship shattered. I picked up only a ghost of his pain, but even that was enough to send my mind reeling in shock.

Another explosion hit the ship, a dull boom against the hull, and the force of that strike shook the Jag like a giant hand. I grunted as it threw me into Daniel, and we slammed against a bulkhead. We all grabbed handholds and hung on, staring toward the cockpit. This was all felt unreal, too fast, impossible, crazy.

The Jag tried again to contact Althor's mind, more care-fully this time, but again he recoiled. I was so tuned to him, and his mental state was so heightened inside the ship, that I was picking up the Jag as well. The ship had a mind, an intel-ligence, a sentience.

It was alive.

Althor's link to the ship was hurting him. His brain somehow interpreted his damaged neural connections with the Jag as pain. He broke the link and spoke out loud in a resonant language I didn't recognize. In response, the bulkhead in front of him glittered blue, swirling with bright lines and speckles, then cleared into a screen, as if we were looking out a big wind-shield to the scene outside. Milcops were backing away, staring at the rumbling Jag with their mouths open. Two of the guards were struggling with a third, the man with the clenched face who wanted to destroy the ship. They fought in silence, trying to wrest away his gun. He flipped one of the guards over his back and knocked the other to the ground, then hurled some object at the Jag. Another blast shook the ship. I grunted as the explosion threw me to the side, and I lurched into Heather, who was gripping the long handle of a cabinet. I grabbed it as well and hung on tight.

Outside, a milcop with dust-blond hair fired his gun—not at the Jag, but at the leg of the man with the clenched face who was throwing grenades at us. The bomber went down with a cry, his face contorting as he clamped a hand around the calf of his left leg. Blood pumped out around his fingers. The guards he had been fighting each grabbed one of his biceps, hefting him back up, favoring his injured leg as they pulled him away from the battle.

The entire time, Althor and the Jag were speaking to each other, brusque words low and fast in Althor's language. The ship hovered at the edges of his mind, extending mental probes here, there, making brief contact, withdrawing if Althor mentally flinched, building the link if it didn't harm him.

Whatever they were doing, it had a dramatic result. A rainbow of light appeared outside the ship, a wave of color that shaded from red to orange, yellow, green, blue, and violet. Then I realized those colors weren't real, but an effect created by the Jag to represent—*what*? When the colors swept across the milcops, they clapped their hands to their ears. I concentrated on the Jag, strengthening our link. Then I understood. The ship was using membranes in its hull to create a noise so painful to hear, it drove away both milcops and dogs. The colors showed the sound waves: red for maximum density, purple for minimum. The Jag was fighting its attackers with a weapon of noise.

The milcops kept backing away, two of them taking the injured man with them. Some of the guards were already out of the fenced area and running for a nearby building, one shouting into a walkie-talkie. I would have run, too. They had no way to know what the Jag was about to do. Attack? Explode? All I could tell was that the ship intended to protect Althor at any cost. His star fighter was majorly pissed.

The ripples of light continued to spread, but when they reached the fence around the hangar, the colors turned into a muddy mess. The mess reflected back toward the hangar and smeared with the outgoing wave until the rainbow faded. I caught a thought from the Jag to Althor: the ship was missing some instructions, "proper boundary conditions," whatever that meant. Its damaged systems were misreading the effect of the fence, interpreting its presence as a command to stop the noise.

If we could have taken off, it wouldn't have mattered. The Jag, however, was going nowhere. It couldn't roll any farther out of the hanger, and Althor's verbal commands had no effect. He tried sending it a mental message, but his neural link to the ship caused him too much pain. He finally ran his fingers across the mesh around his body, manually inputting commands to the ship. Glowing red lines appeared on the forward screen, superimposed on the scene outside the ship. They blazed red as they outlined the edges of the hangar visible on either side of us—

The hangar exploded.

Debris flew everywhere, up and out, hurtling through the air. The remaining milcops around the ship ran like mad or dropped to the ground, protecting their heads while debris flew around them. A block the size of a door came at the Jag from one side, and it looked as if it were shooting straight at us. When it crashed into the hull, it appeared to shatter only inches away from Althor's face.

Then the hangar was gone. The Jag stood free under open sky.

A loud rumbling shook through the ship, vibrating the deck. As soon as it started, the guards who had dropped to the ground outside jumped to their feet and sprinted away. One man tripped over a chunk of debris and fell to his knees, and another hauled him up so they could run. The Jag's thunder built, growing stronger and louder.

Althor swiveled his seat around to the four of us. "Some of the launching routines for my ship are—I don't know the word. Not working. Off-line."

"Can you fix them?" Heather asked.

"They fix themselves. It needs some seconds. Then I take off." He regarded me steadily. "If you want to go, you must leave now."

This was it. He might escape or he might die, but either way he was leaving. He wanted to know if I would go with him. I had to answer, but I couldn't speak. I wasn't like Daniel, ready for the unknown, craving the adventure. I didn't want to leave Althor, but the thought of leaving Earth terrified me.

The others stood frozen, staring at Althor and me. When I didn't respond, Althor's face became an impassive mask.

Turning his seat around, he returned to his controls. Next to me, the airlock snapped open.

"Hurry," Althor said curtly, intent on his panels. "All of you. Go. Now." The rumbling from the Jag's engine shook through the ship.

The others looked like they had no idea how to react, either. I let go of my handhold and stepped toward the airlock. I was making the decision Jake had offered me at Caltech, choosing safety with him over my fear of the unknown. Surely I could live with it: Jake was also an empath, not as strong as Althor, but still like me.

Except I would never forget Althor's words: *It's like starving inside.* Being with Jake was just enough sustenance to stay alive.

I swung around. "Wait."

Althor stayed focused on his controls. He had become a machine again, whether on purpose or because he had no control over the process, I had no idea. His voice was flat. "I have no time to wait."

I took a ragged breath. "Take me with you."

Althor froze, his hand poised over a control panel. "You will come with me?"

"You have to promise." My voice was shaking. "You have to swear you won't strand me in some place I don't know, some universe I've never seen, some alien world where I can't understand anything. You have to promise you won't throw me away."

He swiveled his seat to face me. "I will give you this oath." His English was suddenly perfect and his gold inner lids had come down over his eyes. "If you will give me your promise."

"For what?"

"That you will be my wife."

I couldn't imagine why he wanted a nobody like me, but if it meant the same thing in his universe as in mine, it was the protection against desertion I had asked for. Or it could have a totally different meaning among his people. Or he could be lying. I didn't have time to figure it out. I had to choose. Now.

So I went with my gut. "I promise," I told him.

"Swear that you will connect to no other network," Althor said. "Local or remote."

What? "I don't understand."

"Swear." His voice was metallic, without inflection. "Or I will not take you."

"But you were the one who asked—"

"I was too closely integrated with my emotional functions when I asked you before." He regarded me with his shielded eyes. "In this mode, I have a higher clarity of thought."

He was lying about something. I recognized that orange flicker around his body. But he was in control now and he meant to get what he wanted.

"And you?" I had no idea what I was asking, but I was so "closely integrated with my emotional functions," my clarity of thought had gone to the wind. "You'll promise the same for me?"

"Yes," he said. "You have access to my systems. You are in my mods, nets, memories, files. Your influence has migrated to all of my processors. No virus guard can remove such a thorough invasion of my systems without destroying their integrity. If you come with me, the fact of your presence will continue to rewrite my code, penetrate my memory locations, and alter my processing functions until you are thoroughly integral to my systems."

Good Lord. What was I getting into? But I understood his unasked question and that was what I answered. "You have my word. I won't betray you."

Althor inclined his head. "I trust your word. I will take you."

Then he turned back to his controls. Just like that, a switch in his mind changed from one setting to the other, dropping our conversation as if he were swapping to another mode.

I glanced at the others, then looked away, embarrassed. They seemed confused, unsure what they had just witnessed.

"The rest of you leave," Althor said as he worked. "Now."

"You gave us your word," Heather said. "A ride first, before you go."

He didn't answer, just kept working, but neither did he insist they get off the ship. I was aware of the Jag in the background of my mind, strengthening its mental link with Althor as it found more locations in his neural web that it could access without hurting him. Althor was entering commands by touch, voice, and mind now, like a verbal and mental dance that went too fast to follow. He and the Jag were merging. Except it wasn't only them. I was caught in their link.

The hatch snapped closed and the growl of an engine came from the back of the cabin. I turned with a start. Two panels were folding down from the bulkheads like drawbridges, each about three feet wide and four feet long. White material covered them and filled the recessed hollows they left behind in the bulkhead.

"Get in the cocoons," Althor said. "All of you."

Cocoons. I hoped that wasn't a literal description. As we went toward the panels, I caught a mental message sent by the Jag to Althor, a snippet of communications it had caught from the Yeager base, a man there talking about "ground-based aircraft scrambling from Nellis."

As I reached the panels, and the cottony stuff inside one of them snapped out a ropy coil. It wrapped around my leg and yanked. With a grunt of protest, I fell across the panel. Other ropes from the cocoon coiled around my body and pulled me into the recessed area, hefting me around as if I were a box of cargo. Within seconds, I was sitting in the recess, facing outward. The cottony stuff wrapping me up, fast and efficient, until it covered everything except my face with a silky white cocoon.

"What the—shit!" Daniel yelled as the coils yanked him down on top of me. He sprawled across my legs, his knees thudding into my thighs.

"Hey," I said.

"Sorry," Daniel muttered. His embarrassment left an astringent scent in the air as the coils crammed him into the recess with me. He thrashed around, trying to free himself, but harder he fought, the more tightly the cocoon held him.

"I can't breathe," I said. "You're too heavy."

He shifted around until we were squeezed together side by side. In the other cocoon, Joshua and Heather looked a lot more comfortable with their arms wrapped around each other.

"Daniel," I said.

"Look, I'm sorry," he grunted. "I can't help this."

"I know. That's okay. I wanted to ask you. Do you know what scrambling means? Aircraft scrambling from Nellis?"

He tensed, his shoulder rigid against mine. "Where did you hear that?"

"The Jag told Althor."

"Nellis is an Air Force base near Las Vegas," he said. "I think scrambling means they have chase planes in the air, covering the base and this area."

"Does that mean they'll try to stop anyone from taking off?"

"Hell, yeah." He grimaced. "I wouldn't be surprised if they have a squadron continually airborne. Twenty-four aircraft working in waves, six new to launch every time six land."

"Do you think Althor can get past them?"

"I don't see how."

From where we were sitting, only part of the forward screen in the cockpit was visible, but it was more than enough to show flames blasting the tarmac outside as the Jag tried to take off. Billows of exhaust plumed through the air, accompanied by the roar of the engines. All that noise and commotion, and the Jag was going nowhere. The rumbling became more insistent and the deck tilted, pressing us farther back into the cocoon.

The Jag lifted into the air—and then Althor's link with it slipped, no, *ripped*. He made no outward sound, but his mental groan reverberated in my mind. The ship hung above the ground with just enough thrust to balance gravity. It couldn't seem to go higher, though it moved sideways. Grey and white clouds of exhaust filled the screen, but the Jag barely managed to wobble over the chain link fence surrounding. Then the ship climbed higher, higher yet. It just cleared the next hangar, blasting the roof of that building into oblivion. We kept going, out over a taxiway now—

And the engine quit.

The Jag dropped with a sickening lurch. The engines kicked in for a moment, then cut off again. We hit asphalt with a jarring impact, and it shoved the air out of my lungs as if I'd been socked in the ribs. Althor's hands were flashing over his controls. Apparently the ship could also take off like an airplane, because Althor quit trying to take the Jag straight up and taxied down the runway instead, engines roaring. We sped up until it felt as if a huge, invisible hand was pushing me into the cocoon. The ground fell away—no, we *leapt* into the air.

Static burst out of some device in the cockpit. ". . . immediately!" a voice was saying. "I repeat, land your craft immediately."

"My intent is not hostile," Althor said.

An indrawn breath came over the comm and in the background someone said, "He's speaking English!"

A curt voice snapped out of the comm. "Land your craft and release your hostages. If you refuse, we can only assume your intentions are not to the benefit of this country." With only the barest pause, the man added, "Or to this planet."

Messages flashed by in my brain, almost too fast to catch, data sent from the Jag to Althor. Most of that flood was in another language, but bits and pieces came in Mayan or Spanish. Whether the Jag was deliberately translating or was automatically adapting to my mind, I had no idea. Whatever the reason, the situation was clear: a "ceiling" of fighter planes was holding us down. We were flying in a low circle above the base while the Jag searched for a hole in the ceiling.

"If I land," Althor was saying into his comm, "I am your prisoner."

"We have no wish to harm you," the man at the base answered.

"Why should I trust you?" Althor asked.

"Trust has to begin somewhere," the man said. "You ask us to trust that you aren't hostile. Prove it."

I felt Althor's anger crackle, felt the words *I don't have to prove anything to you* on his tongue. He held them back. Instead he said, "Call off your fighters."

"You have violated our airspace," the man said. "With a heavily armed war craft. You have attacked American citizens and military personnel and taken hostages. If you refuse to land, we will be forced to use whatever means necessary to stop you."

"If you fire on this craft," Althor said, "it will be considered an act of hostility by Skolian Imperial Space Command."

Another voice came on the radio. This man was excited, barely able to contain his words. "We don't want to hurt you! We want to talk to you. What is your Space Command? Are your people coming here? How do you know English so well?"

Althor spoke carefully, choosing his words with help from a

translator that whispered in his mind. "My commanding officers know where I am. If you persist in holding me or my ship against our will, they will interpret your actions as a deliberate act of aggression against my people."

The first voice came back on the radio, clipped and cold. "We have found no trace of another ship. Your craft was damaged and abandoned in orbit."

"I have already contacted the mothership," Althor said.

"No indication exists of either a mothership or that your craft transmitted any message."

"Then your search is too primitive," Althor said. I knew he was stalling.

"Land now," the man told him. "Or we *will* fire."

Throughout the exchange, the Jag sent Althor updates on its systems. Most of the weapons and navigations capability were off-line. With Althor's help, the ship was fixing itself, but it wasn't easy. The Jag couldn't have sent a message anywhere, and the brass at Yeager were calling his bluff.

"They ought to be more afraid of what will happen if they don't let him go," I said.

"You think if they captured a MiG jet fighter from Russia, they'd let it go?" Daniel asked.

I scowled at him. "This isn't a EuroEast airplane. It's from another star."

"And its pilot knows English? Looks human? Leaves his ship spying on the planet? Commits murder and kidnaps a woman as practically his first acts on Earth?" Daniel grimaced. "They must be scared shitless."

"You knew all that when you agreed to help."

He spoke more quietly. "Yes, I did. My gut says to trust Althor, God only knows why. But you need to see why those chase planes will fire on us."

I spoke softly. "Daniel, we could die."

His face paled. "I know."

"But you still wanted a ride."

"Hell, yeah. When would we ever get this chance again? Besides, believe me, they'll do everything in their power to get Althor back alive."

"I hope you're right," I muttered.

In the cockpit, Althor was trying to negotiate. "You've damaged my craft. I may not be able to land."

"Can you eject?" the man asked.

"Not all five of us."

A message from the Jag flashed in Althor's mind, sharp and insistent. I had no idea what it meant, but in that instant, pressure suddenly slammed against us, flattening me against Daniel.

"*Holy shit.*" That came from one of the fighter jets. "Look at that mother go!"

The pressure grew worse, crushing us. Spots danced in my vision. I couldn't think, speak, breathe. Darkness closed in.

The pressure stopped as fast as it had begun. Daniel slumped forward, his head against mine, and a red drop floated past my face. His eyes were closed and blood from his nosebleed floated through the air in wet spheres.

Dazed, I turned my head to see—what? Althor was out of the cockpit and *floating* through the air toward us. It was eerie how he moved, as if he were underwater. His tie drifted, its end curling in the air. I struggled to breathe, but I couldn't gulp in enough air. I looked past Althor to the screen that showed what was outside of the ship—

And I passed out.

10

PSIBER FIGHT

"I think she's waking up," Heather said.

I rose through the darkness toward her voice.

"Tina?" Althor asked. "Can you hear me?"

I opened my eyes. A trio of faces gazed down at me: Heather, Althor, Daniel. They were crouched around the cocoon, hanging onto handles on the bulkhead, their hair drifting about their heads. Daniel's nosebleed had stopped and Heather looked fine. Althor had taken off his tie and jacket, and his contacts and beard were gone, too. The outline of his Jagernaut vest showed under his shirt—and so did fresh blood, soaking the cloth. Although he showed no sign that anything bothered him, I felt the throbbing pain in his shoulder.

From where I sat slumped in the cocoon, a slice of the cockpit was visible, but it showed only a blank bulkhead. The screen there had vanished, along with its view of what lay outside the ship. I so much wanted to look again, to convince myself that the astonishing image I had seen was real.

Earth.

The turquoise ball had hung against the stars like a jewel in the Milky Way's glittering swath. It hadn't been a picture in a book or a painting by an artist. What I had seen had been real.

A mechanical pencil left by some tech from the base drifted by my nose, and my hair swirled in a black cloud, freed from its wig. The cocoon had retracted its cottony ropes. I tried to pull myself to my feet, but instead I drifted into the cabin.

"We're in orbit," I said, disoriented. I was floating.

Althor caught me around the waist. "Just barely."

"Will you turn on the holomap again?" I asked.

Heather blinked at me. "The what?"

"Holomap," Althor said. "In the cockpit. The screen that was showing Earth."

"How did you know to call it a holomap?" Daniel asked me.

"I don't know." It hadn't occurred to me to call it anything else.

Althor held me up as if I weighed nothing, which I guess I did. Using his foot, he pushed against a bulkhead and sent us floating toward the cockpit, our bodies nudging aside the debris that drifted in the cabin. I finally saw Joshua; he was still in the other cocoon, his eyes closed, his face pale.

"Josh?" I asked. When he didn't answer, I spoke to Althor in a low voice. "Is he all right?"

"He was sick," Althor said. "But he'll be fine." He pushed us both into the narrow cockpit. "It happens to some people in free fall. Heather threw up. You and Daniel both passed out. The oxygen mix in your cocoon was wrong. My sorry for that."

"That's okay." It would never have occurred to me to worry about an oxygen mix.

He slid me into the pilot's seat. The ship responded, molding its exoskeleton around my body. The controls shifted in closer and arranged themselves at my fingertips, translucent panels that glowed with lights, some blinking, some steady, some silver, some purple, far too many red, which I gathered meant the same for Althor's people as mine. Trouble. A visor lowered over my head and hieroglyphs scrolled across my field of view. Feeling trapped, I pushed the visor up so I could see the cockpit. Prongs poked the base of my spine and neck, probably trying to plug into my nonexistent sockets. Even without a direct link to the Jag, though, I felt its mind more now that I was in its control seat. The ship was distant. Impersonal. Puzzled by my presence. The Jag wasn't sure what it had caught, but I intrigued it.

Ragged mental exchanges between Althor and the ship murmured in my mind. Although I didn't catch details, this much was clear: the ship wasn't going anywhere without repairs. We had been lucky to make it this far, into what it called a low-polar orbit.

Althor had rigged a temporary fix to the shroud, enough to hide us from sensors on Earth, at least for now. The Jag was also eavesdropping. The authorities at Yeager apparently believed Althor's ship was an armed scout on reconnaissance, checking out our solar system. I caught fragments of an argument, one guy cautioning against shooting us down, that they didn't know what would happen if the craft exploded. Another stated that we had to contact Althor, not shoot him down, that he could herald some of the greatest discoveries in human history, besides which, if his people were as advanced as it looked, Earth would be insane to antagonize them. Another voice said they needed to stop "the hostile," which I gathered meant Althor, from reporting back to his military. He said Earth needed to prepare for the worst threat humanity had ever faced. The argument raged on.

Always in the background, the Jag's report on the FSA

defenses droned in my mind: *Theater High-Altitude Air Defense, Patriot PAC3, Light Exo-Atmospheric Projectile, RAPTOR/ TALON, HEV . . .* The words went on like a chant, the Jag digging up identities of what—to Althor's people—must have been centuries-old systems that might not even have the same names or be the same weapons in this universe. Nor was it only the American military, not by a long shot. Nations all over Earth were trying to figure out what our unexpected launch meant. The FSA had given no warning to anyone, which I gathered wasn't supposed to happen, at least not with peacetime missions. The entire planet was on military alert.

Althor asked the Jag a mental question, but I could no longer tell what language he was speaking. It phased in and out, sometimes Iotic, sometimes Spanish or English or Mayan. The Jag responded, telling him that some missiles were ground-launched, unable to reach us, but others could apparently blow us to smithereens. Some countries were aiming their bombs at America rather than at the Jag. My mind reeled with the deluge. *God please, don't let this start a world war.*

During all of this commotion, Althor remained "standing" in the cramped cockpit, wedged between the forward bulkhead and the pilot's seat where I was sitting. He was facing me, looking over my head toward the cocoons in the cabin. Strange position for a pilot. Then I realized it made no difference if he stood, sat, floated or turned cartwheels. The ship could link with his brain no matter what he was doing. His sockets acted as receivers for the Jag's wireless signals. It wasn't as efficient as when he plugged into the onboard systems, but it worked just fine.

A yellow legal pad covered with notes drifted by us. Althor gave it a nudge and the pad floated away. "Can you clean up the junk in here?" he said to someone behind me. I leaned around the chair and saw the others floating in the cabin, all three watching us.

"Sure," Heather said.

"Put it in the cocoons," Althor said. "They'll transfer the debris to a holding cavity."

"I should help." I tried to push out of the pilot's seat. It had other ideas. The seat refused to let me go.

Althor brushed my hair away from my forehead, where the scaffolding had struck my temple. "I think you need to sit for a while. This is a bad bruise."

"I'm okay."

"Humor me, then." His tone was warm, once again the Althor I knew, and his face looked human now despite the metallic tinge to his skin.

Joshua spoke behind us. "Althor, do you have a bag?"

I glanced back to see Joshua drifting in the center of the cabin, his face pale. Althor took one look, then opened a nearby panel and pulled out a silver bag.

Heather floated over to Joshua. Although she spoke in a low voice meant only for him, the Jag picked up her words and sent them to my brain.

"What's wrong?" Heather asked.

"I'm sorry," Joshua muttered. "I think I'm going to upchuck everything."

"Why are you apologizing?" Red flushed her cheeks. "You held it longer than I did."

Althor floated over to Joshua. "Astronauts with far more training than you two get sick." He gave Joshua the bag. "It's nothing to be embarrassed about."

Joshua managed a wan smile. "Thanks."

Althor nodded as if this was all typical procedure, which made me like him far more than whether or not he sounded like a man rather than a machine. He was thoughtful in how he treated my best friend. He could have been dismissive, impatient, or harsh, but instead he was kind.

He squeezed back into the cockpit and opened the forward bulkhead. The panel unfolded a few inches from my knees. He took out a bowl with iridescent colors swirling on its surface, like the rainbows on an oil slick in the street after a storm. A cluster of small domes attached to its inner side. With methodical care, he fastened the domes to the panels arrayed around us. Then he rolled up his sleeve, uncovering his wrist guard. It was an odd image, a man in a conservative white shirt wearing what looked like a gang member's black leather guard. That struck me as a good image for a Jagernaut: violence controlled by the tenets of civilization.

I concentrated on Althor, trying to understand him better, but I caught only the surface layers of his mood, his concern for the Jag and our situation, his fatigue, and his unease that we would be captured. When I tried to probe deeper, pain sparked in my head. Wincing, I withdrew my mind.

Up until now, the Jag had been only a presence in my thoughts, studying me as if I were a new system Althor had installed. Now it seemed to realize I wanted to know more about Althor. And so it showed me, using its own concepts, what it meant to be a Jagernaut. ISC's elite fighter pilots lived by a demanding code of honor. They had to combine two dramatically different sides of the human psyche, the empath and the killer. It created a dualism that—at its best—produced officers who balanced their highly developed destructive abilities with an ethical code and innate decency that came from their ability to empathize so deeply with people. That was also the reason they had such a high suicide rate: at its worst, turning empaths into such versatile killers was a recipe for emotional devastation.

I touched Althor's hand. "They have no idea."

He glanced at me. "What?"

"On Earth," I said. "Those people down there have no idea what you're really like."

He smiled slightly. "Is that good or bad?"

"They think you're evil," I said. "They're wrong."

"They're just doing what they have to do." He traced his finger down my cheek, the barest touch. Then he went back to work. A prong rose out of one dome, and he pressed his wrist guard onto its point.

"What are those domes?" I asked.

"Web mods." He lifted his hand and the dome came with it, attached to his guard. A red light glowed on its bottom. "The light comes from a laser. It sweeps over a mesh inside the panel, producing a diffraction pattern. The pattern changes if the controls are damaged."

That almost made sense. "So you read the light patterns and see if they have errors."

"That's right." Unlike me, he didn't seem the least surprised I had figured it out.

The Jag told me more, using images as much as words. A dome sent the patterns it read from the ship to Althor. His spinal node read them, figured out which were wrong, and sent corrections to the ship. The ship changed itself until the patterns it produced matched the new ones. Such a pretty way to do repairs. It only worked for simple fixes, though. Serious problems required more work than the Jag could do by itself.

"What do those domes tell you?" I asked.

Althor frowned at hi controls. "That my ship, it is a mess."

"You got away. That's the important thing."

"Boy, did he ever get away!" Daniel whooped in the cabin behind us. "He left those Jinn-19 jet fighters in the dust."

I leaned around the chair to look. Daniel had moved closer and was watching us with a fascination that he was no longer making the least bit of effort to hide.

"I am not away yet," Althor said as he worked.

The Jag continued to murmur in my thoughts: . . . *exceeded range of St-IV . . . Polar orbit, 500 kilometers . . . navigation systems corrupted . . . WARNING: ARROW systems deployed . . . radar directed/inertial update . . . IR terminal homing . . .* Throughout it all, the ship kept poking at my mind like the host at a party searching out the identity of a stranger who had shown up unannounced.

A siren screamed.

The cockpit lit up like a Christmas tree. The panels snapped away from my body and jerked forward to Althor, trying to close around their real pilot. The Jag's damaged systems couldn't control them properly, and they ended up pushing Althor onto his knees facing away from me, wedging him between the forward bulkhead and my calves. He didn't waste time untangling me from the seat, he just yanked the panels around his body. The entire cockpit was changing shape, making him its focal point with me riding piggyback.

Warning, the Jag thought. *Shroud failed.*

"Get in the cocoons," Althor shouted to the others. "Now!"

The Jag tried to strengthen its link with Althor, but his mind recoiled as if it had struck him with a white hot poker—so instead the ship blasted its messages straight into my mind: *WARNING: shroud failed. WARNING: XB-70 aircraft carrying SRAM Rotary launchers. WARNING: air-launched missile approaching.*

The cockpit disappeared.

No! I was in space with no suit, no protection, just me with the stars. I gasped for air, panicked. Then it hit me: I could still feel the pilot's seat under my body. I was in a simulation, one so vivid, it seemed real. Earth hung below me, sea blue and turquoise against the black velvet of space, showing North and South America beneath long streamers of cloud.

A gigantic lattice appeared around me in the simulation, filling space, its gold cells the size of human beings. Data scrolled through the cell on my right. As soon as I looked at it, the cell flooded my mind with data: missile trajectories, weapons construction, tracking systems, Jinn-19, KC-135, ICBM. I couldn't absorb the deluge.

I was also picking up military chatter from all over Earth. I didn't understand all the languages, but I got enough. They all knew our country claimed to have found an alien war ship, but whether or not they believed our story was another question altogether. Everyone wanted to know Althor's intentions, and it sounded like some countries were assuming his were the same as ours in America. I was drowning in all the messages, symbols, and numbers. How did Althor process it all?

Almost as soon as my mind recoiled, the flood stopped. A white beam swept across my "body" as if it were analyzing me the way the lasers in Althor's domes analyzed his controls. The light blinked off and a violet pulse formed in a lattice cell in front of me. The Jag sent me new information, but this time it slowed down the data as if it were adapting to a new mod in its systems. The Tina module. I would have laughed if I hadn't been so freaked.

This new data wasn't about me. The violet pulse elongated into a man.

Height, 194 cm, the Jag thought. *Weight, 114 kg. Eyes, violet. Humanoid class, gamma.*

Ho! It was showing me a symbol for Althor, his body drawn in violet light. He stood looking away from me, facing the Earth that hung so majestically in space. Points of light appeared far away, coming from the Earth. Red blips. *Missiles.* They were hurtling toward us from the planet. When our shroud failed, the American military had located the Jag and launched an attack.

Six minutes to impact, the Jag thought.

Althor was gripping a white orb in his hand. He hurled it at the missile swarm, and the orb streaked through the lattice like a glittering comet. In only seconds, it reached the cloud of red blips. The orb vanished in the same instant that three of the red dots expanded, faded, and disappeared. It was eerie to see them go in silence, with barely a flash of light.

You see very little light because only compounds within the missile contain oxygen, the Jag thought. *No gas exists in space to heat into a fireball or transmit sound. The cloud of debris has a great deal of kinetic energy, however.* Then: *My plasma field has absorbed or deflected eighty-nine percent of the X-rays from the explosions.*

The detonations may have made no sound, but Earth responded with an explosion of words. The pilot of a fighter plane yelled, "Jumpin' crickets, that baby ain't no fucking *scout!*" Althor's "baby" didn't need a mothership; the Jag had its own fangs. Reactions poured in from bases all over the Earth, some urging a stop to the missile launches, others pressing for an escalation, all of them demanding to know what the hell we were doing.

Althor hurled another orb at the missiles. He had trouble with his aim, and this orb went off, missing the oncoming bombs and hurtling away from the Earth, out into space, useless. He threw another, this time with even worse results. The orbs were trying to home in on the missile swarm, but whatever they normally used to find their targets wasn't working.

With no warning, at least none that I understood, a rod in the "roof" of Althor's grid cube coiled down to his body and wrapped around his wrist. When he raised his arm to throw another orb, the coil tugged his wrist, correcting his aim. Yes! The link of his mind with the Jag strengthened—

Althor gasped with pain. The "sound" came from the image, not the real Althor, but agony spiked in his mind, and I felt the real Althor tense against my legs. The coil snapped away from his arm, flailing like a broken rubber band. His image faded, becoming no more than a smudge of purple.

Missile tracking systems failing, the Jag thought.

Jaaaag. Althor's violet image reformed, distorted and blurred. He had a cluster of the orbs in his hand, but he seemed unable to throw them. His thought phased in and out. Traaansferrrr control from navigation to weapons trackiiiiiiiing . . .

Control transferred from navigation to weapons. Then the Jag thought. *Navigation failing.*

Fix iiiiiit . . . Althor struggled to throw more of the orbs, but he was wavering, rippling, fading.

Jag, I thought.

A fiber detached from the lattice and coiled around my head. *Attending.*

Can you show me what's wrong with the navigation system? I asked.

The lattice underneath Althor's feet lit up, highlighting the gold rods that formed the edges of the cube. Except they were no longer rods. They had become great twists of unraveling rope. Althor let go of his orb weapons and grasped the navigation "ropes," clutching the ends to keep them from raveling any further. The orbs floated away from him, meandering around his grid cell.

Navigation control restored, the Jag thought. *Weapons interface corrupted.*

Althor swore, then dropped the navigation cords and grabbed at the orbs.

Weapons control recovered by 21 percent, the Jag thought as his hands closed on the several of the orbs. *Navigation interface corrupted.*

I reached forward. My arms shimmered with blue light as I stretched them across the lattice, longer and longer, until they reached Althor's cube. I grasped the cords at his feet and held together their raveling ends.

Navigation integrity restored, the Jag thought.

Althor spun around. Tina! Get out of the system! It could damage your brain.

Get those blip bombs, I thought as I pulled back to my grid cell, bringing the navigation cords with me. They dragged along my arms until the glimmering skin broke and swirls of electronic bits dripped onto the grid.

Althor whirled around and hurled several orbs toward the oncoming warheads. This time, his shots streaked straight at the red blips, taking less time to reach them. Some hit their targets right off, and those that missed came around and went after the bombs again, homing in with deadly effect. When they finished, only two of the red blips remained.

Missile launchers failing, the Jag thought.

Althor swore and yanked a rod down from the lattice above him. The rod broke in two, one half coming away in his hands while the other half lengthened to reform the edge of the lattice cell. The half in Althor's hands morphed into a massive gun. As it formed, he braced it against his shoulder, aiming at the warheads from Earth.

He fired.

Light streaked out from the virtual gun, and the Jag poured stats into my mind: *focused beam, 2.2 MeV, antiprotons . . . particle penetration into nucleus . . . excitation from bound to unbound state . . .*

The beam hit the two remaining blips and they disappeared. Just like that, as quiet as a night on the high desert. With a mental groan, Althor sagged to his knees, the monster gun lying across his virtual thighs.

A new swarm of red blips appeared, headed toward us from Earth.

Missile launch from XB-70 craft in quadrant sixteen on the planet, the Jag thought.

No! I cried. *Not again!* It looked like the new missiles had come from Russia.

Althor struggled to his feet, hefting up his mammoth gun as if the virtual weapon were too heavy to lift. His image wavered, blurring in the lattice.

Tracking systems inoperational, the Jag thought.

NoOoOoO. Althor's mental protest vibrated, fading in and out.

Switching to backup for tracking system, the Jag thought. Then: *I am unable to access the backup modules.*

I'll do iiiit, Althor thought. He reached toward a cluster of darker cells. His arm pulled out longer, longer—and stretched so thin that it detached from his body and dropped through the lattice like a dead weight. Bits of memory pumped out of his shoulder "stub" as if he were bleeding the 1s and 0s of binary code. His virtual scream curled through the grid and his image smeared into a violet smudge that faded and then vanished. His scream trailed into silence.

Jag! My panicked cry bounced everywhere. I was alone with the warheads.

A thread coiled toward me. *Attending.*

Is Althor dead? That couldn't have happened, not now, not after all we had been through.

Commander Selei has discontinued, the Jag thought.

What does that mean?

Commander Selei has discontinued. Then: *My functions are degraded. I have lost autonomous capability. You must input commands for me to respond.*

I had only one "input." *Get us out of here!*

Navigation degraded by 94 percent. Backup inaccessible. I cannot execute your command.

Then blow up the bombs.

Tracking systems inoperational. Weapons/navigation interface corrupted. Backup inaccessible. I cannot execute your command.

I didn't want anyone executed, including us. *Can you make us invisible?*

No. Shroud nonfunctional. The codes that control it are corrupted.

I had no idea how to uncorrupted codes. *Show me the problem in a way I understand.*

Look up.

I looked. A sky hovered above me. *What is that?*

A representation of the damaged code.

Yes, I saw now. Errors in the damaged code showed like a mess of cracks that turned the sky into a giant, ragged jigsaw puzzle.

Fix the sky, I thought.

Specify "fix."

I had no clue how to rewrite code. I wasn't even sure what "code" meant. All I could think was to tell the Jag, *Make some plaster.*

Specify "plaster."

Like mortar. To repair the cracks in the shroud.

The shroud consists of energy fields, projections at various electromagnetic wavelengths, modulation of hull properties, and evasive maneuvers. It cannot crack.

I pointed at the jigsaw sky. *Make plaster to fix that.*

Specify nature of replacement code.

I don't know how. I thought of Althor's fix-it domes. *Can't you do the repairs? Don't you have some kind of self-repair routines?*

Damage to my internal web has deposited data in the wrong memory addresses and erased crucial mods.

What does that mean?

I am injured. I need help to rewrite my code.

I had no clue how to help. I tried to submerge my mind more deeply into the Jag, lending it my mind to augment its own, just as I had done for Althor when I helped him recover from his wounds. But what could I do for a ship? Well, it had translated the shroud into an image of the sky. If I gave it better directions on how to fix the "sky," maybe it could translate that into whatever it needed to rewrite its damaged code.

The plaster must be thick enough to fill cracks, I thought. *But thin enough not to interfere with how the sky works.*

After a pause, it thought, *With that input, I can only reconstruct part of my code. Probability of successful operation raised from .04 to 11 percent.*

Eleven measly percent was no good. The swarm of warheads was so close now—we couldn't have more than a few minutes—

Estimated time to impact is thirty-three seconds, the Jag thought.

Ai! Desperate, I thought, *Jag, listen, the plaster must be flexible enough to bend without breaking, in case the sky needs to bend, but strong enough to keep the sky together. It must be smooth enough so it doesn't interfere with operation of the—* Of the what? *Of the lattice. And the plaster needs to change consistency so it can adapt to changes in the sky.*

The cracks in the sky went white, filled with putty.

Probability of successful operation raised to 43 percent, the Jag thought. *Estimated time to impact is two seconds.*

NO! The first of the red blips reached my lattice cell—

And disappeared.

What the—? *What happened?*

Waveform modulation reduced to 13 percent, the Jag answered.

What does that mean?

We cannot withstand another direct hit.

What direct hit? *I didn't feel anything.*

We went into quasis, the Jag thought. *Next missile impact in five seconds.*

I heaved on the raveling navigation cords I taken from Althor, yanking hard, kicking the Jag onto a new course. I had no idea where I sent the ship, but acceleration hit us, pressing Althor's body against my knees in the real ship and throwing me to a new lattice cell in the mental landscape. The blip missiles hurtled through space where I had been only a moment ago.

I cannot withstand our present acceleration, the Jag thought. Then: *Air-launched missiles from European quadrant.* Another swarm of red blips appeared.

Madre de Dios! Jag, sand the plaster on the sky! Fix the damn thing!

Replacement code applied.

A cloak of darkness fell over the mindscape. The lattice shone gold against black velvet, and the pack of missiles racing toward us glittered like sparks.

Shroud functional, the Jag thought.

I yanked the navigation cords, kicking us into another course change, gritting my teeth as the acceleration slammed me into my seat. *Can the missiles find us now?*

Yes. Our exhaust is visible. It went on, relentless. *WARNING: navigation systems failing. WARNING: if we continue to accelerate, the stress will weaken my structure past the point of recovery.*

I had no idea what the hell to do, so I asked for everything. *Change our course again, fix yourself, and get rid of our exhaust.*

Commands implemented, the Jag thought.

The force pushing me against the pilot's seat stopped.

What happened? I asked. The navigation cords in my hands were no longer disintegrating.

I stopped firing the engines after the course change, the Jag answered. *So no exhaust.*

Are we safe now?

No. I estimate a probability of 8–21 percent that a warhead will hit us.

That's a lot better than before.

This is an accurate statement.

I let out a choked breath. *Good work, Jag.*

Thank you.

Can I see Althor?

Commander Selei is discon—

I meant, let me out of this lattice thing.

Mindscape simulation released.

The blackness of space faded, and I became aware of the cockpit around me. My mind felt bruised. Althor was slumped over the controls in front of me.

I laid my hands on his back. *Jag, what happened? Is he alive?*

He is discontinued.

I don't know what that means.

His processing units have ceased operation. His brain no longer responds to input.

That felt like a sucker punch to the gut. *You mean he's brain-dead?*

No. His neural activity has not ceased. He is dormant.

That sounded better than dead. *Can we help him?*

I can reboot his brain.

Will that hurt him?

He is already damaged. Each time he overextends himself, it exacerbates his injuries. I can revive him, but that is all. Until he is repaired, his human/psiber interface should be used for no more than amplification of his link with you.

Why only with me?

The interaction between the two of you is natural. It would exist even if he had no biomech. Using that link won't further corrupt his systems. In fact, it may aid his repair processes.

I doubted telling the Jag to make plaster for the cracks in Althor's mind would help. *I don't know how to repair him.*

You do without realizing it. Incredibly, though it was a machine without emotions, its tone seemed to gentle. *You are a healer as well as an empath.*

Why do you say that?

You can exert biofeedback control over your own body and to some extent, through the Kyle centers of your brain, over the health of others.

Like my mother. Somehow, this starship from another universe was telling me more about my mother and myself than I had even known myself. *How much can I help him?*

I do not have enough data to quantify your Kyle rating.

I don't know what you mean by Kyle rating.

I am unable to determine a numerical value.

Oh. That clarified exactly squat. Regardless of my "rating," my brain felt okay. Althor was another story. It sounded like he had suffered brain damage.

Yes, the Jag thought. *He is in trouble.*

How bad is it?

He can function. With proper treatment, he will heal.

Proper treatment. He wouldn't get that here. *If you reboot him, will it damage him any more?*

No.

Do it, then.

The cockpit vanished from my view and the lattice reappeared in space. Then it blanked out. Completely. No grid, no Earth, no sky, no nothing. Just black.

In the cabin, the real Althor groaned. In my mind, white symbols scrolled against the black of space. The Jag spoke in a monotone, words I didn't recognize, maybe its default language. The lattice and Earth reappeared, and data once again poured through the lattice, this time a confusing flood of data rather than the pictures I understood. I was seeing the mindscape at a more fundamental level, what went beneath the interfaces created by the Jag to help me interact with its systems.

Althor's violet image shimmered into view, facing me.

Are you all right? I asked.

He spoke in his own language.

Resetting language mod, the Jag thought.

I blinked. Who was I talking to, Althor or the Jag?

We are the same, Althor said. With the Jag translating, his English was perfect, or at least as perfect as the odd English the Jag used.

How did you repair the shroud? Althor asked.

I guessed, I thought. *The Jag did most of the work.*

Tina, that was an impressive "guess." It saved our lives. His image shimmered with violet light. You should never have been subjected to that battle. I am sorry.

What about you? I didn't want to think what it must be like when he fought people instead of machines. Did he feel them wanting to kill him? Did he feel them *die*?

Althor's image dulled. Yes.

How do you bear it?

Dark hues shaded his image. There was a time when I wanted so much to be a Jag pilot, I could feel it like a hunger. I fast learned that the "glory" means nothing. But it is necessary.

I spread my hand across his chest, blending my blue with his violet. *I have to believe that a better way exists to protect what we love than by killing people.*

He answered gently. I hope someday we will find it.

The attack left us all subdued. For the rest of the trip, Heather, Joshua, and Daniel floated at a portal screen, watching the stars and the Earth reel by outside the ship. Althor worked on repairs and I stayed in the lattice, letting him see its mindscape through my mind to protect his own. All that time, the Jag monitored the communications on Earth. Militaries from all across the world were searching for us, all of them working together, probably the greatest cooperative effort in the history of the human race.

Regardless of whether or not Althor escaped back to his universe, the Earth here had changed forever. Humanity had proof that we weren't alone. The FSA had shown the governments of the world enough to convince them Althor's ship was real, a war craft from another star rather than a new weapon we had created. Desperation built alliances. With a sense of combined purpose that humanity might never have achieved on our own, the nations of Earth would cooperate against the possible threat of a hostile interstellar empire. They wouldn't rest until they mastered spaceflight and figured out where Althor came from. With one visit to Earth, he had changed human history.

We had a much simpler purpose: survive and escape. Althor finished repairing the shroud, and it hid us while he worked on the other systems. After about an hour, he put away his tools.

"Did you fix all the problems?" I asked.

"Enough for us to leave." He let out a tired exhale. "At least I hope so."

"Including the problem that brought you here, to my Earth?"

He shook his head. "I still don't know why that happened. I need to do more work. But I want to move away from Earth, find somewhere safer." He glanced over my head at the silent, awe-stricken group gathered at the portal behind us, where Joshua, Heather, and Daniel were staring in rapt silence at the glorious view of Earth and space.

"First, though," Althor said. "I return my hostages."

"They'll never forget this." Neither would the rest of Earth. The three of them were about to become more famous than they had probably ever imagined.

Althor touched the exoskeleton around my body and it opened, freeing me to leave the chair. "You can ride in the cocoon on the way down. Once we're away from here, I'll fix the co-pilot's seat for you."

"Okay." As I pushed out of my seat, the others floated over to us, listening.

"You're letting us go?" Joshua asked.

Althor nodded. "You're free to go home."

Their uncertainty eased. Given the way Althor had changed the "rules" of our deal at Yeager, they had no guarantees about anything he would do. Their moods were complicated. Daniel wanted to go into space for real now, not just on this one trip. I wouldn't be surprised if he ended up as an astronaut. Joshua was relieved. Heather was fascinated and wanted to know how it all worked.

"Your military will debrief you," Althor said. "Tell them I threatened to kill you if you didn't cooperate. This should protect you."

"Joshua could never pull that off," Daniel said. "He's a terrible liar."

Joshua scowled at him, but he didn't deny it.

Althor regarded them steadily, his gaze steel hard. "It was never a lie."

Even Daniel went pale then. I knew Althor had never intended to kill anyone, especially not the them, three people who had helped save his life and make his escape possible. But he convinced them, and that was what mattered. If they believed it, then whoever questioned them would as well.

The sun was setting when we reached Caltech. We appeared out of nowhere, hanging next to Milikan Library, washed in a sunset that spread a red glow over the Jag and reflected in the windows of the tall library. As we landed, our exhaust battered the lawns and students sprinted away, shouting or pointing. Papers and books were flying everywhere, dropped by their owners or torn from their arms. Clouds of smoke, white and grey, billowed around us and blistered the grass into oblivion.

As soon as we landed, Althor jumped out of his seat and strode to the airlock. We had very little time; the moment he had dropped the Jag's shroud, it was possible for people on Earth to detect us, including the military. It might take a few minutes for them to figure out what had happened, but it wouldn't be long before fighters were on their way.

Althor opened the airlock and warm air flowed into the cabin. Standing up, I felt heavy in the gravity. I looked through the open hatchway. Outside, several hundred yards away, a rapidly growing crowd of people stared at me, silent and still, their shock reverberating off my mind. For now, they were staying back, but it wouldn't be long before curiosity overcame their shock and they ventured closer to the ship.

Joshua came over to me, his eyes glossy with tears. "Tina—"

It hit me then, really hit me. This was it. I was saying good-bye forever. We both reached out and pulled each other into a hug.

"Good-bye," he whispered.

A tear rolled down my cheek. "I'll miss you."

He squeezed me. "You take care of yourself."

"You, too, Josh." I leaned back, dropping my arms, self-conscious with Althor watching. "You say good-bye to the VSC for me, to Rosa and Mario and everyone. Tell them I'm fine." My voice caught. "Tell Jake that I—I wish him everything good in life."

"I will." Softly he said, "Wherever you go, whatever you become, don't ever forget us."

My cheeks were wet. "I won't."

He nodded and went to the airlock. Daniel and Heather were already there, standing with the wind stirring their hair as they watched us, bathed in red-gold light from the sunset.

Althor spoke quietly to the three of them. "I thank you. For my life."

Daniel nodded with a respect that I suspected he showed very few people. "Good luck." He smiled at me. "To both of you."

Heather spoke. "Althor, you gave us a view of the future. It was a gift. An incredible gift."

They lifted their hands in farewell. Then they each jumped down onto the grass outside. I watched as they ran across the scorched lawn toward the waiting crowd. People converged on them, talking, asking questions, pointing to the ship, their voices lost in the thrum of the Jag's engines.

Althor returned to his seat, but he didn't ask me to take the cocoon, not yet. He understood. I needed these last few minutes to say good-bye to my home. As he closed the airlock, he activated a view portal that let me see the scene outside. I stood there, hanging onto a grip in the bulkhead, while the ship slowly rose into the air, more easily now than before. Joshua, Daniel, and Heather watched us leave, their upturned faces receding in the twilight as we left the world of my birth.

11

INTERLUDE

Saturn wheeled above us, a golden giant banded by butterscotch stripes. Hundreds of rings circled the planet like the bronzed grooves on an LP record. Althor put us in orbit around the moon Rhea. I floated at a portal, gazing at Rhea's mother world with her spectacular rings. Sliding my bracelet around my wrist, I thought of my own mother. I didn't know what she would have thought about me going into space, leaving my home forever, but I thought she would have understood.

"Got it!" Althor said.

I turned with a start. His legs and hips were floating in the air, but the rest of him was hidden inside a bulkhead he had opened.

"Did you find what went wrong?" I asked.

"The Jag has a problem in the engines." He floated out into the cabin, his body angled at a slant to mine. "The inversion drives and the shroud were both affected."

It was strange to talk to someone hanging sideways to me. He moved with such ease, so unlike my clumsy attempts to swim through the air. I stayed by the bulkhead, my arm hooked through a handle there while I kept turning my bracelet around my wrist. I always did that when I felt nervous.

"Can you fix the problem?" I asked.

"I think so." He watched me twisting the bracelet. "I must admit, that is much more attractive as jewelry than as a piece of plumbing."

I rubbed my thumb over the metal. "I've always wanted my daughter to have it."

Althor understood what I didn't say. "I have want for a long time to be father. But I can't make promises. It is true that we are similar. But maybe not enough."

"Is there a chance?"

"Possibly. We need to ask the doctors." As he spoke, he touched a square on the bulkhead. Another panel slid open, tall and thin, revealing two slinky space suits hanging within its recess. Seeing them was like a blast of cold wind.

"You're not going outside, are you?" I asked.

Althor ran his finger down the front of his vest. "For a bit." He pulled off the vest, leaving his muscled torso bare to the cool air. "I need to do some work on the hull."

My face heated despite the climate-controlled cabin. "What are you doing with your clothes?"

Althor peeled down to his skin. "I have to change." He hung his uniform in the locker.

"Are you sure you have to go out just now?" Watching him undress, I could think of better things for him to do with that beautiful body than risking his life in the near vacuum of space.

"It won't take long." If he had any idea what images were playing out in my mind, he gave no sign. He seemed preoccupied about the repairs. The slinky suit he took out of the locker didn't reassure me. The thing looked too flimsy for a space-suit.

It's called an environment suit, the Jag told me.

Well that was embarrassing. Just what I needed, a starship eavesdroping on my misbehaving thoughts.

You are inside me, the Jag answered.

I still wasn't used to hearing it so clearly within my mind. *Why is it easier for you to link with me now than before you and I met in person?*

The quantum probability distribution of your brain is maximized in the same spatial location as the wavefunction for the processors that produce my evolving intelligence. As a result, our probability overlap function is large and I am able to affect your neural firings without biomech enhancement.

Uh, okay. I had no clue what it had just said.

It means that when you and I are close enough, I can talk to you without additional technology.

Can you do that with anyone?

No. Only Althor. Or you.

Why me?

Probably because your link to the pilot is so strong.

He shouldn't be going outside, Jag. Can't you fix whatever is wrong while he stays in here?

Unfortunately, my ability to fix myself is part of what needs to be fixed. But it is not necessary for you to worry. The suit will protect him.

How? It looks so fragile.

So the Jag, which quite refreshingly never seemed to think I was too stupid to understand sophisticated ideas, answered my question in detail. First it told me about the "antique technology" of a 1987 NASA space suit. They needed seven layers to function, starting on the inside with a nylon lining, then a garment that removed heat and waste gases by circulating chilled water through tubes, then a Mylar pressure bladder, a

Dacron pressure restraint layer, a Neoprene layer for micro-meteoroid protection, aluminized insulation, and an outer protection layer. The helmet looked like a bulky, high-tech fishbowl.

The gloves were especially cool. They had silicon rubber fingertips that made it easier to handle tools, and they attached to the suit through metal rings with ball bearings that let the wrists rotate. The astronaut maneuvered using a gas-jet-propelled unit that resembled a big backpack, jetting around space. The suit also had cameras, tethers, lights, a solar shield, a computer, a microphone, and boots. But it was *heavy*. Even without that nifty jet pack, it weighed at least 250 pounds. That was what Mario had weighed when he got out of prison, where he had spent most of his time lifting whatever he could use for weights, becoming so large and muscular that no one messed with him.

After the Jag finished amazing me with the NASA suit, it told me about Althor's space threads. His suit was a second skin. The power module fit into his belt, yet it kept him warm in space. The hood hugged his head and was transparent for his face. Nanobots packed the suit skin. The Jag described them using concepts I had learned in high school chem: double or triple bonds in the molecules acted as robot arms; chemical groups rotating around single bonds acted as gears; molecular spheres served as ball bearings; aromatic groups formed plates. A mesh of something called fullerene tubes acted as a muscle system, one far stronger than human tissue. The skin contained tiny pico-chips that linked into a network, creating an AI within the suit. Smart skin. The energy transfers sounded wicked clever. When Althor moved, the skin converted the energy it absorbed from contractions into the work it needed to stretch in other places. It could repair itself and recycle wastes. Its outer surface acted as a solar collector. The skin manipulated the textures of its inner surface so Althor "felt" whatever he touched. Now *that* was progress. He could make love to me while he was in the suit and feel every lingering touch, no matter how soft.

The enhancement of sexual reproduction is not a purpose of the sensors, the Jag informed me.

Maybe not, I said. *But hey.*

I am not sure how the word "hey" applies in the given context.

I watched Althor tugging his "second skin" into place on his sculpted body. *It means Althor wears his suit well.*

I would hope so.

Althor glanced at me and smiled. I had a feeling he picked up only a sense that the Jag and I were communicating, not the specifics. His lips moved inside the helmet. "I'll be back soon."

"Okay," I said, my good mood abruptly doused. Despite the Jag's assurances, I dreaded the idea of Althor out there in space with hardly more than a membrane covering his body.

He took out his equipment, those little domes and other tools I didn't recognize, and hung them from his belt. Then he floated to the airlock. The inner door irised open, leaving behind a soap bubble glimmer in the opening. He passed through the glimmer as if it were no more than a mist. The outer door hissed apart as the inner one closed, but the timing was wrong; I saw the outer lock open *before* the inner door sealed. I gulped in air—but nothing happened. No air rushed out of the cabin, no trauma, no crisis. Althor just went out the airlock and both doors closed.

I blinked. *Jag?*

Attending, the ship thought.

Why didn't the air go out of the ship when both airlock doors were open?

They weren't both open.

Oh. I still didn't understand, but I had a more pressing concern. *Is he all right out there?*

Yes, easily. Then it thought, *Watch.*

Althor appeared on a view screen. It showed him skimming along the hull, his suit glittering in the light from Saturn. The planet hung in the background, huge and golden, like a painting. Except it was real.

Why does his suit sparkle like that? I asked.

The sparkles are my representation of gas-jet spurts made by his suit, the Jag answered. *The suit plugs into his sockets, and he directs them by thinking where he wants to go.*

I remembered Althor's difficulties when he linked to the Jag. *Is that safe?*

He is managing for now. However, the process will probably aggravate his injuries.

Surely he can communicate with his suit in some other way. Like talking to it.

The specialists on Earth deactivated the suit controls when they were studying it, the Jag thought. *The only reason the neural links still function is because they had no idea those existed.* Outside, Althor went to work on the hull, bathed in Saturn's bronzed light like a man in a mythological tale. When I concentrated, I could pick up the Jag monitoring his condition in careful detail, as if it considered Althor its most valuable system.

Yes, the Jag thought. *He is mine.*

His. I hoped the Jag didn't see me as a rival.

The word "rival" has no meaning in this context, the ship told me. *He has a need for you. It is in your best interest to treat him in a manner humans consider appropriate for the mutually agreed upon mating of your species.*

Ah. So. The Jag wanted to make sure my intentions were honorable. It reminded me of how my cousin Manuel had glowered at any guy who had the *cajones* to ask me out on a date.

You have my word, I thought. *I'll treat him well.*

Good. We are understood.

I just wished Althor would finish his repairs and come back here where we had luxuries like air to breathe.

After what felt like eons, he packed up his tools headed to the airlock. The instant he was safely inside the cabin, I launched myself through the air and plowed into him, sending us both into a spin. He grabbed me around the waist with one arm while he opened his face "plate" with the other, laughing the whole time.

"What's so funny?" I growled, hugging him as we spun through the cabin.

He caught a handhold on a bulkhead and brought us to a stop. "I should come in airlocks more often if this is the reaction I get."

I laid my head against his chest. "Don't go out there again."

He nuzzled the top of my head. "If I did my work right, I won't have to."

So we kissed. A lot of kisses. In between, Althor peeled off his environment suit. Very nice. This no-gravity business had its advantages.

Some time later, Althor donned his uniform and returned to the pilot's seat. While I dressed, floating nearby, he ran more tests. Holos scrolled above the panels that clustered around his chair.

Jag, I thought. *Can you bring up the co-pilot's chair?*

Yes. Its repairs are done. Another chair rose out of the deck, squeezing in next to Althor's seat. The cockpit changed shape to make room for both. A silvery exoskeleton lay open on the new chair like butterfly wings. When I slid into the seat, the exoskeleton folded around me, molding to my limbs. It reminded me of Althor's space suit, except this was a flexible framework rather than a membrane.

Althor remained intent on his controls. "Do you know Heather's last name?"

"MacDane, I think." I watched him working, his fingers flicking through holos or tapping menus on translucent panels. An image formed above a panel in front of us, a figure about six inches high showing an attractive woman with gray-streaked red hair.

"Library entry," the Jag said. "Heather Rose MacDane James. Winner, Nobel Prize in Physics, year 2027 according to Earth's Western calendar."

"Hey," I said. "That's Heather." It didn't surprise me that she had achieved the highest award in physics, one so big even I had heard of it. "What did she win the Nobel Prize for?"

"Dr. James developed the James Reformulations of relativistic theory," the Jag said. "Her work made possible Allied development of the inversion stardrive."

I smiled, pleased. "Good."

"It looks like she developed it in my universe without knowing it existed," Althor said. "No record exists of anyone like me showing up on Earth in our 1987." He touched another panel. "Full entry on Dr. James."

More people appeared in the holo: a slender man with an achingly familiar face and three girls ranging from about four to twelve. The Jag reeled off data about Heather's birth, life, education, and work. Then it said, "Husband, Joshua William James. Children: Caitlin MacDane James, Tina Pulivok James, and Sarah Rose James."

Tears gathered in my eyes. "That's—I—it's lovely."

Althor spoke gently. "A good name they gave their daughter."

Another panel hummed in front of him, and he shifted his attention to the glyphs scrolling through the air above it.

"Althor? What about—" I couldn't ask.

He turned back to me. "About?"

"Me."

He spoke quietly. "You married that boy from the house. Joaquin Rojas."

So Jake and I had worked things out. That felt right, or at least it would have if Althor had never shown up. "Did I go to college?"

His face relaxed. "You attended a school called UCLA on full scholarship." He paused, his smile fading. I understood. It was unsettling to talk about what happened to me in a world without him. But *UCLA*! On full scholarship. That was more even than I had dreamed.

After a moment, he said. "Your husband went into business with a man named Mario Vasquez. They owned a 'garage,' which in this context I think means a car repair shop. You were their accountant."

"That's amazing." So Mario had become his own boss. He and Jake would be a strong team. They had always hung together. I had never imagined being an accountant, but it fit with the way I liked math. The life Althor described, it sounded good. I was glad. I wished similar for the Mario and Jake in my universe. Jake was a good man despite his hard edges, maybe even because of them. He would make some girl a wonderful husband.

Althor still had that inwardly directed look. An odd expression passed over his face, as if a spirit had walked across his grave. It came in his mood, too, but he shuttered his mind, cutting me off.

"What's wrong?" I asked.

He shook his head. "Nothing." Then he said, "We need to go."

So. This was it. Time to go. Such a simple statement, but it felt like the whisper of an icy wind in a moonless night.

We moved away from Saturn in a smooth arc. Althor switched on a holo that floated above the panel where Heather's had been a moment before. This image showed the Jag as it moved in space. But wait, no, that was impossible. No one was out there to record us.

"It isn't an actual recording," the Jag said. "I am using my own data about myself to simulate our progress."

"Impressive." That was when I noticed the strangeness. "We're squashed."

Intent on his controls, Althor spoke in his own language.

"What?" I asked.

The Jag answered. "He said you're seeing length contraction."

"Oh." I had no idea what that meant, but I didn't want to keep interrupting their work.

"It's all right," Althor said. "I'm swapping."

"His systems can share time between different nodes at the same time," the Jag said. "Like you and me."

How strange. I was a node in their network. *What is length contraction?* I thought to the ship.

The Jag spoke. "A relativistic effect."

"Oh." I couldn't figure out if the ship wanted me to talk or think to it.

"It's speaking out loud for me," Althor said. "To protect my mind."

Ah. I liked that. Computer TLC. "Jag, you're a sweet ship."

"I am a JG-42 star fighter designed for warfare," it said. "Being sweet has no part of that."

I had no doubt. But if you asked me, the Jag liked Althor. "What do you mean by contraction?"

"The faster we go," the Jag said, "the shorter I become."

"You're kidding."

"It's true," Althor said. "Actually, we seem rotated. It's because at fast enough speeds, light from one end of the ship reaches the observer sooner than light from the other end."

I squinted at him. "You don't look squashed."

He smiled, working his controls. "Compared to you, I'm not moving. So you don't see a change."

"However," the Jag said, "compared to Earth we are going at about ten percent the speed of light."

I was no expert, but that sounded freaking fast. I thought of how it felt when Jake raced in his car, how it pushed me back in the seat. And he had only been going about a hundred miles an hour.

"This may be a stupid question," I said, "but wouldn't speeding up that fast kill us?"

"It is an excellent question," the Jag said. "The answer is yes. Forty seconds ago, I accelerated at one hundred times the force of gravity. That would have smeared you and the pilot into paste if we hadn't gone into quasis."

I touched my arms, assuring myself I was solid. "Quas-what?"

"It is a form of stasis. You know quantum mechanics, yes?"

"Uh, no, can't say that I do."

"I am a system of particles. Atoms. Molecules."

"I'm cool with that."

"Every system of particles is a quantum wavefunction."

"You lost me there."

"Think of the wavefunction as a diagram that tells you how my particles are put together."

"Okay."

"If even one particle changes its behavior," the Jag continued, "the diagram changes. Quasis, or quantum stasis, prevents all changes. Every particle in me—including those in you and the pilot—continues to vibrate, rotate, and otherwise behave as it did during the instant the quasis started, but none of them can change what they are doing."

Althor glanced at me. "It means the ship and everything inside becomes rigid. Nothing can deform it. Hell, we could be hit by a nuclear warhead and nothing would happen."

"Is that why we survived that missile hit back at Earth?" I asked. "The Jag put us in quasis."

"You are correct," the ship said. "No quasis is perfect, however. When the missile struck us, some of my particles changed state."

"Is that bad?"

"It damaged my hull."

"Are you all right?"

"I can survive. Assuming no one else decides to try blowing us up."

"Tina, look." Althor indicated the forward view screen, which showed the stars in the direction we were traveling. "Watch."

I watched. Nothing happened.

"Oh," I said.

He smiled. "Wait for it."

Suddenly the stars jumped forward. The color of one I was watching turned from red to green.

"Hey," I said. "What happened?"

"We just went in and out of quasis," Althor said. "We're now at 40 percent of light speed."

"I didn't feel a thing!"

"Your neurons can't change state either," the Jag said. "So you can't think a new thought in quasis. That's why you don't notice anything."

I was quite suitably impressed, but it seemed like one little detail was missing. "Jag, how can you bring us out of this quasis thing if you can't make any changes after we go into it?"

Althor laughed softly. "That's a one huge detail."

"My atomic clock," the Jag said. "On the atomic level, particles continue to move. So the clock continues to keep time during quasis. I tell it before we go in when to bring us out."

"That's amazing."

"Thank you." The ship sounded pleased. It might be a machine, but I'd have bet the bank that it liked being called amazing.

The stars jumped again, drawing toward a point in front of the ship like an army with torches converging on their target. They were dimming, though. Some had turned a deep violet and others were too dark to see. I caught something from the Jag about a "Doppler shift" that caused the color change. The display now read sixty percent of light speed. The strangeness of that view was like nothing I had ever imagined, but that actually made it easier to deal with. None of this felt real.

"Have we inverted?" I asked.

"Not yet," Althor said. "We need to push as close as possible to light speed first."

"Why? Doesn't that use more fuel?"

He glanced at me. "As a matter of fact, yes. But it's safer to invert from higher speeds."

I regarded him uneasily. "Safer why?"

"Think of light speed as an infinitely tall tree blocking the road," Althor said. "You can never go over something that high. But you can go around it." He motioned at his holomap with its Doppler-shifted stars. "For us, 'going around the tree' means entering complex space, a universe where our speed has both real and imaginary parts. It's better we don't spend too long there."

"So we go as close to the tree as we can so we can get around it faster?" I asked.

"That is indeed what he meant," the Jag said. "Although his tree analogy is strange."

Althor smiled at its opinion of his physics. Outside of the ship, the stars jumped again—

And the Jag turned inside out.

12

INVERSION

"*Madre de Dios,*" I whispered. Yet somehow we were still inside the ship—because the rest of the universe had turned inside out with us.

On the holomap, the stars jumped apart, shifting toward redder colors. None of the constellations looked familiar—no, wait! They were all still there, but flipped around.

"*That,*" Althor said, "was inversion."

I felt as if someone had rolled me through a clothes wringer. "The stars are in the wrong place. Is that why you call it inversion?"

The Jag answered. "The term in this context comes from a conformal mapping in complex variable analysis. On your world, Mignani and Recami proposed it during the mid-twentieth century for generalized Lorentz transformations in four dimensions."

"Oh," I said, for lack of a more intelligent response.

Althor smiled. "It means, yes, that's why it's called 'inversion.'"

"So how fast are we going?" I asked.

"Not much," Althor said. "Only about one hundred thousand times light speed."

Only? "That sounds pretty fast to me."

"No upper limit on speed exists here."

"And we are going into the past," the Jag added.

I'd swear that damn ship was teasing me. "Yeah sure, we could go back, land before we took off, and really confuse those poor milcops at the base."

Althor laughed. "It's not actually possible to arrive before we left. But we can get close."

"Errors always accumulate," the Jag said. "But I estimate we will arrive back in sublight space fairly soon in time after we inverted."

"Arrive where?" I asked.

"Epsilon Eridani," Althor said.

"Is that where you live?"

"Well, no." He seemed startled by the thought. "It's not a station run by my people. The Allied Worlds of Earth set it up. Your people."

"Then why are we going there?"

"It's only eleven light years from Earth. A quick jump." After a pause that went on too long, he added, "That's all I'm willing to risk on this faulty engine."

I could hear what he didn't say. "And if doesn't work?"

He spoke quietly. "We could end up in a universe where neither of us belongs. Or the ship may just blow up when we return to normal space."

We fell silent after that. All too soon it was time to return to "normal space," if anything about this trip could have been described as normal.

As we slowed down, the stars contracted to a point. The universe turned right side out and—

* * *

—we were alive.

I gulped in a breath. *Alive*. But where? An orange sun lay in front of us, its brightness muted by whatever filters the Jag used. I saw no sign that humans had ever been here. We could be lost in a universe with no one to help us. We could invert over and over, searching until we ran out of fuel and became a tomb drifting in space—

A voice burst out of the comm. "Imperial Jag, this is Epsilani Station. Identify yourself!"

Althor's relief flooded me like water pouring out from a damn that had burst. He couldn't even answer. He just closed his eyes and sat with his hands gripping the arms of his seat.

"Imperial Jag, respond!" The voice crackled, speaking English with a strange accent. "We are a civilian base. I repeat, we are civilians! Please state your intent." The fear in the man's voice told me far more about how Jags and Jagernauts were viewed in this universe than anything that had happened in mine.

Althor drew in a deep breath. "Epsilani, this is Commander Althor Vyan Selei, Jagernaut Secondary, ISC Sixteenth Squadron. My intent is peaceful. I have a damaged ship and request permission to dock at your station."

The man's voice quieted. "Are you requesting quarters also?"

"Yes," Althor said. "Repairs too."

After a pause, the man said, "We'll do what we can, Commander. But we're just a science station. We've never even seen a Jag out here."

"I understand." Althor touched his bandaged shoulder. "Do you have a doctor there?"

"We can have one meet you at the dock."

"Good." He paused. "One other thing."

The man answered warily. "Yes?"

Althor glanced at me as he spoke into the comm. "Can anyone there make a marriage?"

Silence.

"Could you repeat?" the man asked. "I'm not sure we picked up that last bit."

"A marriage," Althor said. "Can anyone there perform one?"

"Well, uh—yes, I'm sure we could set it up with the chaplain."

"Good." Althor watched the lights blinking on his controls, green and blue dots flashing over his panels. "I am receiving your docking signals. We're coming in, Epsilani."

"We're sending codes for your docking protocols," the man answered.

"My thanks." Althor tapped a panel and the comm went silent. He reached across the small gap that separated our chairs and took my hand. "We made it."

I managed a shaky smile. "It's like finding a magic harbor in the middle of nowhere."

"Like you," he murmured. "Or a jewel hidden in the least expected place." Gently he said, "Let's go home, Tina."

Appendix I

CHARACTERS AND FAMILY HISTORY

Boldface names refer to Ruby psions, also known as the "Rhon." All Rhon psions who are members of the Ruby Dynasty use **Skolia** as their last name. The **Selei** name indicates the direct line of the Ruby Pharaoh. Children of **Roca** and **Eldrinson** take Valdoria as a third name. The del prefix means "in honor of," and is capitalized if the person honored was a Triad member. Most names are based on world-building systems drawn from Mayan, North African, and Indian cultures.

= marriage

Lahaylia Selei (Ruby Pharaoh: deceased)
 = **Jarac** (Imperator: deceased)

Lahaylia and **Jarac** founded the modern-day Ruby Dynasty. **Lahaylia** was created in the Rhon genetic project. Her lineage traced back to the ancient Ruby Dynasty that founded the Ruby Empire.

Lahaylia and **Jarac** had two daughters, **Dyhianna Selei** and **Roca.**

Dyhianna (Dehya)
= (1) William Seth Rockworth III (separated)
= (2) **Eldrin Jarac Valdoria**

Dehya is the Ruby Pharaoh. She married William Seth Rockworth III as part of the Iceland Treaty between the Skolian Imperialate and Allied Worlds of Earth. They had no children and later separated. The dissolution of their marriage would negate the treaty, so neither the Allieds nor Imperialate recognize the divorce. *Spherical Harmonic* tells the story of what happened to **Dehya** after the Radiance War.

Dehya and **Eldrin** have two children, **Taquinil Selei** and **Althor Vyan Selei. Taquinil** is an extraordinary genius and an untenably sensitive empath. He appears in *The Radiant Seas, Spherical Harmonic,* and *Carnelians.*

Althor Vyan
= 'Akushtina (Tina) Selei Santis Pulivok

The story of **Althor** and **Tina** appears in *Catch the Lightning.* **Althor Vyan Selei** was named after his uncle, **Althor Izam-Na Valdoria.** The short story "Avo de Paso" tells the story of how Tina and her cousin Manuel in the New Mexico desert and appears in the anthologies *Redshift,* edited by Al Sarrantino, and *Fantasy: The Year's Best, 2001,* edited by Robert Silverberg and Karen Haber.

Roca
= (1) Tokaba Ryestar (deceased)
= (2) Darr Hammerjackson (divorced)
= (3) **Eldrinson Althor Valdoria**

Roca is the sister of the Ruby Pharoah. She is in the direct line of succession to the Ruby throne and to all three titles of the Triad. She is also the Foreign Affairs Councilor of the Assembly, a seat she won through election rather than as an inherited title. A ballet dancer turned diplomat, she appears in almost all of the Ruby Dynasty novels.

Roca and Tokaba Ryestar had one child, **Kurj** (Imperator and Jagernaut). Genetically, **Kurj** is the son of his grandfather. **Kurj** married Ami when he was a century old, and they had one son named Kurjson. **Kurj** appears in *Skyfall, Primary Inversion,* and *The Radiant Seas.*

Although no records exist of **Eldrinson's** lineage, it is believed he descends from the ancient Ruby Dynasty. He is a bard, farmer, and judge on the planet Lyshriol (also known as Skyfall). His spectacular singing voice is legendary among his people, a genetic gift he bequeathed to his sons **Eldrin** and **Del-Kurj**. The novel *Skyfall* tells how **Eldrinson** and **Roca** met. They have ten children:

Eldrin (Dryni) Jarac (bard, opera singer, consort to Ruby Pharoah, Lyshriol warrior)
Althor Izam-Na (engineer, Jagernaut, Imperial Heir)
Del-Kurj (Del) (rock singer, Lyshriol warrior, twin to **Chaniece)**
Chaniece Roca (runs Valdoria family household, twin to **Del-Kurj)**
Havyrl (Vyrl) Torcellei (farmer, doctorate in agriculture)

Sauscony (Soz) Lahaylia (military scientist, Jagernaut, Imperator)
Denric Windward (teacher, doctorate in literature)
Shannon Eirlei (Blue Dale archer)
Aniece Dyhianna (accountant, Rillian queen)
Kelricson (Kelric) Garlin (mathematician, Jagernaut, Imperator)

Eldrin appears in *The Final Key, Triad, Spherical Harmonic, The Radiant Seas, The Ruby Dice, Diamond Star, Carnelians,* and *Lightning Strike/Catch the Lightning.* See also **Dehya.**

Althor Izam-Na
  = (1) Coop and Vaz
  = (2) Cirrus (former provider to Ur Qox)

Althor has a daughter, Eristia Leirol Valdoria, with Syreen Leirol, an actress turned linguist. Coop and Vaz have a son, Ryder Jalam Majda Valdoria, with **Althor** as cofather. **Althor** and Coop appear in *The Radiant Seas.* Vaz and Coop appear in *Spherical Harmonic.* **Althor** and Cirrus also have a son.

Del-Kurj, often considered the renegade of the Ruby Dynasty, is a rock singer who rose to fame on Earth after the Radiance War. His story is told in *Diamond Star,* which is accompanied by a music soundtrack of the same name cut by the rock band Point Valid with Catherine Asaro. The songs on the CD are all from the book and are available online. **Del-Kurj** also appears in *The Quantum Rose, Schism,* and the novella "Stained Glass Heart."

Chaneice is Del's twin sister, and is the only one who can calm him down when he becomes agitated. They come as close to sharing a mind as two Rhon empaths can do without becoming one person. **Chaniece** appears in *Diamond Star, Schism,* and *The Quantum Rose.*

Havyrl (Vyrl) Torcellei
  = (1) Liliara (Lily) (deceased)
  = (2) Kamoj Quanta Argali

The story of Havyrl and Lily appears in "Stained Glass Heart," in the anthology *Irresistible Forces,* edited by Catherine Asaro, 2004. The story of **Havyrl** and Kamoj appears in *The Quantum Rose,* which won the 2001 Nebula Award. An early version of the first half was serialized in *Analog,* May–July/August 1999.

Sauscony (Soz) Lahaylia
  = (1) Jato Stormson (divorced)
  = (2) Hypron Luminar (deceased)
  = (3) **Jaibriol Qox** (aka **Jaibriol II**)

The story of **Soz**'s time at the Dieshan Military Academy is told in *Schism, The Final Key,* and the short story "Echoes of Pride" (*Space Cadets,* ed. Mike Resnick, 2006). *The Final Key* tells of the first war between the Skolians and the Traders and **Soz**'s part in that war. The story of the team **Soz** led to rescue colonists from the world New Day, where she met Hypron, is told in the novelette "The Pyre of New Day (*The Mammoth Book of SF Wars,* ed. Ian Whates and Ian Watson, 2012). The story of how **Soz** and Jato met appears in the novella, "Aurora in Four Voices" (*Analog,* December 1998). **Soz** and **Jaibriol's** stories

<caption>APPENDIX I</caption>

appear in *Primary Inversion* and *The Radiant Seas*. They have four children: **Jaibriol III, Rocalisa, Vitar,** and **del-Kelric.**

Jaibriol Qox Skolia (aka **Jaibriol III**) Emperor of Eube
    = Tarquine Iquar (Empress, Finance Minister, and Iquar queen)

The story of how **Jaibriol III** becomes Emperor of the Trader empire at age seventeen is in *The Moon's Shadow*. The story of how **Jaibriol** and **Kelric** deal with each other appears in *The Ruby Dice* and *Carnelians*. **Jaibriol III** also appears in *The Radiant Seas* as both a small child and a teenager.

Denric is a teacher. He accepts a position on the world Sandstorm to build a school for the children there and teach them. His harrowing introduction to his new home appears in the short story, "The Edges of Never-Haven" (*Flights of Fantasy*, edited by Al Sarrantino). He also appears in *The Quantum Rose*.

Shannon is the most otherworldly of the members of the Ruby Dynasty. He inherited the rare genetics of a Blue Dale Archer from his father, **Eldrinson**. He left home at age sixteen and sought out the legendary Archers, thought they were believed extinct when he went looking for them. He appears in *Schism, The Final Key, The Quantum Rose,* and as a child in "Stained Glass Heart."

Aniece
    = Lord Rillia

Aniece is the most business-minded of the Valdoria children. Although she never left her home world Lyshriol, she earned an MBA and became an accountant. Lord Rillia rules a Lysjrioli province which includes the Rillian Vales, Dalvador Plains, Backbone Mountains, and Stained Glass Forest. **Aniece** decided at age twelve that she would marry Rillia, though he was much older and already a king, and she kept at her plan until she achieved her purpose. **Aniece** and Rillia appear in *The Quantum Rose.*

Kelricson (Kelric) Garlin
- = (1) Corey Majda (deceased)
- = (2) Deha Dahl (deceased)
- = (3) Rashiva Haka (Calani trade)
- = (4) Savina Miesa (deceased)
- = (5) Avtac Varz (Calani trade)
- = (6) Ixpar Karn
- = (7) Jeejon (deceased)

Kelric is a major character in *Carnelians, The Ruby Dice,* "The Ruby Dice" (novella, *Baen's Universe* 2006), *Ascendant Sun, The Last Hawk,* and the novelette "Light and Shadow" (Analog, April 1994). He also appears in *The Moon's Shadow, Diamond Star,* the novella "A Roll of the Dice" (Analog, July/August 2000), and "Stained Glass Heart" (*Irresistible Forces,* ed. Catherine Asaro, 2004).

Kelric and Rashiva have one son, Jimorla Haka, who becomes a renowned Calani. **Kelric** and Savina have one daughter, **Rohka Miesa Varz,** who becomes the Ministry Successor in line to rule the Estates of Coba.

The novella "Walk in Silence" (Analog, April 2003) tells the story of Jess Fernandez, an Allied Starship Captain from Earth, who deals with the genetically engineered humans on the Skolian colony of Icelos.

The novella "The City of Cries" (*Down These Dark Spaceways*, ed. by Mike Resnick) tells the story of Major Bhaajan, a private investigator hired by the House of Majda to find Prince Dayj Majda after he disappears.

The novella "The Shadowed Heart" (*Year's Best Paranormal*, edited by Paula Guran, and *The Journey Home*, edited by Mary Kirk) is the story of Jason Harrick, a Jagernaut who just barely survives the Radiance War.

Appendix II

TIMELINE FOR SKOLIAN IMPERIALATE

Circa	BC 4000	Humans moved from Earth to Raylicon.
	BC 3600	Ruby Dynasty founded.
	BC 3100	Raylicans achieve interstellar flight. Rise of the ancient Ruby Empire.
	BC 2900	Ruby Empire declines.
	BC 2800	Last interstellar flights. Ruby Empire collapses.

Circa	AD 1300	Raylicans begin to regain lost knowledge.
	AD 1843	Raylicans regain interstellar flight.
	AD 1869	Aristos created in Rhon genetic project.
	AD 1871	Aristos found Eubian Concord (aka Trader Empire).
	AD 1881	Lehaylia Selei born.
	AD 1904	Lehaylia Selei founds Skolian Imperialate.
	AD 2005	Jarac born.
	AD 2111	Lahaylia Seli founds Skolian Imperialate.
	AD 2119	Dyhianna (Dehya) Selei born.
	AD 2122	Earth achieves interstellar flight.
	AD 2132	Allied Worlds of Earth established.
	AD 2144	Roca Skolia born.
	AD 2169	Kurj Skolia born.

AD 2203   Roca marries Eldrison Althor
                 Valdoria (*Skyfall*).

AD 2204   Eldrin Jarac Valdoria born (*Skyfall*).
                 Jarac Skolia, Patriarch of the Ruby
                 Dynasty, dies (*Skyfall*).
                 Kurj Skolia bcomes Imperator
                 (*Skyfall*).
                 Death of Lahaylia Selei, the first
                 modern Ruby Pharaoh, followed by
                 the Ascension of Dyhianna Selei to
                 the Ruby Throne.

AD 2205   Majr Bhaajan hired by House by
                 House of Majda ("The City of Cries"
                 and *Undercity*).
                 Bhaajan founnds Dust Knights
                 (*Undercity*).

AD 2206   Althor Izam-Na Valdoria born.
                 Major Bhaajan solves second case
                 for Majda (*The Bronzed Skies*).

AD 2207   Del-Kurj (Del) and Chanience
                 Vladoria born.
                 Major Bhaajan solves third case for
                 Majda (*The Vanished Seas*).

AD 2209   Havyrl (Vyrl) Torcellei Valdoria
                 born.

AD 2210	Sauscony (Soz) Lahaylia Valdoria born.
AD 2211	Denric Windward Valdoria born.
AD 2214	Shannon Eirlei Valdoria born.
AD 2219	Kelricson (Kelric) Garlin Valdoria born.
AD 2220	Eldrin and Dehya marry ("The Wages of Honor").
AD 2221	Taquinil Selei born (first son of Dehya and Eldrin).
AD 2223	Vyl and Lily elop as teens, creating a political crisis ("Stained Glass Heart").
AD 2227	Soz enter Dieshan Military Academy (SChism and "Echoes of Pride").
AD 2228	First declared war between Skolia and The Traders (*The Final Key*).
AD 2237	Jaibriol Qox II born.

AD 2240	Soz meets Jato Stormson ("Aurora in Four Voices").
AD 2241	Kelric marries Admiral Corey Majda.
AD 2243	Corey assassinated ("Light and Shadow").
AD 2255	Soz leads rescue mission to world New Day ("The Pyre of New Day").
AD 2258	Kelric crashes on Coba (*The Last Hawk*).
AD 2259	Soz Valdoria and Jaibriol II meet and go into exile (*Primary Inversion* and *The Radiant Seas*).
AD 2260	Jaibriol III born, aka Jaibriol Qox Skolia (*The Radiant Seas*).
AD 2263–73	Rocalisa, Vitar, and del-Kelric Qox Skoia born (*The Radiant Seas*).
AD 2274	Aliana Miller Azina born (*Carnelians*).

AD 2275	Jaibriol II captured by Traders and forced to become puppet emperor of the Trader Empire (*The Radiant Seas*).
	Soz bcomes Imperator (*The Radiant Seas*)
AD 2276	Radiance War begins, also called Domino War (*The Radiant Seas*).
AD 2277	Traders capture Eldrin. Radiance War ends (*The Radiant Seas*).
AD 2277–8	Kelric returns from Coba and becomes Imperator (*Ascendant Sun*).
	Jaibrio III bcomes Trader Emperor (*The Moon's Shadow*).
	Dehya stages Imperialate coup (*Spherical Harmonic*).
	Jason Harrick crashes on Thrice Named ("The Shadowed Heart").
	Vyrl goes to planet Balimul and meets Kamoj (*The Quantum Rose*).
	Vyrl returns to Skyfall to lead planetary protest (*The Quantum Rose*).

AD 2279   Althor Vyan Seei born (second son of Dehya and Eldrin).
Del sings "Carnelians Finale" and nearly starts a war (*Diamond Star*).

AD 2287   Jeremiah Coltman trapped on Coba ("A Roll of the Dice" and The Ruby Dice).
Jeejon dies and Kelric returns to Coba (*The Ruby Dice*).

AD 2288   Kelric and Jaibriol III seek a way to work together (*The Ruby Dice*).

AD 2289   Imperialate and Eube ty to negotiate peace (*Carnelians*).

AD 2298   Captain Jess Fernandez goes to Icelos ("Walk in Silence").

AD 2326   Tina and Manuel return to New Mexico ("Ave de Paso").

AD 2328   Althor Vyan Selei meets Tina Santis Pulivok (*Catch the Lightning*; also the duology *Earthborn: Lightning Strike, Book 1* and *Starborn: Lightning Strike, Book 2*).

Acknowledgments

I gratefully acknowledge the readers who gave me input into both this book and the original version titled *Catch the Lightning:* The Aly Parson's Writer's Workshop, William Barton, David Burkhead, James Cannizzo, Louis Cannizzo, Al Chou, Paula Jordan, Frances and Norm Miller, Lyn Nicols, Nicolas Retana, Joan Slonczewski, Bud Sparhawk, and David Truesdale; the Dream Weavers: Juleen Brantingham, Jo Clayton, Suze Feldman, ElizaBeth Gilligan, Lois Gresh, and Brook and Julia West; the people in the research topics on the GEnie SFRT and the Internet who answered my questions; Caltech students Bradey Honsinger, Stacy Kerkela, Jeffrey Miller, Divya Srinivasan, and Shultz H. Wang; and the members of my Patreon page who gave me input on the revised version. My thanks to Eleanor Wood, Kris Bell, and Justin Bell of Spectrum Literary Agency; to Shawna McCarthy and Russ Galen at Scovil Chicak and Galen, to Tad Dembinski at Tor, and to my editor, David G. Hartwell. A special thanks to my husband, John Cannizzo and my daughter Catherine, for their love and support.

About the Author

Catherine Asaro is the author of thirty books, ranging from thrillers to science fiction and fantasy. Her novel *The Quantum Rose* and novella *The Spacetime Pool* both won the Nebula Award, and she has been nominated for multiple Hugo Awards. Asaro holds a doctorate in chemical physics from Harvard; her research specializes in applying the mathematical methods of physics to problems in quantum physics and chemistry.

Asaro has appeared as a speaker at many institutions, including the Library of Congress, Georgetown's Communication, Culture, and Technology program, the New Zealand National ConText Writer's program, the Global Competitiveness Forum in Saudi Arabia, and the US Naval Academy. She has been the guest of honor at science fiction conventions across the United States and abroad, including the National Science Fiction Conventions of both Denmark and New Zealand, and served as president for the Science Fiction and Fantasy Writers of America. She can be reached at www.catherineasaro.net and has a Patreon page at www.patreon.com/CatherineAsaro.

LIGHTNING STRIKE

FROM OPEN ROAD MEDIA

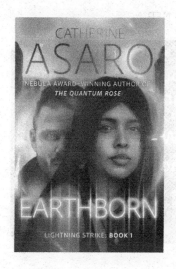

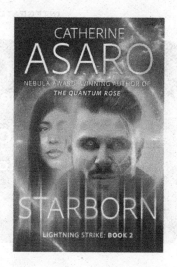

OPEN ROAD

INTEGRATED MEDIA

Find a full list of our authors and
titles at www.openroadmedia.com

FOLLOW US
@OpenRoadMedia